Maybe Someday

Your Hand in Mine

Zulfi Sayyed

PARTRIDGE

A Penguin Random House Company

ISBN: Softcover   978-1-4828-5192-2
             eBook   978-1-4828-5193-9

Print information available on the last page.

To order additional copies of this book, contact
Partridge India
000 800 10062 62
orders.india@partridgepublishing.com

www.partridgepublishing.com/india

Acknowledgements

This could have never been possible without the names written below. I can't stop showing my gratitude and in the alphabetical order would like to thank-

- Aamna- For being my super cousin whose motivations have been the most helpful and for reading a part and calling it "Breath-taking."
- Afifa- For being my best friend, sister, companion, classmate and everything I could ask for. You're someone whom I can just not live without.
- Anjani ma'am- For teaching me all the outstanding words which you will come across whilst reading. You made my ninth standard hard to forget. I miss you and I wish that retirement could have never happened. Even now, I get dreams in which you have come back to teach us English. This book begins with your class!
- Ikku- For making me aware of my writing skills through constant encouragement and support and also for tolerating me and keeping calm in my worst. Do I have to say more?
- Khizer Bhai- For being a believer of silence. I know, we hardly talk but your involvement and not-so-showy concern means a lot.
- Mommy- you for being the most open-minded, cool and honest person I have ever come across. Your simplicity makes me fall for you every single day.

- Nanna- For all those times when you have publicised my writing skills although they left me in a state of complete embarrassment. I feel lucky to be your greatest love!

- Nanu- For making me believe that none could beat you in your education of both mind and heart, your smartest looks, astounding English, urdu, Arabic, Persian. Your college books have helped me endlessly for archaic words.

- Shahrukh Khan- For being my favourite and for acting in such films which have taught me the meaning of love. You're one sheer inspiration!

- Sister Lily- For being one wonderful principal of my lovely school. Your words in the morning assembly give me a lot of hope and strength.

- Sweetu- For being an editor though you hate to correct me and for shedding tears in the end. We are miles apart but still my heart belongs to you. Your undying love and care has brought me here. I can't thank you fully even if I get seven lives for it.

- Tajji- For your support in the form of sisterhood without which I am no one and for all those times when you've listened to my story with all your heart and showed sympathies with the protagonist.

- Tehreem Api- For being a beauty of my life and as you say that my writing has come from you.
  P.S. Writing is surely in our blood!

- Zenab api- For being a sister from different mother. I feel proud to make you proud!

- Zoheb and Fuzail- For being my younger brothers and well, I couldn't write both of you apart so now, breaking the rule. Zoheb, you do know the story and I remember that you both wanted your names.

The greatest thanking goes to my Allah (s.w.t), the most noble, beneficial and exalted. And only you know that how you've made me a writer. I'm going to thank you always, no matter what time it is, good or bad, until my last breathe and even after!

Chapter 1

"SShhh! What's the word?"

"I heard but I have forgotten, Hugh! Why didn't you hear?"

"Oh, so is it my mistake? These people are making so much noise at the back, I couldn't hear properly." Amirah said exasperatingly.

"Then why do you sit here? It is your fault. Now who will tell us?" Kyara sighed.

"Kyara and Amirah, what is happening there?" They heard.

"Oh, we are sorry ma'am. Actually, we could not hear what you said after 'stop being'."

"Oh, Okay! I said 'stop being nincompoop'. Do you want this?" The teacher asked.

"Yes! Exactly. Thank you ma'am. What does it mean?"

"It means a foolish person," she smiled.

"Thank you!" they said and wrote on a page.

"When an insect gets trapped in hot mud, it gets buried and leaves its body print on the soil. The dead remains of plants and animals are called Fossils and from this, you get fuels.

"Buried. Did you hear?" Kyara said turning her head.

"Yes, she is pronouncing it as 'Beried."

"I thought it is pronounced in the same way as it is written."

"She is always right. It must be 'beried'." Amirah tucked her hair behind her ear.

"Unquestionably! So burial as 'berial'." Kyara smirked.

"Aaahh! So the bell has rung again and time flies in her class."

"You're so right. I wish she could have spoken a little more. You know, her speech is conjuring." Kyara spoke calmly.

Never getting enough of that class of their English teacher Mrs. Veronica, they knew that she was their only inspiration and one of the most competent persons they had ever met. She, who had the fetish of the English language, had been working in their school, for the ten consecutive years and had secured reverence and approbation in the Convent institution. Unlike both the girls, the other learners had no deep penchant for her due to her sternness and strict demeanours. The mass seemed to put out their language, when they heard her. She lectured as if, there was no one else responsible for the architecture of the English tongue but just she, who painted novel words upon the ears of people. She had that accent and desirability in her speech, which won over the girls who were fanatical in learning English Literature. Being zealously persuaded by her, they looked forward for her period to get nearer. She was an educator who trained them to lose the world to get vanished in those multi-faceted poems of Robert Frost and ceaseless dramas of Shakespeare. Putting so much sentiments of her own into those lessons, which sometimes looked monotonous, it appeared as if she was the writer of every written account as she dreamt up more than those genuine writers did.

Both the girls carried a pen and paper to note down all those new words, which she handled. Never speaking simply but always-using synonyms of words, she had all the effortlessness in the language as she was born to do so.

"Well, I will be coming at your place at five of clock so for god's sake don't hibernate as usual." Kyara pressed Amirah's hand.

"Hibernate!" Amirah screamed.

"Oh yes! I am sorry. I forgot that elephants don't hibernate," she joked.

"Very funny, huh! I hope I don't see you and you die before five." Amirah pushed her away.

"Hoping for your own death is bad. You know I won't ever leave this world without you," she laughed.

"Trying to convince? But I will take revenge in the evening. Now get lost." Amirah said walking down the lane.

"Goodbye. Take care that this ground doesn't break apart by your weight," she put her tongue on her upper lip.

David and Jonathan's or Damon-Pythias closeness was much more than being friends. The proud destiny made them sisters from different mothers as they had same habits, same interests, and same looks and were like penumbra without each other. Calling themselves as "Twins", they believed that there was nothing in the mankind which could ever take them away. When they were hand in hand, the planet for them was below their feet.

Glee lied in each other's joy, twinge controlled over in each other's ache. Amirah Iman was essential to her as night is to thief. Always caring for her like an elder sister though she was just six months older, she was a brother frankly. Wiping her tears when she cried, her odium was for those who did anything unjust with her.

'Kyara', a name which was incompletely sated assumed that her life was made for those star-studded dresses of Alexander McQueen and Elie Saab, shoulder bags of Gucci and Moschino, stilettos of Jimmy Choo and Christian Louboutin, Fragrances of Giorgio Armani and Chanel and scarves of Burberry and Louis Vuitton. Stella McCartney, Donatella Versace, Prada, Valentino, Christian Dior, Hermes, Ralph & Russo, there was no other international identified mark which she was uninformed about.

Uncovering the authentic desires of her tiny life of fifteen years, she saw her clothes to be petillante to add to her idealism.

"Who has kept my maxi dress in this section? You know I hate when someone opens my cupboard." Kyara said.

"I have kept your clothes because you were in school." Mommy replied remaining engrossed in cooking.

"Why? I don't keep this in this section. Oh god! How can I explain? It's just...aaaaaa!" she said banging the door of the cupboard.

"Don't bang the door Kyara. Your cupboard already is overloaded. Have pity on it." Akira said.

"Akira, don't you think you should keep your extra special comments till yourself? When they come out, they act as ferocious pollutants."

"Oh really! Mommy, don't you think she is becoming ill mannered day by day? She needs some special attention of yours."

"Heard what she said? You don't have to over react in every situation." Mommy spoke grumpily.

The immediate tyranny of a present emotion made the elusively charming tears to fall drop by drop, without any sound showing that they possessed an emotive power. Akin to the pearls, shining even in the dark consisting of her lacerated feelings, they were an illustration of her innocence and indomitable pride Her mystic meaning water with less hydrogen and oxygen but more feelings, continued for hours, until her eyes turned red like fire. Without food in an echoless silence, she went to Amirah's house walking towards the east which frowned with clouds.

All over again everything got back to being perfect in the presence of her source of ecstasy and emotional warmth and she could ask for no greater blessing. The stream which had forgotten to smile was again having curves in the charming air of vitality.

Sitting with her undying strength that she considered a part of herself only, they had neither competitions nor differences. Undersized fights could not exceed more than a day which had made them the role models of friendship which was something to pride upon. They could have easily won a "nonstop speaking competition" due to their infinite talks about books, fashion, films, politics, food, places, people and everything trending at that time.

"I am hungry. Go get something."

What do you want to eat? I think we must go and make some noodles." Amirah said.

"We? You will make. I don't even know to light the stove. How can I make?" Kyara said with an expression of self-conscious innocence.

"Ya ya! You are no less than an infant. But lighting a stove is as simple as ABC. What will you do after your marriage?" she asked sharply.

"Marriage? Who has thought about it? You have even started thinking about it," she laughed. "After marriage mmm, I will ask your brother- in-law to make food. As I will be too busy shopping. I will ask him to shift to Paris, then you very well know darling what I will do. Oh my god! All those sparkling stores will be in front of my eyes. Can't wait."

"Oh god! This girl's life starts and ends at clothes. We were on food, I suppose."

"Yes, we were."

"And why do you wear such clothes. You are a Muslim. Don't you think you are too old to wear shorts and skirts huh?" Angrily, said Amirah.

"Ammz I will stop one day," she winked.

"But when? Don't you fear god? You will be burnt in hell fire if you won't stop wearing these 1 cm clothes."

"Centimetre! I expected millimetre from you," she said.

"And this is not at all funny, I am serious Kyara."

"Okay!" Kyara said in a funny way.

"Okay I'm not a fool to waste my energy on such a person who doesn't even care for her after life. You must not wear all this. Beauty lies within us. Dressing modestly is what our god likes." Amirah uttered softly.

"See the noodles are ready. Let me eat first then I will solve your problem. Would you like your friend to be hungry?" Kyara asked innocently.

"You are so wicked in changing the topic. Let me serve my infant."

"Awwwww," she paused. "Why do you serve me?"

"Why do you ask the same question to me always?"

"Thank you baby! I love you more than you love me." Kyara said.

"Obviously not. It's the opposite."

Next morning, she went to school and got astounding news of being elected as the class' president. It made her rocket fly high as she actually deserved it but some were happier and those were all her friends, they loved her completely. Being the limelight of her group, she listened to all, helped all, and loved all. An impartial girl, believing that uncovering anybody's secrets or bad habits would lower down her standard, she was a confidante in everyone's lives because she made them feel secured and significant. Lies were always on her hating list and even maintaining a distance from those who spoke them. Judging people by their clothes never made her shameful of talking to the poor. One unique character that considered herself the best and supposed that she had everything she needed. Akin to that bird that prides on her beauty and intelligence, she was. Her sweetest misconception was that there was no one in this world who could control her mood or steal her happiness. Having all the necessities in overload; a loving family, a beautiful friendship, and she, her favourite, she believed that God had spent an extra time to design her.

Her incorruptibility was her off putting quality in the 'Me' world. Thinking deeply about everyone and loved to bring a smile on each face, she never made one weep; neither had she hurt a single soul. She cherished to sacrifice for her loved ones and always had sympathetic thoughts. Her infrequent attitude did help her to win many hearts but isn't it said that the sweetest person has gone through a lot. She was small, she was immature, and blindly she felt that good was in the air everywhere. Little did she know about other hearts? Having the slightest idea, she was just joyous in her own existence, which she supposed to be like a typical Hindi film, where there was everything pleasing; an actress, an actor who will come at the right time, some friends and a perfect family. She pictured as if there were hidden cameras watching her all the time and reviewing her attire and attitude. Like those childhood fairytales, which she had heard from her grandpa and grandma, she believed that in her life too, there will be a prince, who will love her madly and they will live happily ever after. She was not into all this stuff as she knew that acting of her age was also style. She believed that she would marry the one whom her family would approve of. Being cheerful to imagine this, she never thought of herself being mad for any other person. She did believe in love stories but even thought that extreme tales are a waste of time and just exist in "stories." Waiting for the upcoming years to experience life more; in a group of sentences; "She was a personification of love, beauty, human emotions and if correct to say, perfection!"

One fine day sang itself into evening, when the chirping of birds reached her ears, the sluggish zephyr touched her brown, long, lusty hair and she sipped her black coffee gently, she rushed to complete the last chapter of her novel. It was not understood by her that why wasn't she able to focus on it. She was constantly getting distracted despite of having entire mood to read. Unknowingly she did not want to. It was something else which was taking turns in her mind. It was an incomprehensible feeling and so to make her mind calmer, she decided to dress herself well as she felt good when she was in the best of her clothes. Suddenly she heard, "Kyara, some guests are visiting us at eight, so can you get ice-cream from the nearby shop"?

"Mommy, how can I go alone? I will feel afraid. Ask Akira." Kyara complained. "She is busy. That is why it has been said to you. And afraid? Give me a break. Maisha is going to accompany you." Mommy said.

"Okay! I will go with her but let them come first else ice-creams taste bad if we bring them before time"

"From where do you bring your own new philosophies? Alright go whenever you want but do bring," pleased mommy.

"Okay mum!" She replied in a cute tone.

She went in her room and started listening to her favourite singer. "Brazil, Morocco, London to Ibiza, straight to L.A, New York, Vegas to Africa! Lalalalalalalala". She was extremely happy without any reason; she called Filiz, her friend from Delhi whom she had met first time in her wedding in 2011. Filiz was her friend because they loved each other's company and had spent great time in Delhi. Steadily they had become really close friends. Filiz was a kind of teacher to her. She used to share everything with her and she was a director in her life that she trusted the most. Her advice before anything was as important to her as it was to arrange her cupboard every week. She was much elder than her but they always looked at one another as the best of friends. Being immensely beautiful, she possessed a childish innocence which was the most attractive thing. She was not like those married girls who restricted themselves into a house and tended to forget the outside world but an outgoing person who was still the same after such a huge change in her life. She was open minded and an outstanding interior designer. Designing was a craze for her so much so, that she renovated all her relatives' houses. She was made up of a mixture of mad genuine elements. They shared the same taste in clothing, hobbies, and even personalities. Her better half M.R Ayan Shah was one of the leading businesspersons of Delhi. He was terrifically smart and a heart robe but Filiz was no less. They both loved each other and had an arranged marriage. Like her friend, she too believed more in her parents' choice.

"Did you see the latest pictures of "Lakme Fashion week"?

"Oh ya! I did. I liked Tanma and Meeta." Kyara spoke.

"Certainly, Zavi was good too and I loved what Miranda wore. She is a doll, isn't she?" she stated.

"Undoubtedly. I love her, alike a Barbie, so sleek and so charming".

"Kyara, see its seven suddenly," she laughed. "As always we have talked long, I guess you should see whether everything is arranged for welcoming the "so called guests." We will chat."

"Yes thanks for reminding me. I forgot that I have to get ice-cream for the guests. Bye. I will send you a picture of the ice cream."

"Get our favourite flavour."

"Surely," she cut the phone.

"Mommy, I'm going. Where is Maisha?"

"Here I come Kyara, let's get it going."

The sun had lost its shine, the moon was about to rise. The sky appeared blue which was discrete in its colour. It had all the shades of life as if it was going to tear apart and beyond those skies rested a mesmerising abode.

"Kyara, I need to get a packet from one of my friends. He will come at the shop."

"Oh okay," she said while walking down the lane.

An enchanting voice came from behind. "Is that your sister?"

She did not notice for a while; as she was too busy talking about the flavours of ice-cream. There was utter silence at that place. It appeared as if not even the air was blowing. All the processes had stopped for a second and it seemed as if life had ended for a moment. Kyara did not like that stillness, she did not even turn to see the speaker. After a flash when she paid to the shopkeeper, she turned back.

With a swift twist, her long hair, which was on her left side, came to the right and her black mini dress took a smooth round with the blowing air. She saw a boyish creature in his car looking at her. Maisha was holding the packet so she understood that he was her friend. She did not know him but she experienced a peculiar feeling to see him. As if he was known, somewhere. He had a striking smile on his self-indulgent face and at that time, his exquisite eyes, which had a blistering charm in them, met hers. She was perplexed by his interrogative behaviour.

"That's Kyara." Maisha smiled.

"Yes Kyara, hi! You have grown up, I mean I saw you last when you were small, really small."

"Hi! Really?" she enquired. *"Who's he?"*

"He's Rehaam." Maisha said. *"That guy who visited the Sunderland apartments so much. I know him."* Good Elf, her angelic inner voice and Baddie, her evil inner voice sighed together.

"I have to go," he said starting his car. "It was so nice to meet you."

"Same here," she ended softly.

"Okay so he's the one?" she said.

"I had told you, I guess." Maisha replied smiling.

"Yes but you didn't tell me that you were talking about him," she said. "How's he?"

"He's good," she said. *"How would I know? I saw him last when I was so small."*

Though this was an extremely ordinary meeting, it had something intensely distinctive. Those sixty seconds had affected her in a way. She did not know the reason but she was happy. She thought about him first time and not in a different way but in a usual manner. He was like all other strangers to her. She did not think that whether she would see him again or not. It was just like that stormy wind, which had passed by, and she did not think of him ever again. It reminded her of all those times which she had spent in Sunderland apartments. He did not live there, but visited frequently. He was someone who helped all and had a nice thought for everyone. A well-off boy, who belonged to an affluent family of Himachal, had shifted with all his family to her city nine years before. He was not among all those boys who prided on their wealth but someone who was down to earth and extremely generous. When she was ten years old, he was 18. He was not thin but not even huge and averagely heighted who had a normal haircut, little beard on his chin and light moustache. It was all, that she knew about him and after a thought of five minutes, she forgot it all.

The next morning her vacations were going to start off and she was tremendously keyed up. She planned that she would play badminton with Amirah every morning in their neighbourhood park to keep herself in shape. The vacations were passing like hot air balloons. They went briskly and finally just the last nine days were left. Both the friends had decided to watch a movie on the last ninth day. They were awfully excited and had planned to sport same kind of hairstyle. Tickets had been booked and everything was in place. Their friends had come to pick them up at sharp two of the clock. The four friends gorged on all the drinks, snacks, sips, and dips and as usual, Kyara had all the magnetism in herself that day too. She was looking exceedingly elegant and people had to turn back to see her exquisite vogue. She really enjoyed all that and loved to be in the limelight. It was like a dream for her to be the best-dressed person in the globe. She desired to be on cover page of fashion magazines and always aspired for giving advices regarding trends.

She had been really busy in completing all her pending work as the schools were about to begin. She had logged in her account on a social networking site after many days and saw the pictures of that "mall visit" uploaded. She loved them all and suddenly read a status of her friend on which a serious discussion was going on between people. That status was about a Hindi film song; some people loved it while some did not. She had commented on it to show her liking for it and suddenly she saw a name, which had liked her comment. That name was none other than "Rehaam

Alhamd" and she did not understand that why he liked her comment. It was irritating for her and then she heard a sound after few minutes, 'trrr-trrr'. That was her ringtone for notifications and then she switched on her phone and saw something which she was expecting somewhere within. She had received his friend request and she didn't know what to do with it. Honestly, she wanted to talk to him because he attracted her in an unusual manner but not in that way. She didn't have any different thoughts, she didn't even know him neither did she like. However, for humanity's sake she did accept his request because she remembered that after all he was a nice person.

"Hi! How are you? Thank you for accepting my request," he messaged.

"What is the point in thanking for this?"

"Hi, I'm good, thanks. How about you?"

Good. What's up? In which class are you?" he asked.

"I am in the ninth standard. What do you do?" she asked.

"Well I work; you know my dad's business so I handle it," he replied.

"Who doesn't know about Richie rich?"

"That's nice," she replied.

"So are you doing something? I hope I didn't disturb."

"Oh, no no. I am just sitting idle, no work to do," she responded.

"Why? Haven't your school started yet?" he asked.

"No, they'll begin from first of July so just waiting waiting."

"Waiting? Who waits for school? I have heard of this first time."

"This boy hates school. I could have an idea."

"Why first time? I wait; all of my friends are waiting. You know these vacations were a bore."

"Really, why were they boring? Didn't you go somewhere out?"

"I did go to Delhi but just for five days in the beginning of May. After that nowhere else, so they are dull."

"Ohke, I see. Well how's everyone at home? Do you know that I know all of you?" he wrote.

"Everyone is nice, busy in their own lives. How do you know us?" she asked. *"How does he know everyone?"*

"Because I frequently visited Sunderland apartments. I had friends there."

"Great that is! I didn't know you, just heard your name," she replied.

"I thought you knew me," he said. *"Why?"*

"I knew you, but not so nicely, now I do."

"Ya, now I do too. It is prayer time; can I catch you in five minutes?" he asked.

"No!" "Actually, even I am going offline. I'll catch up with you soon," she replied.

"Oh, Okay. Bye, take care."

"Bye! Take care," she said. *"He's nice for Maisha. Isn't he? Kinda cute"*

That was their first ever conversation for such a long time. She loved it. She never talked to any boy this much before. It created a sense of trust in her. She wanted that conversation on random topics to go on and on, and she never wanted to say bye but she had to. She didn't want that person to have any wrong idea about her. She was just simply attracted. She had started considering him as her friend.

"Hello! Cutie pie," he messaged her.

There was no reply from her in spite of being online.

"Kyara, are you there?" he texted constantly for five minutes.

"Hmm," she replied. *"Not now!"*

"What 'hmm', what has happened, why aren't you replying?"

"Because I don't want to reply, I am sad and I don't want to talk to anyone."

"But why? Won't you tell me what's wrong? I am your friend right?"

13

"No, I won't say to anyone, I am crying," she sent.

"Kyara, stop crying. How can you cry for small things?"

"Small things? How can you say it is small?"

"Then tell me what is it?"

"Hmm, mommy shouted on me," she messaged.

"Oh, this is indeed a small thing. You should not mind all this. Your tears are very precious, why are you wasting them? Now smile for me, your pretty face won't look good while crying."

"Oh! Why does he behave like that?" "Hmmm. Thank you for your consolation. You have all the abilities to make someone happy, right?" she asked.

"No, these abilities have just come for you. Now make a promise to me."

"What kind of promise?" *"Ahmmmm?"*

"You will never cry, and you will be happy always, Okay promise?"

"Ha-ha okay," she said. *"I am happy now."*

This had been the start of their new friendship which made them talk to each other too frequently. Always wishing well for each other, Rehaam had remained busy in his work and Kyara too, worked hard for her first semester exams which made her pass them with flying colours. The days were passing rapidly and suddenly it was the Rehaam's day of birth. She had his phone number but she didn't find it right to call at night because they had never before talked on phone. She decided that she would call him in the morning after passing the night impatiently.

"Happy birthday," she shouted.

"Whose this?" he replied in a serious tone.

"Kyara," she murmured.

"Oh! Thank you."

"How're you?" she asked.

"Fine. Thank you," he responded sternly. *"I don't know why I am talking."*

"Well, we were talking about that film," she started.

"I will call you," he said and cut the phone.

"Gosh! I want to cry now." She spoke in her mind and began sobbing. *"I am never talking to him again."*

She believed that he hated her voice and disliked everything about her. Not wanting to interfere in his life anymore, she assumed that he loathed it. His rudeness had affected her in such a drastic manner that she didn't like talking to anyone for some time. She logged in her account to distract herself and saw a green dot in front of his name which hinted that he was online and then she believed that if he had been actually busy at that particular moment then he could have called a little later but he just wanted to avoid the conversation and so he did that. She never wanted to text him first nor did she want him to. His discourtesy was too high for her soft-heartedness.

"I'm so so so sorry. My mum and dad were just sitting in front of me and I didn't know how to respond to you. I'm very sorry. I had to call you but then I saw that you called from your landline and if I had called then somebody else could have picked up so can I call now," he messaged.

"No! It is all right, you should not say sorry on your birthday. Rather, enjoy it."

"Hmm no, I am sorry. Well thanks a lot."

"All the pleasure is mine. What gift do you want for today?" she asked.

"Ha-ha! No gifts, your wishes mean more to me," he replied.

"No, don't act silly. I wait for my birthdays for gifts and I will give to you too, don't worry."

"Ha-ha no! Well what are you doing?" he asked.

"I am talking to you," she replied.

"Seriously Kyara, I didn't know."

"Ha-ha! What are you doing?"

"I am just sitting."

"So where are you celebrating? Are you going somewhere?"

"Nah! I rarely celebrate; I have grown up *na*."

"So what? Birthdays should be celebrated. See my photo; I was dancing in the wedding."

"Oh! That sounds great, let me have a look"

"Wait, I'll send you the link."

"WOW! You look stunning here," he sent.

"Thanks," she replied.

"You are so beautiful, why did you change your display picture?" he asked.

"I don't know, wait I'll put that itself," she said.

"Ya this one is awesome. You know, I have to tell you something."

"Okay what?"

"You know I am committed to a girl and I will marry her soon, *In Sha Allah*," he said.

"Tell me something new."

"Ha-ha! Let me tell you, I know this," she sent.

"How do you know, no one really knows," he asked.

"Well, I know everything. It is so nice that you will get married to Maisha, and then I will dance on your wedding."

"Oh, okay! So, someone knows her name too. That is impressive."

"Someone knows everything. She is my cousin, actually a sister as she lives with me. Do you know?"

"Ha-ha. Of course I know. I thought that she didn't tell you so that is why I didn't tell before."

"Well, she shares everything with me. I know a lot about you," she laughed.

"Really? It is time for prayers; I will catch up with you later," he wrote.

Moreover, their conversation had ended. She knew it from before about Maisha and Rehaam and she was ecstatic. She always wanted good for everyone and she wanted them to marry soon. Rehaam loved her girl and even Maisha loved him. They had a very cute love story whose beginning she was unaware of. Maisha was fantastically charming and engaging. Kyara and Maisha were cousins and she had been living in her house because she only had her father in her family who was always out. She was open to all and used to discuss Rehaam with Kyara too often. She too enjoyed talking about him, as he was her friend too. Maisha was of Rehaam's age and obviously, Kyara was like a mediator when they fought and acted like a typical problem solver for both of them. Trusting on her in their personal issues, Kyara like a good friend helped both of them.

The day had at last come when Kyara was turning a year older. Her friends had planned a surprise party for her at night at her own house. She was incredibly thrilled about her day, when she felt the most special. She had worn a cute, black, mini dress in which she looked like a doll. She had received many gifts and the best gift was from Amirah. She gifted her, a T-shirt that had a picture of both of them and had a title "I could have asked for a much normal sister, but not better than you". All her friends were in her house at night and her birthday was made the most memorable one. She even had a call from her friends and Rehaam, which had made her day. She had given her phone number to Rehaam, and they had talked too often in twenty- four hours on messages.

"Good Morning birthday girl," he texted.

"Good morning!" she replied.

"So, how is your birthday going?" he asked.

"It's just morning. Ask me when it will end."

"Okay! So how will I give you your gift?"

"Which gift? I mean, why you have bought?"

"It's my cutie pie's birthday. I had to buy. Now don't interrogate and tell me where you will meet?" he asked.

"Ha-ha! I am going to hotel Caesars palace at four P.M and Maisha would be there too. So I would love if you will come."

"Well, four is high time; I have some office work in that area. I will come, but just for five to ten minutes.

"Ohh, that's bad. Thank you for five minutes."

"Ha-ha! Let me come first. It depends on your luck."

"Well in that case, my luck is too good," she wrote.

She, along with her friends had reached the place at four, and had ordered whatever they wanted to eat. Rehaam was not picking up his phone and Kyara did not know about his arrival. Maisha too, was not sure of him.

Finally, a boy in a dark blue, full-sleeved shirt, whose sleeves, he had folded up till the elbow, was seen coming. He had his hair gelled and they were short. He had little beard and moustache. All the eyes in the room were on him, as if he was some celebrity. It appeared as though everyone took some time off to see his peculiar yet stylish walk. He was walking in a very different way as if he was on red carpet. His saunter had that appeal which very few people possessed. His personality was not like everyone else. It had that charm, and it had that sophistication. His amble had so much classiness that even her eyes were stuck on him for few seconds. Everyone was asking her except Amirah, that who was he?

Then she was explaining everyone about Maisha and Rehaam and all were happy to see them. He had a very cute gift for her, a teddy bear that was purple in colour. "Best Friends" was written on that teddy bear's tummy. Her birthday was booming and she was so happy but at the end of the day, she was not feeling good. She was missing someone; she wanted her time to be spent more with him. She did not want him to leave but she wanted to stay with him and talk endlessly. She loved to talk to him; she always waited for him to text her. They were friends by choice and they missed each other much often. Kyara was in love with their friendship and she talked so much about him to Amirah. She never called him by his name but always addressed by "*woh*," while talking to others about him. When she talked to him, then she gave a lot of respect and always said "*aap*" and even he used to reply in the same manner.

Being youngest in the family, Rehaam Alhamd was born with a silver spoon and still had it in his mouth. A Corporative who considered his work the most important part of his life, he was an expert to handle his love life too.

He always gave a lot of time to Maisha, and she never complained to him. They were so pleased with each other and he was especially severe about their relationship. He was not cheating on her and had all the blissful plans to get married to her in the coming years. Both the families were thoroughly favourable and cheerful about them. Rehaam considered her, his world and himself, fortunate to have her. Maisha was too relaxed and thought of everything lightly. He was just a small part of her happy life. She was with him, because she liked him. Love was something, about which she claimed but she herself did not know its meaning. There was love, but still it was missed. She never really felt to be in love though she felt him. However, Rehaam was undoubtedly in love but still, not actually. They both never devoted themselves to each other. They were together despite of being apart and met each other despite of being distanced. They were each other's habits; they both were extremely possessive about each other but never cared much. She always liked to do what Rehaam said, but she never left anything because of him. Even if she left, she left it in front of him. It was a sense of showing off between them. They showed that they bothered but they were burdened. There were restrictions on both of them and had rigid conditions. Rehaam was an orthodox; he hated, when she talked to someone else; and even Maisha disliked if he talked to somebody. They both had thought that being possessive about each other means love. Little did they know it was much more?

It is just not the story of these two; but there are billions of youngsters, who remain with each other just because of their likings and desires. They tend to be in love because they gain from it, it is akin to a time passing element for them. They sing, they dance, and they live and do what not. They get into marriage too. Nevertheless, what would be the consequences of such a marriage where there is no concern? They will live with each other, they will have a family, and they will fulfil all their desires. However, for how much time will they enjoy all this? Do they ask themselves that are they truthful? Are they not doing anything that will hurt any life?

All their wishes, all those requirements will end in some time and they do not know that after that, it will hurt a lot. Youth is transitory in which everyone is a fool. They imagine and dream but forget that on one day, they all will get bored of all that stuff, which made them excited and energized. They will surely get to know that this world is just not for some useless stuff or relations but it is that beauty, which requires a very dissimilar eye to see and heart to feel. It is like a promise to us made by the supernatural being. We are sent not just to spend our lives with joy and glee but also to understand what pain is and how dependent we are on the natural processes, which do not stop. This life is a comedy, it does not only end here, but goes on and on even after when the beats go off. In fact, that is the time when actually it sets off, where there is no pain, no tears, no agonies and just bliss. Where people are marked on their behaviour and they can't close the eyes to. They have to pass through so many divine checks and they are bound to pass them acceptably. That world consists of a dreamland, which has all kind of good filled in it. Where delight flows in rivers and fortune makes up the hills. Where land is a gift from Ishtar and stock of luck is with all.

Every human dreams of living in it but do they work to attain it. They act in that heinous way which can only take them to the place of torment. That place has fire and blood in it. Where lives the devil of devils. The bodies are burnt and do not die. They are immortal so that their pain doesn't end in any way. All that soreness is the result of their own deeds. They hurt. They kill, they grab, and they chill!

'We wish you a merry Christmas; we wish you a merry Christmas; we wish you a merry Christmas and a happy new year!' sang Kyara.

"Oh god! Why do you sing all this?" Amirah interrogated.

"Because it is Christmas," she smiled. "Does anyone sing this song on Eid?"

"Obviously not; we do not celebrate all this and you will not sing it now."

"Ok, Okay! However, will have to wish him, after that, I will stop."

Nonetheless she never texted him as she wanted him to text first. She was dying to talk to him but did not want to seem annoying. She waited and waited but he never messaged. He was online all the time, which was making her so sad. She didn't know why, but she was sad, really sad. It appeared as if he had forgotten her, he was happy in his own life. Then at New Year's Eve, she texted,

"Hi, are you there?"

"Hi! Yes," he replied.

She never liked his one-word replies; they showed her that he was least interested to talk.

"I want to talk to you."

"Oh, so talk *na*."

"Why are you not talking? You know, I don't feel good if we don't talk," she wrote.

"Awe I have been busy, you know. I'm so sorry, my cutie pie."

"It's okay. Happy new year to you!"

"Yes, to you too. So what are you doing on new year?"

"Nothing really! What about you?"

"Well, nothing yet but should I come to meet you?"

"Han? No, I mean, how can you come?"

"Ha-ha I can, if you want, or we will go for a drive maybe."

"Wooosh! Drive!"

"Drive! No, some other time."

"Ha-ha okay! So how was 2012 for you?"

"It was really nice. See I met you!"

"Ya, seriously, even I met you, my best friend, ha-ha. Such a small best friend. I met my wife too this year, it was fantastic."

"Wife? Is he married?"

"Yes, I am waiting for your marriage. And then I will dance."

"I am waiting to see you dance. We will dance together, Okay?" he added. "So tell me something about Maisha, you are her good friend right? She talks so much about you; you know she loves you a lot."

"Yes, she's one of my best friends. You know, she loves you very much. She is a sweetheart. I think I am always incomplete without her. We are no less than twins. We do same things; speak in the same way and sometimes even our thoughts collide. We both are exactly same."

"Yes, I know, she doesn't have siblings *na*, so she tells you everything."

"She does. She has me."

"Actually!"

"I am going to Delhi, the next morning. We' l talk all day else I will get bored."

"Sure! I am sleeping now, good night."

"Yes, sleep, Good night."

That comfort was like chalk and cheese. She was not the same girl anymore who just had herself in her life. He was unknowingly becoming important to her and she never wanted that sensation to be altered. He was becoming so dear to her that she did not know what she would do if he had left or changed in some way.

Then those examinations arrived, which made her tensed drastically. She had to score greatly because she was the president, and she had to maintain her grades. Exams were like torture to her, she hated them whole-heartedly. She had to study so much and not because she was enforced to study, but she studied for herself. Studies and good marks made her very happy. As she considered herself perfect in all the fields, she was bound to get good marks, which made her believe that she was actually perfect. She had to wake up at seven in the morning to study until late. Whole of her schedule had changed for fifteen days; she had forgotten everything and had just concentrated on her studies. She was splendidly well in all the subjects, and feared a lot before appearing for exams. Having the least of confidence in herself, despite of regarding herself faultless, she knew somewhere, her weaknesses. No human was her strength or weakness, but she herself was. She feared so much so that she used to get sick before one night of exam; she was scared of teachers, papers, questions, answers and everything. She had a kind of testophobia. She fainted, vomited, was fevered and what not happened to her. She had forgotten all the people of her life. There was no Rehaam, no Amirah, no Filiz and neither Maisha. All she had was her mind and her books. She had even stopped using her cell phone for a month and did not even miss it much. She was truly, a very extremist person and did everything excessively. Love, liking, studies, clothes, friendship, family, and everything that affected her, was done in an incommensurable way. All of her exams went very nicely. Could anyone believe? She did not say a word to Rehaam and she was stunned to see that he did not care even. She had started forgetting him because at a point, he was not that important to her and it actually did not matter much. She was all right in this way and neither she was sad with him. She viewed him, as "Maisha's husband," and she knew he was her friend but she never expected much from him. Her exams had come to an end and she was so keyed up to visit her grandparents who lived in Bombay. He was angry with her, she believed so to make him normal again, she thought to talk to him once.

"Have you forgotten your best friend? I am really sorry, because I think you are angry with me. You even had cut my phone that day when I called you. Is there something like this? If it is, then I apologise," she messaged.

"Oh, No- No! How can I forget my pretty girl? Don't say sorry, I can't hear it from you. You know, I am being so busy these days that I don't have time to talk to anyone. By the way, how are you? You must have started with your exams, right?" he messaged.

"No, still, I am sorry. I am fine, how about you? My exams have ended. Tomorrow I am going to Bombay at nana-nanny's place."

"Oh, Okay! By train?" he asked.

"By air. My flight is at seven in the morning. You know Filiz shall be there too," she said.

"Who is Filiz?" he asked.

"I guess, I have told you about Fila. Her name is Filiz."

"Oh, Yes! Well that is great, enjoy there, you know Maisha is going to Paris, Huh!" he messaged with a sad emoticon.

"Yes, I do. Don't be sad, she is going just for a twenty five days."

"Yes, I won't be able to see her for so many days. Isn't this sad and bad?"

"It's going to be fine, don't worry."

"Hmm, tomorrow you are also leaving. I will be left here, all alone."

"As if?"

"You have so many friends; they'll take care of you."

"Friends? I don't meet them too often."

"Why? You should now. Go out with them, enjoy! Else you will miss this time, in future."

"Ha-ha! Who has so much time to enjoy and who will have the time to miss? You don't know how busy I remain throughout the day."

"Okay, if you don't have time, then I am sure, you will not miss both of us so much. Don't worry."

"Hmm," he ended.

It was evening, when the doorbell rang. Her maternal uncle and aunty had come for dinner. Kyara was as usual dressed in a short mini skirt and a short top. Her hair was tied up in a messy ponytail and she was looking utterly modish. She smiled at those relatives but they never smiled at her. They were just staring at her attire. They had an awful expression on their face that Kyara hated thoroughly. She felt an impartial discomfort to be with them. She just wanted to run away from that room, and never see them again. She was very scared because she did not want them to comment on her clothes in front of everyone. She stood up to go from that place but suddenly -

"What kind of clothes are you wearing? Is this the way in which a girl should be dressed? It is so small, how can you even sit with your family? Don't you feel ill at ease?" An expected voice came.

She was conked down, to hear that. She never knew that her dressing could affect someone so much. She was infuriated but she didn't reply to her because the one who replied in a bad mood was not her. She never said anything to anyone; if anyone appreciated her, she just thanked, and if someone criticised her, she even smiled at that time. Her smile was so constant, which left everyone spellbound. The beam she had was everlasting and it was for all. She was never partial in making anyone happy. She wanted the world to get happy by seeing her smile. She smiled at those, who were considered untouchables by others, who were unprivileged and ignorant in themselves and who never received any sympathies from a person. She had her condolences with all, and never used to comment on anyone. Maybe, she never thought of hurting a soul, she certainly did not want to give even a pinch of pain to any heart by any means. This is hard to believe though, but she was there, somewhere, who was striving hard for other's happiness forgetting about her owns. Her miseries, her problems, they did exist because after all that perfection, she was a human first. She tended to forget them all because they acquired a cheerless second place in her life. First was, for all those, who were in her life and made it more beautiful for her to live in it. Tears in any eye, broke her from inside. She appeared to be that sunshine, for the needy, which even a sun, would need one day and that soothing smell of which even the flowers would be deprived.

At the spur of the moment, she was in her room, weeping as always. She had not had food that day and those bitter remarks had badly saddened her.

"Hi, what are you doing, did you have food?" Rehaam messaged at that time.

"Hmm, I am good. I didn't have, did you?" asked Kyara.

"I had, why didn't you have?" asked Rehaam curiously.

"Hmm, I don't want to," she said.

"Why don't you want to?" he asked.

"Just like that, you say, what did you have?" she asked to change the topic.

"I had chicken briyani. Now you go and eat something, right now!" said he.

"Nice! Who cooked? Nah, I will not eat," she messaged with a sad emoticon.

"Mommy had cooked. Kyara, don't be stubborn. Eat means eat, simple," he said.

"No, don't you understand once? HUH!" she said.

"What's wrong? Why is my cutie pie being so angry? Tell me, did someone say something to my Kyari?" he asked.

His usage of "my" before her name always made her extremely glad. Her mood used to change in moments, when he used to talk like that.

"Hmm," she replied.

"What hmm? Now tell me quickly. Won't you tell me?" he messaged with a crying emoticon.

"Hmm, one aunty has come to my house, and I'm wearing short clothes, so she had so many problems. She started saying anything. I am so sad and I am crying. I don't want to eat anything," she said.

"Awe, you are so innocent. Firstly, someone is breaking the promise of not crying. Kyara, you are very gullible, you get hurt by anyone. You know, you should just ignore all such things. Your own family allows you to wear, so you should not mind anyone else's opinions. Everyone has differences and you should wear what you like. If you will listen to everyone, then when will you listen to yourself? And please, you are not even that small, that every time you sit and start crying. I will say that you must ignore such people, and do whatever you like. Now please, smile for me. Can't see you crying, you know that very well. Still, you do, HUH; my small Kyari doesn't think about me *na?*"

"Ha-ha I do care for you, Okay?" she texted with a smiling emoticon.

"Now go and eat, then only we will talk," he said.

"No, I don't like what is been cooked," she said.

"Oh, then? What you want? In fact, I should get you something," he said.

"No, please no. why would you. I will eat that only," she said.

"Okay and don't talk to me," he said.

"Han? Why?" she asked.

"Ya, I am no one to you, right? You don't allow me to do anything for you; this means you don't consider me your friend. Huh! It will be better if we stop talking."

"Oh god! Are you mad or what? There's no need to bring anything, I will eat two- minutes-noodles or something else."

"You like unhealthy? I am bringing something for you, and without any more questions, you are coming down in five minutes."

"Really, someone has gone mad. I don't want, if I would have, then I could have said to you directly."

"Okay, you don't want, but I want to give. No more discussions related to this topic are. So how are you? How's life, Miss Kyara?"

"Ha-ha-ha good I am. What about you? It has been so long, we didn't talk," she wrote closing her eyes and shaking her head.

"I'm good."

"Don't seem like."

"By the way, come and just leave. Don't begin your talks," she wrote shyly.

"Oooh, I see. Someone knows how to command," he replied.

"I can sense your frown."

After five minutes, she received his text and she went on the road in front of her house. There was no one, so she asked him, and he told that he was on the adjacent road. She walked promptly towards that road. It had a low turn to go there, and then she veered and saw an already seen car. She was not able to see his face from the distance as there were sunbeams falling on the mirror of the car. She became so nervous and cautious that she started staring at the ground. She felt so bashful that she just wanted to reach to him in a moment, but she had to walk a little. She had changed her clothes and was then wearing a simple peach top with a pair of ankle length jeans. Her hair was as usual, tied up in a sideward braid held up by a cute hair clip of red colour. Her mind had no thought and she was being so anxious. She wanted to see him, but she did not want him to see her. She was focusing so much on her walk, because she somewhere knew that he must have been looking at her. De facto, he was! His eyes were all on her, and he was taking pleasure in seeing her walk. He was attracted by her shy mannerism because he himself was a very shy person, which she was aware of. That road was a very usual on which no one really used to go, it was a short one but he stayed at the end of it and the whole road had to be walked upon by her. It was such a less distance, but for both of them, it appeared as if it was miles. She was stuck to the left side and was walking at her best as if there was someone to impress, as if there was someone about she cared. Finally, she halted and then she first saw, those eyes, which made her, forget everything of this world. She had never seen so charismatic eyes, which had a distinct shade of brown. She never saw him fully, because she used to stop when those eyes used to come to her sight. It appeared as though, they spoke. They told a tale of themselves, a saga of him. They had lustrous water in them which had magic, an unexplained enchantment, and a dream like illusion. She had a feeling of happiness, which she had never experienced before. She was so so so contented that she wanted that time to be endless; she wanted to spend all her life looking in those eyes where she found her fortune to end. There was a sheer stillness when they looked at each other. He saw in her eyes that were speaking so much, as if she wanted to tell him something. According to him, her eyes were truthful; they depicted something that was untold. She had an apparent virtue in them, alike a newborn child who has not seen the world, but still relies on the one whom it loves. He was struck somewhere, because it was new to him too. It was not at all understandable that why were they not speaking anything? Attraction to him was her long hair. They were godly as they were so long, touching her laps when in front and beautiful. He had understood that she was being shy in front of him, but he was continuing to stare in those deep eyes, whose importance was known to him. At another moment, they both looked down in embarrassment and she had held the door of his car for comfort. Again, their eyes had risen up and suddenly they met and connected themselves. A delightful smile had stroked both of their faces. Every little fraction of them, was smiling and they smiled in a very reserved way. She was habitual of raising her eyebrows while giving such a smile and she did so. Rehaam was fascinated by that raise of her and then he had thought to speak something to end the discomfit between the two.

"Hi, Kyari," he shouted in a pleasing way.

"Hi!" she said in a formal tone.

"What were you doing?" he asked.

"I was talking to my," she paused. *"Why am I saying this? No stop! Please don't. Stop! Stop! Stop!"*

"Ha-ha, my Rehaam?" he asked informally. *"I didn't mean that. I meant a friend. Did I?"*

"Ya, only mine," she said and hugged herself bashfully. *"This statement was not given by me."*

"Take this and eat it please, Okay," he whispered giving her an eerie but comfortable smile.

"Bye!" she said.

"Han, bye!" he said and drove away.

She went back to her house and ate that pizza which had been brought by him. She told her mommy that Rehaam had brought for her and she did not react much to it because she knew that he was with Maisha. She was keeping busy in packing up the clothes for their visit to Bombay.

"When is Maisha leaving?" mommy asked.

"She will be leaving, today at eight at night." Kyara said.

"Okay! Where is your baggage, Kyara? Bring it to me," she asked.

"Yes, I am. Here it is," she said.

"So many clothes! Why are you taking whole of your closet for five days?" she asked in an astonished voice.

"They are so less, I was thinking to keep more," she added.

"Have you lost it? Take some out. Don't make your bag so heavy. You will have to drag it on the airport, and then it will cause a problem," she said.

"No! No! I will carry, don't worry. These are needed. What if I go short of clothes there? It's better to keep extra, you know," she said.

"You can't listen, right? Your choice, but I shouldn't hear that it's too heavy and you are unable to carry it."

"Okay," she smiled.

"So, my Rehaam?" he messaged and her blood started running fast to be first in the race.

"Ha-ha," she replied after ten minutes. *"I'm sorry. I just didn't mean that. You're taking it wrongly."*

"Why?" he said.

"I don't know."

She had just said it for some reason, which was not at all known to her. She had no answer to his questions and for a moment even he had become serious and he curiously wanted to know the reason behind her words. Yes, they were words, just a combination of letters!

"Have you eaten?" he asked.

"Yes, I have, thank you," she replied.

"Huh! Bye."

"No. I'm not at all thankful," she texted

"Better! So long, hair you have. You know you look so small, just like a doll," he sent with a winking smiley.

"Was that a compliment or something else?"

"Why small?" she asked narrowing her eyes.

"Because you tie your hair that way, as if you are a small kid."

"Oh! So how should I tie?" *"He doesn't like my hairdo."* She spoke forlornly within herself.

"You must tie a ponytail. I have never seen you in that."

"Nah, you have seen, I remember," she said.

"You remember everything but I don't. So tomorrow you will go *na*, should I come to drop you?" he asked.

"No. Thank you. My whole family is going to be there, and just mommy and Akira know you."

"I can, if you want," he asked.

"Thank you but no."

"I miss you," he wrote.

"Why?" Good Elf and Baddie pouted.

"Aww, miss you too. I should sleep now, tomorrow I will wake up early," she said.

"Yes sure, I will also wake up early for you, good night," he said.

"Whoa! Informality at its best level."

"Why would you? No you will sleep. I will message as soon as I will reach there."

"Did I ask you?"

"You're so disgusting at times. Good night, sweet dreams!" she wrote.

"Am I? Good night, take care," he said.

They ended up their talk at night. She was mesmerised by his care, which he showed her every second. She attached herself so much to a person as if there were just two of them, putting out everything from her tiny mind. She had started dreaming, she had begun to visualise her talks with him. She imagined of all that stuff, which she would tell him. She wanted him to know every detail about her. In fact, she talked to him for all the hours of the day. Sometimes she really talked to him, and sometimes she just imagined of doing that. She was getting so much attention from a single person that he hypnotized her. He was all on her mind, when she ate, she drank, she sat and even when she slept. There was no one else in this vast world who had taken away Kyara's beauty sleep and her odd thoughts. She had regarded him as her best friend, someone who knew her the most, someone who cared for her the most, and someone whom she trusted the most.

Ding ding ding ding! Her ringtone made a rigorous noise and she woke up at another moment. It was at four in the morning.

"Get up, Kyara! If you will wake up late, then how will you dress yourself up?" he messaged.

She was expecting him to wake her up and so he did. She was ecstatic and she woke up without any complaint.

"Good morning! Ya, I should get ready."

"Good morning! Has everyone woken up?" he asked.

"I don't know. Let me see."

"Oh, so what will you wear?"

"I will wear a grey skirt with a white top and a pale black jacket with a pair of black boots," she messaged in perfection.

"Oooh sounds great! Do send me your picture after reaching there, in these clothes."

"Yes, I will," she answered.

"Now, go and get ready. Do eat something before leaving and text me when you leave."

"Okay I will," she replied.

It was sometime in March when she had left the house for the airport with her family. A chilly breeze was blowing and was touching her hair, which were tied up in a ponytail! She had already told him, and he had wished her a safe journey. He wanted her to keep him updated all the time as if she was going for some sort of war! She had reached the airport, and suddenly all the people had their eyes on her. She walked so stylishly holding her orange "Jimmy Choo" bag in her hands as if she was on an elongated ramp. Alike those models whom she saw on 'fashion TV'; she used to leave everyone awestruck by her poise and grace. She had boarded the plane and had thought of him all through the journey. She was just going for five days but still she was taking them as one twenty hours or seven thousand and two hundred minutes. She thoroughly missed him because she was unable to talk to him while in air. She didn't speak a word to her mommy or her sister. Being lost in her own thoughts about him, she was enjoying that distance from him in some way because she wanted to know how much he could miss her.

She was in Bombay after some hours of her journey and she always loved to be there. She loved everything about that city which had been very close to her heart. She had been going there since her early days and was greatly obsessed with it. She always liked that place's atmosphere, which was of her type. It appeared as if, the people, the places, the trains were all running before their time. They just wanted to reach somewhere, about which they did not know. They had everything with them but still they wanted more and more. There was not a single creature that was empty in some way. All were stuffed with anomalous thoughts, pushy dreams, and a life, which carried a great weight. The time of that mind-bogging place used to pass much more quickly than others and so to match up with it, the populace also made itself faster than anyone. People dreamt of living in that city, as if it was not just a common spot instead something else, which would act as a hen to give their success to them as eggs! That air of it had an influencing quality, which gave people aspirations and motivation. Whoever stood on its soil imagined himself to be a superstar. Moreover, why will they not feel so? It was badly true that it had that magic which could turn an ordinary man into a star overnight!

A city of dreams or a city of fashion, none can ever hate living in it. Even the common "*dabbawalas*" who had been a speciality of it were millionaires in themselves. This was that uniqueness in it, everyone was rich; Prosperity used to begin from the residents of hundred storey apartments of *Worli* to the small slums of *Sion*. Where the multinational companies and the filthy huts of low class people shared the common roads, where the billionaires parked their cars and preferred to travel by local trains to avoid long hours of traffic and where twenty-four hours were much lesser for them to hunt their imaginings.

She went straight and hugged her grandparents who had been waiting outside the airport since an hour. She loved them tremendously, because they loved her more than anyone did. She was an apple of their eyes, and they always missed her the most. Her grandfather was a retired officer from the army and was a disciplinarian who covered a huge respect in her eyes. He was the one who taught her to speak and to walk as she lived mostly with them when she was small. Getting well with all the relations, he was an obedient son, an adorable brother, a doting husband and an unsurpassed father. All his qualities made him an idol of all his grandchildren, which were ten in toto. Being the most religious person, he kept his faith above all the human aspects and had a firm belief in the Almighty, the most beneficial and exalted. His knowledge in every facet no matter which language, which religion or which issue was the most extensive. From the reigns of the Roman Empire to the histories of small towns like Amravati and from the rules of the new British English to the local politics of Nations, he had it all! It was a mind, which was one of its kinds as those years in which Asoka lived to the rise of Nazism; he knew their years of occurrence by heart.

And her grandmother who was far more intelligent than every one really thought. Her major interests just lied in shopping, travelling, and looking after herself. She was a woman of Mumbai! Always fast, always ready to go anywhere and an open-minded person although she belonged from a small town in Haryana! She was one of those kinds who never used to think much before doing or saying something. She did whatever she liked and used to hate cooking and housekeeping and her mind was never into being religious. She was just enjoying her life largely in her small family with her husband and her son who was a bachelor. It seemed as if her grandpa used to offer namaz and read verses for her too, as he always did it in an extreme manner. They had a typical love marriage; he had gone to see Haryana and there his eyes were just stuck on a girl who was as simple as a drop of water. She was sixteen and he was twenty- four. There were no troubles in their love, like a determined brave heart, he directly went straight to her father and asked for her hand. Her father was too impressed with him as he had that quality to impress everyone in a single glimpse and so they were together for fifty years, and the best part was that love had not died. They romanced, they shouted, they cried and they convinced. Like that couple which enjoys the first few months of any new relationship and they had spent so many years doing so. They were madly in love with each other; a perfect case of being each other's better halves, it was.

They were different undeniably but they were one. They had different choices and priorities, yet they could not set apart each other. They truly justified that opposites do attract one another. The thing, which is highly needful, is to ignore the differences and appreciate the similarities.

Chapter 2

Click* click!

"You know, it is not coming nicely."

She texted him, as soon as she reached the Oberoi apartments of a posh locality of 'Lokhandwala'

"Have you reached?" he asked after two hours.

"Yes of course!" she replied.

"Okay, then show me your picture," he said.

"That is what I am saying that I am not looking good in the photo, so you can't see it. Hugh!" she messaged.

"Oho, just show, I will decide that. You look good anyhow, now send," he said.

"No, Okay, see," she replied and sent the picture. She was so scared and worried that she kept her phone on the silent mode and locked it. She did not have the courage to hear that sound of the message or even to open it. Having the least idea about his perception, she pressed the button of her phone and closed her eyes. She did not want to see that greenish sign of the message, which used to come on the left top of her phone. After a pause of ten seconds, she opened her eyes and saw it. Her heartbeats were growing faster and faster, and that feeling was not at all understandable. She had never feared so much in the past for just showing someone her picture. Finally, she had decided that she will unlock her phone to read his message. She gradually made the pattern to unravel the mystery of his thought process.

"Wow, Beautiful! Grey suits you so much," he had messaged just after she had sent the message and then he asked her repeatedly that where had she gone.

"Ya, I am here. Thank you!" she replied.

"Oh, so what are you doing? Well, send me the picture of your hands too; you have applied nail paint, right? I want to see."

At another moment, she sent the picture of her hands having yellow nail colour on her long nails.

"Great! You have such long nails."

'Whom are you talking to?" she heard.

"Me! No one. Just like that," she said in a rather nail biting way.

"What? Tell me." Mommy asked.

"Oh! Rehaam," she replied.

"Oh, Okay! Why do you talk to him?" she asked in a typical 'mother' tone.

"He's a friend and of course a future brother-in-law, you know."

"Ya, he is nice, isn't he? I saw him last on a general store, he was buying something. He didn't know me, but I knew him. He looks good *na*." Mommy said.

"You know he is asking, what has been cooked?"

"Ha-ha, he wants to know everything, I suppose. You must tell him then that there's chicken for lunch," she replied.

"He's mad! Well I will tell. Are we heading towards somewhere today?" she asked.

"Yes, we will go to Atria and then from there to your favourite place if time supports us."

"Oh, Okay, time will. I will get ready after lunch and this time we will leave until three else you know what happened last time on that road. Annie Besant gets heavy with traffic in the evening," she said.

"Okay, we will. Wear proper clothes, because Mumbai's heat is harmful, you will get a tan, so dress yourself accordingly and tell your sister too. By the way, where is she?" mommy asked.

"She has gone for swimming in the pool, you know, I suppose that is why she comes here," she said.

"Oh, why haven't you gone? Go and enjoy, why do you have to stare at your phone screen all day? Don't become so precocious day by day," she said.

"No, I am not, I am tired. Let her swim and why should I swim? I feel scared, so many alien species must be there, and so I will feel weird," she said.

Sea, it was. A sprawling water of Arabia she saw and those stones, which she admired the most. A point of 'Nariman' had been her most beloved and wanted place. It was the one of the lush ones, those high buildings of glass made her look over the top. She loved to hear the stories and the histories of each building, which had been in Colaba and the nearby places. Being seated on the raised ground just before those similarly shaped huge rocks, which were built by the English to reduce the effects of high tides, she glanced at that water which appeared black due to the illness of sunlight but still that reflection of moon and those glittery stars made it meaningful and gratifying. At that place, where nothing stopped, where nothing waited and where there was no silence, she found herself the most comfortable and secured. She thought that in a city like this where everything changes in a jiffy, there was something that never altered; its sea. As if, it had a life, it had seen every transformation of the place, from the initiation when the outsiders started building it then that 'Bombay' where streetcars were there and then that 'Mumbai', a town of 'Sachin Tendulkar', a place of films and the moneyed. A Sachin Tendulkar fan is ought to be in love with his city as she was. From swearing upon his straight drive shots to celebrating twenty fourth April, she did it all! Shahrukh Khan and Sachin Tendulkar were the two "S" acting and playing vitally for her.

"Mommy, when are we going to go to the hill road?" she asked.

"We will go there tomorrow, as the market might get closed till we reach there."

"No, today itself, I want to go to Mannat," she said.

"What? Is Shahrukh waiting for you?"

I do not know, but what if he comes out and waves, Can you imagine? And what if I faint? You said we will meet him, I think you are not that big fan of him, what say Akira?" she said.

"I am a bigger fan. I am seeing him, even when you were not in this world. Hugh! I don't know about you but if I faint then let him wake me up, you don't panic. But what if I don't faint? Well, I will pretend." Mommy replied.

"Mommy, pretend, really?" They laughed noisily.

"Well girls, I will ask your Nauman uncle to plan our meet with him. You know, how good his place is in the industry, I am sure he will do something. Today if we will go at his house, then of course we will not be able to see him nicely and he will think we are not his genuine fans. You know how cheap it is, to stand insanely in front of his house. I mean, that's not our thing. So we will meet him for a longer duration," she assured.

"No-No-No." Kyara pouted.

"Why don't you understand at once? Mommy is saying something, and we will have to do that. Stop arguing unnecessarily else we will not take you when we will meet him." Akira said.

"Oh, please! I will meet him first. But what am I going to say? Ha, I will sing a nice song for him and then he will marry me," she blushed.

"Marry you! Do you know your age? Break your castles. He will marry me because I am elder than you and maybe we will just have twenty- six years difference. You will have thirty three years difference." Akira laughed.

"Hugh! Age doesn't matter when there is true love, Okay," she said.

"Ha-ha. As you say, so his eldest son will be elder than you," she continued.

"Whatever! Don't irritate me. See mommy," she said.

"Okay, cut it." Mommy said.

"You know, I will meet my favourite 'THE SHAHRUKH KHAN'. Oh my god, I am badly eager," she messaged him.

"LOL Okay, great but why?" he asked.

That was a pretty unusual question, which was put before her. She thought that he would react in a different and a rather happy way but his stupid questions made her think a little.

"Did he just say why?" Baddie frowned.

"Why is little eerie. I don't think someone can need any reason to meet him. Don't you know I am his greatest fan?" she asked in an irritated mood.

"Ha-ha Okay, go on! What else?" he asked.

"He is just not interested." Good Elf said putting herself under the blanket.

She was round the bend about that one person. She used to stop even when a small interview of his came on the television. All his movies, from 'Deewana' to 'Jab tak hai jaan', were thoroughly learnt by her. All the chat shows, reality programmes and even that first serial in which he worked was seen by the little girl who had a dream of marrying him. Thinking about her married life with him, she was so illogical that when he got hurt artificially in the films, her tears fell. His hobbies were her hobbies, his favourite colour, she wore, and his favourite food, she ate. Whenever anyone talked about him, her ears used to get very active. She thought as if he was her personal property. Believing that she was deeply in love with that person without even knowing him, she liked him since her childhood but she was not that crazy for him from the start. She suddenly started liking him too much in those days. Everyone used to ask Kyara about his working schedule and future projects. She loved that attention which she gained when she informed everyone about him and was truly possessive about him. Liking him was deeply respected and she gave it a very high place in her colourful life. Being unaware of the meaning of love and devotion, she was with him in a certain way!

Four days had passed in the hush-bush of the city and finally the day had come when she was going to meet him. She dressed herself up in a grey jumpsuit and curled up her hair. Her hair was straight so she loved the curls in them and they always looked marvellously magnificent. She was so thrilled that she did not even know how to react. The meeting was fixed in the evening and she was ready at three.

Tring Tring!

"Hello!" Spoke mommy. "Hello, this is Nauman, how are you?" he asked.

"Hi! I am good, what about you?" she asked. "Ya, fine pretty much. Well, I was saying that today suddenly Shahrukh had to go out of town. Can I arrange the meeting tomorrow?" he asked.

"Oh, that's a bad luck. No, you cannot, as we will leave the city tomorrow morning. Well, maybe next time," she said in a sad tone.

"I am sorry, you know but next time I will tell you about his plans in advance so you arrange your arrival and departure accordingly,"

"Yes, better luck next time. Ha-ha. Well, wish me luck, as I have to deal with Kyara now. I know, she will not understand and begin to cry," she sighed.

He said, "Oh that is sad, well I will call you. Good-bye for now!"

"*Allah hafiz!* Take care," she stated.

"Akira and Kyara, come here!" She shouted.

"Yes mommy. How am I looking?" Kyara said.

"Beautiful! Like always. Akira, where are you?"

"Yes, I am here. What has happened?"

"Actually he is out of town and we are not meeting him today. Nauman uncle just called me and said so." Mommy said without pausing.

After hearing this, there was a sheer silence in the room for two seconds. None of the girls said anything and everyone was staring at each other. Even her grandparents were in a state of shock as they were more bothered about Kyara's reaction more than anyone else's. Didn't it seem like a classic Indian daily soap in which every character's faces are zoomed in with a standard sound of jolt and their bodies are shown from top to bottom when such a situation occurs?

"Kyara, don't begin to cry, I beg of you." Mommy said to end the silence.

She had already begun without thinking of anyone. It was an absolute heartbreak for her as it was her dream. A dream, which was in her mind for so many years and it had broken into small pieces in front of her eyes. She was so happy, the happiest actually. On cloud nine, she imagined herself to be. She even had thought that what she would do after seeing him. What would be her first sentence? What would be her expression? In addition, what kind of words would she use? She even framed her sentences. It seemed like an important, life-changing interview to her. She had thoroughly prepared herself up and that entire plan had just crashed. She was so sad that she cried and cried for the whole day. Everyone was sympathetic towards her but no one really could understand her pain. She did not know what to do. It was the worst day of her life, as she was just one-step behind meeting him. That was her biggest anguish. Being not able to meet her favourite superstar could make her feel so testing and upsetting. The biggest stress of her life until then was that. Immaturity was irrefutably personified, as she never wanted to be practical in her life. Level- headedness was missing somewhere, as she never imagined anything going not in her way. Everything had to be according to her needs and pleasure and even the slightest sadness affected her so much then. It was such an idiocy of her and that is why maybe god had to teach her something useful, something very functional and so there was a change. It had to occur to give a certain meaning to the existence and to make her know that life is not easy; it is a cluster of sniff, giggle, grumble, triumph, falls, and spite and at last love!

"Kyara! See who has come?" Akira smiled.

"Fiilliizz!" She shouted loudly.

"Kyyyaaaraaa." Filiz shouted even louder.

"Oh my god! How are you?" she said and ran to hug her tightly.

"Aww missed you so much. After one full year, I am seeing you. I am fine."

"I missed you too, so much. Where is Ayan? He was coming too, right? How are your in-laws? And Fila, why are you looking so slim, how?" she asked.

"Calm down! So many questions in one go. Let me answer now. Ayan has work so he could not come. Mom and dad are wonderful, I told you *na*, they have gone to Bangkok to my sister-in-law's house, and why am I looking slim, that I also don't know. Ayan teases always that I am looking fat, so I guess I have lost some weight because he makes me realise every day. You see words matter a lot," she laughed.

They continued their talks for constant three hours. It was six in the evening, when they decided to go to the beach and then for shopping. Filiz actually belonged from Bombay so she spoke very quickly in that 'bombayite' tone. Her sense of English was remarkable and she had a great taste in almost everything.

"Shopping or Shakespeare? Choose one." Filiz said.

"Though that is a tough one, I guess Shakespeare because the other one I did yesterday only." Kyara replied.

"Okay, then we will be going to the theatre. I have the passes of the play hamlet. Shall we go?" she asked.

"Of course, that will be such a great one. I have always wished to see all this but my city does not have such theatres." Kyara sighed.

"Oh, that is heartbreaking. So, we ought to make it before eight. Let us leave now as it will take half an hour to reach there," she added.

She had loved the drama of Hamlet as it had been like a dream for her to watch all those characters performing live on the stage in front of her eyes that she had read about. All those vivid dialogues, tempting costumes, and that whole atmosphere of that theatre was winning. It had engaged her in something, which was literary. She loved Shakespeare and his archaic words; she wanted herself to become like him one day. A writer, yes! That is what she wanted and the movies in which the leading lady was a writer inspired her to a great extent. She had all her mind into writing, but she asked herself over and over again that about whom would she write? Nature, life, profession, family, friendship, and maybe love were the topics in her mind. She was not that environmentalist, as she never paid so much attention to it. She just thought that nature was a natural thing which is god gifted and there is nothing special in it to exaggerate. Writing about life was a tough one for her because she had a perfect one. She never saw the bad side of it and she had a firm believe that god won't ever keep her in a tough situation due to her goodness. When she thought about writing about profession, it sounded funny as she was so small and she never really paid attention on it. She had a family, but writing about her family was too mainstream and her friendship, that was a good one but there was no reason for her to write about it. In truth, she did not enjoy doing so. She did not like writing about so random topics about which most of the best sellers write. According to her, they personified a lot and she did not have any good imagination to do so. The fact behind this was that she always got what she imagined or dreamed and she believed that a writer needed pain, tears and a little passion. She did not know of anything about which she was passionate. She could have written about her favourite actor but without any basis, she was unable to do so. She thought of love but there was no one in her beautiful life to make it more beautiful and truly, she did not even long for any kind of partner or a lover. She never really thought about all that stuff because she considered such relationships unlawful and she could not imagine troubling her family and lying to them just because of a single soul!

"Kyari, how are you, and where are you?" Rehaam sent.

"Yes, very good! I was with Filiz," she said.

"OK, did you meet your actor?" asked he.

"No, I couldn't. Some things went wrong and you know he is not in town and he will come tomorrow. Everything was messed up," she wrote with a crying emoticon.

"Oh, that was a miserable one, but why do you have to worry? I am sure you will meet next time, you know everything happens for our own good."

"Ya," she replied.

"Well, tomorrow the city will become more beautiful as before," he sent.

"Really why?" she asked in surprise.

"Fool! You will come here tomorrow to add on the beauty," he replied in a happy mood.

"Ha-ha Okay! You know, I have bought a gift for my best friend," she texted.

"Oh, for Amirah?" he asked.

"No, she is my sister."

"Then who? Me?" he asked.

"Yes. See you know, my bff."

"Ha-ha! What have you bought and what does bff mean?" he asked.

"Bff means best friend forever and gifts are not to be told before."

"Oh, I will wait till tomorrow. Marry me," he said suddenly and she never understood that statement so she asked rapidly in a rather shy and a furiously confused way, "What?" Baddie and elf were silent too, first time.

"Marry me!" He typed.

Make it funny Kyara. Baddie said exhaling.

"Ha-ha, then what will my sister do? You are so older than me, do you know?" she replied in a funny way and she never took that proposal solemnly because it was not at all grim. *"He's so mad. Maisha I need to tell you this."*

"Ha-ha Maisha will marry someone else, you marry me *na*. I am just seven years elder than you, it will be fine, right?" he wrote.

"Ha-ha, someone has gone mad. By the way will you wait for me until I grow up?" she asked in a serious way.

"Yes, of course! I will wait for you for my whole life."

"Ha, you will have to wait for ten years from now," she said.

Then he sent with a laughing emoticon, "Okay, I will. We will be in a relationship till then," he said.

"Such a long one! Ha-ha. What if you leave me?" she asked. *"He's getting serious and I hate it."*

"I will never leave you, I PROMISE," he said and a complete silence followed. She started thinking about this conversation, which she just had with a boy whom she called her friend. She did not know about the weightiness of it but suddenly she thought of its impossibility as it could never happen. He had to be her brother-in-law after marrying Maisha and she knew how sincere both of their relationship was.

She answered, "No, maybe in the next birth. We will marry, Okay?"

"Oh Okay, but I am waiting for the rest of my life."

"Ha-ha, no don't wait. Concentrate on Maisha. I am remembering Samar of my actor's film; you know he had waited for his love for ten years. You should also wait like him," she joked.

"Ha-ha. Okay! I will be like Samar," he replied and then they both went to sleep. She did not understand the precision at the rear of this behaviour of him and she liked all that without any complaints. She was being so much attached to one person as if she was alone before him and he, he just flew with the flow! He trusted her so much so that even she had become an important part of his busy life. In his thought process, after Maisha, her sister's thought came or maybe even before Maisha, he did care about his new relationship, which had some boundaries, had some walls. He was a brotherly friend first, but somewhere inside he wanted to know every little detail of her. Wanting her to talk to him every time and give him the account of pettiest facet, an attraction or enticement was seen in his attitude and no one could know why that feeling came. A feel of concern, an idea of longing, an itch of getting closer and a yearn of that tiny girl who did not even know the meaning of all this because she had never experienced an ache for anyone, was boiling in his heart. Undoubtedly, she also liked him within the boundaries indeed. Any other idea never flickered in her mind or even if it did, she erased that because she knew that for him, she is a best friend and just a sister nothing more. Both of them had been confused and they were not able to grip the outlandish feelings, which they both were subjected to.

The next very morning she had reached her city, which had waiting for her. She never liked that place much and always cursed it because she thought that it was too boring and slow. She accepted that there were no clothes of her level in the outmoded markets of the city, which had more cows than shops and she hated going in places, which had Indian clothes. She had a very dissimilar view about Indian dressing sense, as it was too defunct and behind the times. What is the need to cover the whole body when there are shorter clothes, which make you look prettier and smarter? That was her question to all those who just dressed traditionally and she unknowingly regarded such as outdated and people who do not know to match up with their surroundings and society.

She was all focusing on that gift which she had brought for her most special. She just wanted to give it to him at the very second she reached there. Nothing really had made her electrified so much before as that photo frame which did not have his picture but it was of brown colour and had a boyish essence. Packed up in a rectangular box of the same shade, it was tied up with a ribbon of blue with the dots of purple.

"Come and take your present now," she messaged.

"Now?" he asked.

"Yes! Come quickly," she replied.

"Okay, I am coming till eleven."

In that wait of twenty minutes, she was panicking so much as though she had to experience some war at eleven. Her hair was wet and she had her pink pants on with a mismatching t-shirt. In that long time, she had to change her upper and she was so confused about them. She quickly decided to wear a purple inner inside with a grey shrug out. That was a total fashion disaster and she had no idea about it. She was concerned for sure, but all she wanted at that moment was to see him, after six days which were like six ages! He came at that time which had been specified and she ran down the stairs carrying that pinkish paper bag which was so enchantingly cute. She went to his white, lavish car and she again started seeing down. Urging her hair to go behind her right ear, which were not ready to move, she walked fast. He just looked casually at her wearing his white shirt and having short gelled hair of a different hair style. She handed it to him and they both looked at each other and smiled.

"How do you like it?" she asked uneasily after an hour.

He said, "I love it! It is so cool. I will put a picture of both of us in it. Thank you sweetie,"

"Ha-ha, picture of both of us! And then what will your mommy think?"

"I will tell her that I am marrying you," he replied.

"She will kill me then."

They talked and talked and talked all day long. His day started with her and her day ended with him. There was no topic of this world about which they both hadn't shared their thoughts. He knew everything about her and she was aware of each fact of his life. They had become so close that it never appeared that Kyara was so younger than him. Time was passing and they were getting closer and closer day by day. Sometimes Kyara did find his questions very informal and eerie but the comfort level which they both shared with each other was rising higher. They had somewhere forgotten that the world knew them as having a relationship of 'brother and sister'. They had a different relation between them which did not have any name and of course it couldn't have any because he was with someone else and that someone was her own so called sister. Their liking was actually expanding and they were getting carried away. Sinking in the desires of two different souls, they did not really know anything. They couldn't stop themselves and in point of fact, he couldn't break off. He did not know but was he in love? How could he be in love? Was this really love? He had no thought of leaving his would be fiancée and be with a girl who was so small, who was so immature and who had not even begun her life. All he knew was that he liked her and that was not a simple kind of fondness for a girl though it had some meaning which was odd.

"Don't you think we are getting too close?" he asked.

"Yes," she replied in a hesitant manner.

"Ha-ha you are my sister," he said.

"Ha-ha yes!" she said.

"Then, just a sister?" he asked and Kyara was expecting that but was a little shocked but calmed from within.

She replied, "Yes, what else? You are my best friend."

"Just a best friend?" he asked and she had no little thought that why was he questioning so much. "Hmm yes," she replied but she did not want to reply that way but at the same time she did not want herself to be shown as a too quick responding girl.

"Maybe more than friends?" he said in a serious way and at that time she was dealing with shocks in her heart and her heart beat was running like a jaguar.

"*Why do you say this?*"

"Hmm," she replied.

"Actually we are everything. You know, we behave as if we are in a relationship we talk as if we are married and sometimes we behave as if we are siblings," he joked.

"Ha-ha seriously, what is wrong with us?"

"I don't know about us, but something is really wrong with me. I need a psychiatrist."

"Yes! Do visit one. Even I need. We must go together," she replied normally.

"Together? No, my problem will increase if I will see you."

"*Goodnesssss!*" Baddie and Elf cried.

"Haw, why? Am I a problem?" she asked.

"Na, just understand. So from now, are we everything?"

"Are you kidding me?" she asked in a severe manner.

"Why would I? Hugh," he replied.

"Ha-ha how can we be everything?"

"Listen, we are already," he said in an exasperated mood.

"*Did he order me?*"

"What?"

"Everything," he wrote again. "And I hope you keep your phone till yourself. If anyone gets to know our stupid talks, we both will get killed."

"Yes, of course! By the way let me sleep now."

"No, send me your picture first."

"No. I'm in bed. Lights are off."

"Hugh! You don't even listen. I am angry now," he sent with sad emoticons.

"Oh god! Wait I will give. Mad person," she clicked and sent her picture.

"Wow!" he replied.

"It is bad. You know I have to oil my hair now and mommy is asleep. Now who will oil?" she asked.

"Don't worry, I will."

"Ha-ha how will you? Come now and do for me."

"Should I?" he questioned.

"You have gone mad, I am sleeping now. Good night!"

"Okay, I will sleep too, good night!"

"Good morning pretty! No electricity, are you awake?" he messaged at eight in the morning. She kept on sleeping and she saw his text after an hour.

"Does he even sleep?"

"Yes yes, I have woken up. Here too, no electricity. Hugh!"

"So, did you think?" he asked.

"What?"

"About me?"

"Excuse me?" she replied abruptly.

"So maybe about your favourite actor, you do think about him all the time, right?"

"What are you saying? Is it a game?" she asked sharply.

"No! Did you have breakfast," he asked in order to change her mood. She answered, "No, I am still half asleep, did you have?"

"Yes, I had 'potato sandwich and mango milk shake," he replied.

The sun had taken its place straight above and shadows of her curtains were falling on her face. She was jovial to feel that feeling which was new to her, which made her feel more beautiful as time passed. Someone who was not even known by her was all she wanted. Her happiness began to lie in his dim-witted questions, his simplicity to lead his life, his humourless statements and his infinite care for her.

It was in the evening when her pink nail colour was still wet, she thought to talk to him, but did not want to message him first. Alike that typical girl's character, she never messaged him first and the saddest part was that even he did not say anything.

"Listen listen listen! You know what?" he texted immediately.

"Yes, what?" she asked.

"I am so happy. You know, my mom just had a great talk with Maisha. She just told me that she loved her and wants to meet as soon as she comes back. Isn't this wonderful?" he said happily.

"Oh, that's so nice! Wait I will just talk to Maisha. I will be right back. I am so excited to know," she replied.

"Maisha, are you there? I heard something big. Did you talk to your would be mother-in-law? Wow, sounds so great. What did she say? How was it? Oh my god, I am much more anxious now," she messaged her.

"Yes Kyara, calm down first. You know, she is such a mild and an easy going person. First I was a little worried but then she comforted me with her normal talks about food and travel. She told me that Rehaam is so shy in front of her and he doesn't say anything if she doesn't ask." Maisha messaged.

"Really? That is a good start. What else did she say?" she asked.

"She asked about my return and invited me to her house and said to give my mother's number to her. Isn't this going too fast?" she replied.

"Indeed, it is. I am so happy for both of you. Now quickly give the number and maybe you get married this year only," she said.

"Ha-ha! This year, NOWAYS! I am so young now. Well, can I catch up later! I am getting a call of him, bye!" Maisha said.

"Should I ask something?" he messaged her after an hour.

"Yes, of course," she said.

What he asked was the most life changing question for her and maybe she never knew that he would be concerned so much about her feelings. That question came up so suddenly and it was of the essence. The main motive behind it is still not known. If it had not been asked, the whole figure would be a contrast of what is it. The most amusing thing ever asked to her which changed everything. It is such an irony that people search for meanings and answers all their life. They change places, they change people, they change relations and they even change themselves. Only a few fortunate people succeed in their search but most of them, not come up to scratch. Do they know that if they empathize, they can even find an image of god in a soul created by him?

"Are you happy?" he asked.

A five minute silence was there between them. She did not say anything then because she herself did not really know what it was. According to the regulation, she ought to be happy. She was her sister and she had always searched for her happiness in Maisha. It was one of the most special days of her, and Kyara had to be a part in her celebration. She was wonderstruck for a moment as she had gone insane. She had no idea of her reply but Rehaam was keen to know her reaction as in some way, his future too depended on her answer.

"Happy? In what sense?" she asked as if she did not know what he was asking.

"You know in what sense," he said.

"No, tell me, I don't," She replied hastily.

"Hmm, my mom has talked to my future wife so are you happy?" he asked again.

"Yes, why not?" she said at once.

"Oh, Okay," he said.

Listening to some music, she was just trying to smile but was unable to. That was a happy song of her favourite and then she got up and started dancing in her room with her head phones on. A peacock dances, when it gets those showers of blessing from the lord. Therefore here it was not a dance of bliss rather a rapid ballet of despair and gloominess. She did not talk to anyone at that time, not even Rehaam. She wanted to share her heart with Amirah but she had just gone to Mecca for *Umrah*. Filiz was her another option but then she thought that why should she discuss it with anyone and trouble all? It was her look out and after few hours, she was a little fine but then she did not want to talk to him to add more to her sadness. She was poignant and she felt like crying but then it was such a baffle for her to experience such kind of feeling first time. She was sharp enough to think to give time to herself and convince her mind that it was not the way she supposed it to be and it could be all right.

Chapter 3

Next day was a Friday when Rehaam had told her that he would be busy till two of the clock as for the special namaz of the best day. Kyara could easily think that how religious he was! He never missed to pray five times a day whereas she had not even done ablution once in so many years. She told everyone about his values and ideas about his religion. He showed himself to be a model of deep faith which she highly treasured.

"Am I in paradise?" screamed Akira. "Ha-ha, please." Kyara rolled her eyes.

"You are wearing proper clothes; I mean *Salwar Kamiz*! How?"

"Okay, now don't be so astonished. I wore it two years back too, if you remember in an *Iftaar* party. Leave all that, you tell that how am I looking?" she asked.

"Marvellous! Why don't you tie a sideward braid?"

"Hmm, thinking to! But NO, that I just can't," she said suddenly remembering his taunts on such type of hairdo.

"Why but? That could have looked good." Akira said.

"Well, no reason! I am in no mood; I will just tie a pony," she said. "As you wish, just come out and show everyone your change. I am sure, you need a doctor." Akira said.

"Will you leave?"

"Guess what am I wearing?" she texted.

"Mm, show me your picture," he answered.

"Oh so curious to see me always,"

"No, first tell me."

"Okay, but I don't know. You tell me."

"Indian!" she wrote.

"Wow! Show me."

She clicked her picture in that yellow outfit and sent it to him. He loved it and then she asked him to give his picture. He then sent his picture and all it looked like a game. 'Photo sharing' one! She could never take her eyes off those eyes and she stared at them for minutes. That white jacket was adding to his appeal and his eyes were brown but they were appearing to be dark blue. He had slightly brought his lashes closer and looked as if there was sunlight which made him powerless to open them wide. He never really smiled but gave an obvious look every time. It seemed as if he was actually in front of her. He looked at her in a very different way which his eyes could state. They did bring out certain things which his lips did not. Alike a that deep well of his feelings set on his left, those eyes were a source to show them up to people who had a curtain on their eyes but she could see as she knew him in every way and at the back of her mind, she was unknown of her rightness.

"You look..." he messaged after some time.

"What?" she asked surprisingly.

"Beautiful. You know, you look like a baby. There is an innocence which is the most appealing in you," he said.

"Ha-ha thanks and you look too good. Maisha is so lucky," she said. *"Phew! What did I just say to him?"*

"Kyara, I was thinking about you all the time and why did not you talk to me yesterday," he asked.

"I slept too soon," she replied uneasily.

"Have you noticed that you are too bad in lying? Tell me, did I do something or am I thinking rightly?" he asked.

"Ahmmmm, what are you thinking?" she asked in a scurry.

"Well, you have to be honest in this case. Promise?"

"Okay, what are you thinking?" she typed.

"See, I told you that Maisha talked to my mom and you did not like it. Now accept it as you have promised."

"Hmm," she wrote as she did not really know how to respond to his open enquiry.

"Be definite and tell me," he sent.

"Yes, I did not like and I did not sleep early because even I was thinking about you and I don't know the reason behind all this. I have never experienced such a query in these years and I don't know what is wrong with me. I am sorry if I hurt you but you asked me and so I have told the truth."

"Some evil spirit has gone inside me which makes me say all this. Hugh!"

"Mad girl! Why are you sorry? Even I am going through all this. I am unable to think about anyone else because you cover whole of my mind. You know what it is?" he asked in a serious tone.

"No!" she typed at once. *"It is very much."*

"Well, then know it."

"You are getting married and I don't think we need all this. We are friends, Okay? And if this is going to happen so let us not talk."

"HUH! It seems as if you are the only one. Let me tell you I am in the same problem and you cannot deny that you like me. But if you don't want to talk then I am no one to force you, bye!" he wrote angrily

"That capitalisation!"

"Stop being angry, I like you and yes you are no one to tell me to talk to you or not. The fact is that all this is totally funny," she sent.

"Hmm, it is not funny. It is about us. Why are not you understanding? Look, I like you!"

"I can sense his tone."

"I understand but how can it happen? I mean you are so elder," she laughed.

"That does not matter. So what do you understand tell me? You are big enough and you should sort it out."

"Are we in love?" she messaged and threw her phone on her bed. She was cold and started breathing heavily. She had no courage to open up her phone and see what his reply was. Being horrified by the thought of his answer, she trembled for a while. She was eager to switch her phone on and after a few seconds, she saw!

"I am in love with you."

Those songs of Hindi romantic movies started up in her head and she smiled like a complete idiot seeing herself in the mirror. She had no idea of her reply but she had never felt so much happiness in the past. It was like a joy jolt which made her feel to be the luckiest and the prettiest girls of all. She started humming and then realised something which was unacceptably true!

"Maisha! What about her? Am I mad? No, this cannot happen. Oh my god, what should I do?"

"Say something please," he texted.

"Maisha!" she replied.

"Hmm, do I have to cheat on her for us?" he asked.

"Cheat? Did he use that? If he can cheat on her then he can cheat on you too, in future." Her inner devil, Baddie wearing a black and red dress with dark lips cried. *"Go away, you baddie."*

"Of course not, her happiness matters more than mine. You know, how much I love her and this is cheating and it is wrong."

"Kyara, I don't really know what to say. I did not know that all this will happen. Tell me, do you love me?" he asked.

"Do I love this man?" She asked to herself.

"*You have fallen for him. He will make your life a torture.*" Baddie laughed.

"*You love him Kyara! There's no right and wrong in love. In it, everything is fair. You're getting your love. Don't miss it!*" Good Elf whispered.

"This is wrong," she agreed with Baddie and ignored Good Elf.

"Yes, but maybe it is not. I am so happy, I love you!" he said.

"Hmm, I don't know. Maybe," she replied and smiled. "*You win Good Elf!*"

That remarked the day in the history of this world of love where it has always been easier to start any relation but not so cool to carry on with it. Two people who get attracted to each other in many ways that cannot be said to be in love while it has a much deeper meaning. This miserable time when all have become so less altruistic and egocentric think that talking all the time or meeting too frequently or even living with each other makes their love truer. It is a wit that if they see their lover once in dreams, they imagine everything. They have given love certain boundaries and a rule book which all need to tag along. It ought to begin at this then it should come at that point and when it comes to something bad, then just end it up. It seems like a humour where love begins and ends in some time. They say, "They were in love." But it was not known that love could be of the past and if it was, then it was not really. Some show an upright tomfoolery to mistake it for longing while it just doesn't consist of few steps but it defines itself to be a step towards a much meaningful life. These four letters which come on every mouth thousand times a day seem to be unfussy and effortless but only some feel it rightly. Love just doesn't happen between two people of different genders but it has its meaning when that mother who has carried the child for so long, loves it without seeing. It is when that father who has been ill, works for an extra hour just to get a pleasing present on his son's sixteenth birthday. When that grandmother feels dissatisfied when her granddaughter does not eat food and isn't god the loveliest exemplar of love as he does everything for our own good? Why the love of the lover is considered the greatest? We need someone to complete us, and god himself has parted us in this world so that we find our soul mates on our own and humans are designed to be in love with everything! Everyone goes through that mystifying phase when we feel as if we are flying high, we don't sleep and just think about that one person who rules on our mind and body and even if we sleep then the dreams appear to be boring than the reality. We imagine them around us all the time and when we see them, we just smile as if it is the first time. Love is just not a feeling but it is a way of life which works towards our betterment as it comes. Everyone is trying to correctly define it, but it is something which is beyond the words consisting of twenty six alphabets. It occurs and changes the person, makes him an angel or mistakenly a devil too. Sometimes at the right time with the wrong one and rarely with the right one at the off beam stage. It can be another word of inanity as we don't know what we are doing and how it should be and it just goes on and on. Few people know how to live with it while some just make fun of it by saying to each other that how much they love but it is unexplainable in real. Those pointless definitions of gifting stars and hanging moon on the windows or sending red roses every day; is this it? It lies in small bits of our living, maybe it increases when we need someone to bear us in our worst and appreciate in our best. Not really a gift, as it is impossible but laying on the grass all night just to gaze at those sparkling balls of fire and trying to figure out each other in them. When that one changes everything by their presence and when those two eyes meet then this world stops the rotation.

Her love was at the beginning and it was as magical as any other love but she never found out how important it was to her so early. She was cherishing every moment with him and everything had become more perfect in her perfect life. Rehaam was the one who never liked Kyara to change for him as he loved her without conditions or demands. They laughed, they fought, they teased and they loved! She knew that she loved him but still, was it love? Couldn't it be an attraction or a simple liking which could have an end? Lost in his thought, she woke up and there he was too striving to sleep but that one image took turns in his mind. They were involved with each other a bit too much as if, there was a single soul in two frames.

Long text conversations, low volume phone calls, frequent pictures and two video calls, this made up their day. It was like a fairy tale where there was no sadness or no villain but just a hero who had a beautiful heroine and their love story which was being endlessly lovely but there was someone whom she did not think of, but he did. He loved Maisha and he loved Kyara too. Was that possible? How can a person love two people at the same time? How could he think of that? Kyara's mind did have many questions like this but she never paid any heed to them because her importance lied in her love. She felt sad that she was wrong and she shouldn't have done this to her most valuable sister but it was unfair to blame her for everything. She never knew that she would fall in love with her sister's future husband and it was a two sided relation. It was dire to think of this love triangle which suddenly happened without any depiction.

"Hey love! What are you doing?"

. "Nothing much, you say," she replied.

"Me? Missing you. We did not talk since morning. I was busy as some guests have come from Shimla," he typed.

"Oh!"

"What has happened? You are sounding dull baby," he asked lovingly.

"Hmm, I was thinking something."

"Tell me quickly, what is wrong?" he asked.

"You will marry Maisha and then?" she wrote in fear.

"Then what?" he replied

"Then, what will happen? Will you leave me?" she asked.

"HUH! Don't even think of all this now. After my marriage too we will be the same, I have told you already," he sent.

"He wants to have an extra marital affair! I didn't know that Himachal people were so broad minded."

She asked, "How can this be possible? You will get married, then you will not have much time for me, you know I fear it will end," she sent sadly.

"Don't say that *na*. I will always have time for my cutie pie. Whenever you will say, I will meet you and it is going to be the same. Marriage won't change anything and I will be yours forever."

"Well, that time will tell," she typed smiling.

"And then we will go to so many places together. You know I saw you in my dream last night. It was so wonderful," he wrote.

"Really, what you saw?"

"No, I won't tell," he replied timidly.

"Why? See I was in it, tell me now," she asked crossly.

"Ha-ha. Curious girl! We had gone to Goa, you know."

"Then what happened?" she asked willingly.

"It was so much fun. We were at the beach and it was all empty, just both of us."

"So romance at its best form in the dream,"

"Oh nice! Did you see my clothes, what was I wearing?" she asked hopefully.

"Mmm, I guess a skirt. You looked soooooo...... good!"

"Oh! So I want to go there. I wish it gets true!"

"Ya, so we both will go," he stated.

"How can we go alone?"

"We will," he said unintentionally.

"Hmm, no!" she replied.

"Why? You don't want?" he sent with a sad emoticon.

"I do, but how can us, you know, go alone?" she asked hesitantly.

"Oh, not even if I marry you?" he said and then her beats increased as if somewhere he did want to get married to her but was not able to or there could be some other reason. He was an unpredictable personality and no one could ever understand him fully, not even Kyara. He was a pleasing gentleman in everyone's eyes. For Maisha, he was amorous and thoughtful but heated at some points. For his family he was a small child who was treated as an unripe fruit. For others, a total business person and Kyara, without understanding him, without seeing his all sides, without knowing anything of his past and future, she had just started considering him her world which at first was bright but isn't it destructive if we go in the depths of making that one person everything?

"Marry? Ha-ha. Have you thought to marry twice?" she asked jokingly.

"We will go there, we will get married and then if you want to get rid of me after that, you can."

She hated that statement of his and asked, "Getting rid of you or will you like to get rid of me?"

"He's mine and he's not mine. What is he?"

"What are you saying? Just a joke, it was. Let us change the topic. I love you!"

"Oh my flatterer!"

"Hmm," she typed.

"What? Are you angry? I am sorry baby, it was a joke. Why would I get rid of you? You know, you are everything," he texted and then she smiled.

Quite some days had passed when he was hers and she was his. They did forget something which was in their lives but seemed to be overlooked. Their story had just begun and it was not appearing to discontinue but things cannot come up in our support always. At times the angels of fate want something diverse which cannot be comprehended by the uncomplicated psyche of helpless humans who are tied under the sturdy ropes of fortune.

"Aren't you going to the airport?" asked her mommy.

"Airport? Why?" she asked without looking at her.

"Oh god, what is wrong with you? I had told you in the morning that your sister is coming back from Paris tonight. So tell me, will you go?" asked mommy irritably.

"Oh, ya," she said softly and feared a little. She stopped talking to him at that very moment and thought modestly. She could never know the reason of that slight thought of fright which had just crossed her mind. That sister, whom she loved the most, was coming back after so long and there was no ecstasy in her heart. The incentive at the back of this was indubitably Rehaam, but then she thought that was her beautiful sisterhood so weak that it could change her sentiments for her most treasured girl? At once, she had decided that whatever happens, whosoever comes, no one can change their relationship with each other. Her golden heartedness made her realise that Maisha was her dearly loved sister and her feelings would never change for her at any rate.

"I know, I love him the most in this world, but I love my sister more than myself. I can never come between them, they will get married happily and I will be pleased because my sister will be happy with him and he will be happy too. It all starts and ends at his happiness."

"Mommy, I will go. Is Akira going?" she shouted.

"No, she is not." Mommy said.

"We will be going to her house for the sleepover. Okay Kyara?" Akira stated.

"Yes why not? That will be excellent."

"Kyaraaa, how are you. Oh my god! Missed you." Maisha said.

"Hey, I hope that bag is for me or did you just buy for yourself, Hugh." Kyara replied.

"Oho, it's all for you. Let us get home. At least do not begin here. By the way, what is cooked? I am so deadly hungry and dying to have home-made food," she said.

"Ya, just eat and become an elephant. You know, you and Amirah are same." Kyara said.

"Oh ya, has she come back from Mecca?" she asked.

"Nah, in five days, she will," she said.

"Oh, so you are alive without her? You know, Rehaam was saying to come to the airport, but it would have been so embarrassing. He is really mad. I wonder is he going to like his things, which I have got." Maisha excitingly told.

"Oh, what have you got for him?" she asked uneasily.

"Well, some formals as he wears them more often, two watches though he hates and few perfumes for his family. In fact I have got two pair of shoes for his mamma and a clutch."

"Wow! Nice!" she spoke.

"So our Maish is already behaving like a married woman. See she thinks so much about her in-laws." Akira taunted as they reached home.

"Ha-ha." A perfect example of a fake laugh was shown who had become cheerless to know that someone else had bought presents for someone on whom she thought to have complete authority. Possessiveness is a damaging emotion which not only destroys us mentally but also socially. The most heinous fact was that despite of loving him so much, she could never show her love publicly. Even if, it would last forever, it has to be hidden as if it is a lie or an erroneous thing. The joy of talking about him to everyone would never be felt by the little girl, who had stupidly planned all her future with that person whom she could not even call her own.

Those in-laws who were someone else's would never be hers because she would not have any relation with them. That mother, whom she had never met, but just heard about, had a very distinct place in her life. She always thought that how lucky was she to have born the one who means life to her. The parents of that quite nonsensical love of her were the most blessed in her sight because if they had not been there so Rehaam would never come in this world for her. This impression on her understanding could not be explained or underscored. The thing was, she did not know his family, but still she loved them immensely because they were 'his' people and the hitch was that despite of being considerate about them, she could build no relation with them by any means.

The next morning had come up with another source of help in the psychological and the emotional growth for her. She could have never imagined herself to be in such a query which not only changed her but also increased her level of patience at a point.

"Good morning," she wrote to him at ten. His last checked time was too before, at eight in the daylight.

"Kyara and Akira what are the plans? Would you like to recommend any movie to me?" Maisha said brightly.

"No plans." Akira yawned.

"Recommendation of movie? Are we going? Wow!" Kyara said unexpectedly.

"Owe! Not really we. Actually I wanted to go with Rehaam. You know, it has been so long and he is being furious."

"Furious? He never gets furious when you don't meet him." Baddie sighed.

Ha-ha. So guys, any new movie? Actually I had no touch with cinema there, so don't know any new release." Maisha said with pride.

"Get out of here. NOW!" She spoke to herself rubbing her forehead.

"I don't know, ask Akira. I will just get back in minutes." She said in a low pitched, dull voice and got out of the room to avoid the conversation. She saw her phone and there was no answer from him which made her feel too snappy.

"Kyara, see this is for him, and family. How is it?" Maisha asked.

"Very good," she replied.

"So we are going at two. I wish you both could have joined but I guess, he would mind. Some another time," she said in a weird tone.

"He will mind my presence. Could anyone say anything worse than this?" Baddie said with a knife in her hand.

"No, we don't want to join either. By the way, I am going back as I am being so bored here. I have to do my homework. So Maish, we will catch up later and yes, enjoy to the core," she said sarcastically.

"In fact, I will directly come at your house after the film. What's say?" she said.

"Sure! So we are leaving." Akira ended.

'Seeing your love, love someone else.' What could be worse for that powerless girl who could not do anything to stop all this which was affecting her in so many ways? At a point, she thought that she should not mind these minute things, but without wanting, without asking for and without permitting, they were causing her a huge distress. Sometimes, it is fine if a boy cheats on his girl for someone else and that girl is unknown of everything. I put that unfamiliarity and mystery much above than that specified and heard issue. At least, it does not ruin the life of someone who sees its love with someone else. It requires a lot of tolerance and a great deal of devotion to live in that way. She was literally dying somewhere inside, because despite of her endless love, at the end, she had to share him with her own blood relative!

It is well if that person is matured enough for such dealings, but irony is that she did not even cross sixteen and the world's exertion was on her small shoulders which did not even grow fully till that time. Her inner beauty was something which was beyond the humanism and supreme mannerism. Controlling all her dark emotions, she started focusing on how much she really loved him and love made her serenity and poises superlative and matchless.

"Yes, Kyari," he sent in the evening.

"Hmm. Got time?" she replied.

"My Baddie is still with a knife."

"Han."

"Good for you. Don't text me now."

"Ha-ha. You are angry because I went with Maisha. Right?"

"Was that a tantrum? What are you up to?"

"Oh my god! What kind of person are you? Is this a game? Why would I be angry? The fact is that I am your nothing and she, everything. Please understand this as soon as possible because if both of us will delay then I fear, this world will become a tough place to live in. Get it," she wrote at once.

"Hmm, don't be so angry na. Send me your picture," he said tranquilly and she sent a big no.

"Mr. Ice wants my picture at this time of war?"

"Huh fine. Bye," he sent.

"I suppose, I was angry."

"Why?" she asked.

"No, I do not want to talk."

"Then I am sending the picture, you send too. Let me see how my cutupie is looking," she said lovingly.

"Ha-ha! What is that?" he asked.

"Your new nick name. My cutuuuuuu..." She sent.

"Nice. Click click then I will."

"Kyara! Kyara! Kyara!" Maisha shouted.

"Yes, I am here. Why are you shouting so much?"

"Leave all that see this. See our pictures of today," she said showing to her and she did not even have a look of them and suddenly said, "Perfect. I will just go and get water for you," she said while walking.

Maisha and Akira talked for a while about Paris, Eifel, markets, parks and hotels. Kyara wanted to join the chatter but then she thought that if they would get to the topic of 'Rehaam and Maisha', 'his family' or something linked with him, she would once more begin to feel difficult and discomfited. Then she went in her room and soundlessly began to read a new book 'laughter tricks' and in five minutes, she received a message from the Delhi girl!

"Kyaraaaa," she texted.

"Filaaaaaa," she replied enthusiastically.

"What are you doing? We did not talk since yesterday. How?" she sent in surprise.

"Just started with a new book. Yes, we didn't. What an unpropitious thing *na*?" she sent with a laughing emoticon.

"Yes, totally. By the way, which book?" she asked.

"Laughing tricks by Emma Bartolini. Isn't the author's name enticing?" she wrote.

"Yep, it seems to be. So how is it going? I mean is it a tale or really some tips and tricks are given?" she replied.

"Hmm, truthfully, it can be a sheer source of one's boredom."

"Really, then why are you wasting the time in it? I am reading 'Did I know Tin' of Roberto Tisdale. It is a mystery, going pretty well until now."

"Whoa! It sounds secretive," she added.

"Beautiful little girl." Suddenly came on her chat bar.

"Yes, where is my thing?" she asked to him.

"You just sent me your thing," he taunted.

"Aaa, your picture will be my thing. You are so mad."

After two minutes he sent, "Look."

"Ooh, nice that is. Why do you always click your pictures in the mirror? I just want to see your face, I mean click from the front camera," she ordered.

"Ok, as you say," he said and sent a mind blowing picture after some wait of few minutes. He had worn a white- shirt in that picture again which had to be of his night suit as it was a sleeveless one. He was not so dark like other macho men but not even that fair which mostly girls hate. A boy has to be darker than the girl and he had that tint like wheat. Not so broad from above, he had left his exercises for few days due to work. His left eyelids were brought closer which could make one to close his eyes forever and his right eye, that was wide open and both of them were looking at the camera and she felt as if he was looking at her directly and he was not somewhere else but right in front of her and looking her starry-eyed. His hair was not gelled like always but they stood straight without touching his small forehead. His nose seemed the same but she could make out a tiny difference in it as it was somewhat leaning towards the right and was puffed in and his slightly dark pink lips which had no particular shape but were broad and they were not smiling but were together as though they were spell bound and words and smiles were lesser to convey his gratitude and devotion for her. His whole personality depicted his innocence and virtuousness dissimilar to those guys who thought themselves to be too over confident. Despite of living in the twenty second year of his, he still looked as if he was just a sixteen year old school boy who was stubborn, readily following the footsteps of his father and new in love! Someone was just needed to recognize him, to comprehend every beat of his heart and to complete him. His splendour could be seen by the whole world's eyes, but god made that one heart along with him which was his but couldn't be called so.

She was falling in love with him more and their closeness was being personified as time passed. They knew each other and loved from the bottom of every particle of their heart and being ready to cross all the boundaries, they were neglecting the whole world.

"To see him was her only desire and to feel her was his lone thrill. They were in love truly but it was intensely immoral for all!"

Ultimately that day for which she had been waiting for had started and Amirah's flight was landing at sharp four in the evening. Nothing could lesser her anxiety of meeting her sisterly friend after such a stretch. She was in her cheery mood and was dying to go to the airport to pick her up. As she stayed near to Amirah's house, everyone thought of her to stay at home and make some fruit drink for the family's greeting. She was dropped at her home by two in the afternoon and her house was actually loaded with people. Three sisters of her father along with their husbands were present. The eldest had three boys who had completed their studies and were planning to get married soon. The second one had a son who was studying and two pretty daughters. The elder daughter was married and the younger one was one year older to them. The youngest sister of her father was married in Qatar and she had especially come to meet them. She had a daughter of nine years and a younger son. All their names were so varied that it was impossible to know each one of them. Her grandfather was married thrice and so the paternal family seemed to be endless. Coming to the maternal ones, they were no less but two brothers of her mother who had two children each and two elder sisters in which the younger one had one friendly daughter of eighteen and a son of the same age as the girls. The elder sister's children were not known because they did not come at that time. She was getting so confused looking at the crowd of the house that she went and began to arrange Amirah's room which had been jumbled by the kids.

"Will you all get out and stop shouting?" she shouted.

"Ha-ha, if you have problem, then you may leave." Kids shouted in a much louder voice.

She felt very embarrassed and said helplessly, "Please, don't mess up here. Go out and play. Won't you like to welcome your amu api? She will be so sad to see this hotchpotch."

"Nooo!" They shouted again.

She left the room at another moment and started walking down the stairs being red in anger.

"Kyara! What happen?" Haira, Amirah's eldest sister asked.

"Oh, Nothing Haira api," she smiled.

"Oho, these kids must be troubling you, wait I will tick them off. Come on," she said.

"Done Kyara. You can clean now without any disturbances. I wonder what is wrong with all these kids these days. I don't think we were so horrible at that age," she sighed.

"Really, Haira api! They all have lost it. Anyways I should clean in a quick. Call me down when the fruits come." Kyara said.

While grinding the mixer, her heart beats suddenly grew. She panicked and her blood flowed in a faster speed. She was panting and there was something inside which was making her feeling uneasy. She did not know the reason but she was going through something which she had never experienced before so abruptly. She stopped the mixer for some time and drank some water but she could not drink that too properly because she was unable to focus on anything around her as if there was something within which lied reasons and they were unknown to her. That was such an unusual feeling and it was for such a short period. She wanted to know the cause behind it. She feared to suffer from any disease so without completely making the juice, she thought to talk about it to him.

"Listen, are you there?" she messaged and he replied after ten minutes. "Yes I am. *Kahiye,*"

"Hmm, where are you?" she asked.

"On my way to home."

"Why, where were you?" she asked.

"I had gone to buy curd from the Lloyd store."

"Oh my god! Lloyd store, you mean at the end of this road of Amirah's house. When were you here? You should have told me. I would have at least seen you," she wrote.

"Oh, next time. I was there just ten minutes before. What were you saying?" he typed.

"Hmm, nothing much. Go, eat your curd," she added.

"Ha, I will at night. And has your friend come?" he asked.

"Nah! The flight must have landed; we'll have to wait for another half hour," she told.

"Take care, I hope you don't faint," he joked.

"Very funny. Oh so you hope well for me, I did not know," she wrote.

"Not really! But sometimes, I am good at humour, you see," he laughed.

"Haw, bad person. Take this," she sent a cartoon of punching hand.

"Ha-ha, when will you meet me?" he asked genuinely.

"Ahmmmm, we will, we will," she said uninterestingly.

"But when?" he asked powerlessly.

"Whenever you like, okay baby? Now tell me, how is your mommy? Does she even know me?" she asked.

"Hmm, okay. We will meet tomorrow. Mommy is good and she does not know you."

"Why doesn't she know? You did not tell her about me. So bad that is."

"Oh Okay, I will tell. By the way, does your mommy know me?" he asked impatiently.

"Yes, of course. My mommy is a mother to Maisha, she tells her everything. You know *na* when she was born, her mother expired so she lived with us only all the time as her father is too busy working. There is no one in her house and her paternal relatives are too greedy and cruel. So you know, we have a difficult family with easy relations. Ha-ha. Isn't that like a speech?" she typed.

"Yes she told me all this before. Such a nice family. Any way, you know mommy wants to meet Maisha and so she will be coming home on Sunday," he sent.

"Oh, great that is!" she typed without any feeling.

"Hmm," he said.

"Well, maybe she has come; I will message as I reach home," she ended.

She rapidly ran to the front door which was cramming with relatives but anyhow she managed to go out and saw her friend trying to take out her *dupatta* clinched at the window of the car. She ran to kiss her and helped her take it out. Amirah's eyes were full of tears to see her younger sister after so long as they did not get much time to talk when she was out. They both hugged each other for ten seconds and began to cry. Everyone was standing amazed to see their emotions and whole of the atmosphere became touching. She then greeted all of them and kissed her mother and elder sister. She went to take the water melon juice and all the relatives initiated there talks and laughter.

"How did you manage for so long?" Amirah halted her silence and asked in a soft voice.

"I managed but it was too hard and problematic. By the way how are you? I mean we haven't asked this before but yes now it seems that you were actually far from me, in fact quite distanced. So many things have happened and there is so much to share. I mean, really another month is needed for all this," she said in the blink of an eye.

"Really! Okay let us start from now. Why don't you stay here tonight? Common ask mommy," she said.

"Hmm Nah. I mean I can't. Some another day maybe but now you tell me that how was *Umrah?* How was your first experience?" she asked.

"In a word, it was paradise. Seriously Kyara, I can't bring into words that how it feels to stand in front of the house of your creator. I mean, I was feeling scared but then I thought that my Lord has given me such a superb chance to be so near to him. An unforgettable journey, it was. Then Medina, it was like a dream to walk on that ground upon which our prophet walked. You know I prayed all the time that may the time stop and I just don't leave that place," she said.

"Sounds so beautiful,"

"It was the most beautiful and by the way what's up with you? You didn't cry much, I hope," she said.

"How can I cry without you? These days are just so nice. You know I am so happy," she said blushing.

"Han, you blushed. Tell me fast, what has occurred and for god's sake Kyara, at least today you could wear proper clothes. We have come from such a pure place and just look at the size of your dress. I mean, shameless."

"Aaa, not at least today. It is so long ya; I intentionally wore a longer one. Please now don't criticise this," she said in order to convince.

After a few hours of chats, feast and gifts exchange, the crowd began lessening and she decided to return. While sitting in the car with Akira, who had come to pick her up. Her brown hair which were half tied came to her face and as she endeavoured to aside them from her eyes, again she underwent a striking feeling which could make her forget all her living surroundings and flew her to a new world of hyperbole. She could sense a new fangled melody which was inaudible to all and sundry, as if it was just meant for her to be acquainted with. At another tick, she saw a sight which had really made her vivacious and becoming a spring of the evaporation of all her agitation, it had caused her eyes to spread wide enough to see him taking a soft turn in his white car in that bluish shirt. She went unnoticed by him, but the central thing was that she had got all her answers and keys. As soon as she again moved away, normalcy of her spirit trailed. *"Is this real? Getting vibes when he is around, Am I in a movie?"* This was the most unrealistic thing ever happened to her. Feeling presence of the one, who was known to her albeit one year was drastically harsh to have faith in. It was unfeasible and there was no practicality in it but she loved in the way which was not just love, but more than that. What if she told anyone about this? It would not be corrupt if it would make people have hysterics. Labelling it to be a "love of tales", they would just giggle on her and criticise her so much, that she herself would lose self-belief and the power of her love which was bona fide. Such ninnies in reality, ridicule themselves by having such a shoddy interpretation because it is been pretended that they scoff at the supremacy of the undying feeling of affection for someone when in verity, god has not granted whole of the human nature to love with that much intensity and might.

"You know, I love you," she messaged.

"I do too, very much," he replied.

"Hmm, I saw you," she sent.

"Where? I didn't see you," he said sadly.

"At the dickens circle, you turned towards the greenwoods apartments and I was coming back home," she explained.

"Oh, so how is your friend?" he asked.

"Pretty fine. She came today and started shouting. She is a bit mad," she wrote.

"Oh, why?" he asked and she replied, "I wonder. I wore a normal Jumpsuit to her house and she minded that. You know, funny that was."

He said, "Okay, show me what you wore and yes now you click your mirror picture."

"Yes, see," she messaged with two photos.

"Pretty. That is short Kyara. Will you listen to me?" his reaction was least expected by her and she said, "Yes, what happen?"

"Don't wear it again. It looks good but just don't," he said at once.

"Oh, you don't like so I will not."

"Ha, I don't. You can wear jeans, ankle length pants, long skirts but not this. You can wear when I'm there but now you are grown up so avoid short dresses. I hope you will not mind."

"No, why would I? I will do as you say," she said calmly.

In the utterly dimness of the glistening moon, she began glancing at those small stars which gave her eyes soothe and draughtiness despite of being made up of sizzling flames. Being engrossed in their influencing feature, she was with them but saw someone else's silhouette which was beholden by the light of reflection. Submitting herself in the other hands, gradually she was being taught that this humanity is no less than a puppet which fancies that their destiny works according to them. It then mocks them every time by turning the tables upside down of each point. She wanted the days to pass in a blink of her eye because each day made her closer to him. At every happening, she firmly believed that even if the world would get against her; that love for which she was living wouldn't leave. Dashing in the restful meltem, flouting the values, they overlooked what could be the upshot of whole of this. For them, it was love, but for others it could be a sheer brazen, loutish relation which had no worth or connotation.

"You know, it is such a special day after a week," she messaged.

"Really? What is it?" he asked.

"Don't you know? Last year, we became friends on this day and did we ever know that it would turn out in this manner."

"Really? Wow! That is so perfect. So you remember the date. Terrific!" he exclaimed.

"If I won't remember then who else will? I am so happy, you know. I will wear new clothes on that day and what will you wear?" she asked.

"Okay, whatever you will say to," he typed. "Wait, I will text after some time." She ended.

"Kyara, I am craving for a blue berry ice-cream. Come on, let us go." Maisha said cheerfully.

"Oh, okay let me change," she said hurriedly.

"No, we don't have so much time and you look so good. Just come, it is not so crowded," she said.

"Okay, let us go."

"In fact, I have something easier. I will say to Rehaam. As it is late," she said unhurriedly and she nodded. After half an hour Maisha called her to tell, "Kyara, please go to that road of mango trees. Rehaam will give you the ice-cream."

Then Kyara became too cautious of her look as her pony tail had become a little messed up. "Kyara, hurry up. He is standing there." Maisha said and Kyara left the house at another second without getting the knots out. Her restless yet pleasurable walk could easily show how jubilant she felt. Walking a little, at length she spotted him sitting in his car and this time, she was not diffident but they both shared an unreserved smile which was an apparent instance of their compatibility. After a silence of five seconds, he handed over the packet, touching her hands. Being overwhelmed by his amorous gesture, she began to look down but he never discontinued staring in those eyes, which were not setting on his.

"Kyara." he said tenderly and then she looked at him with a very distinct smile and this time it was just not only her lips, but every component of her enthralling face smiled too. Her eyes were in a constant attempt to articulate and they were giving some divine expressions which were matching to those indications that the nature gives out in the form of the amplified blow of air and the swish of grass when those foremost drops of purity fall. Exceedingly having the same liquid of fondness, they had words to put across but it was their mind which made them conscious of the time which could not be hindered. Breaking the wave, she started to move backwards facing him. "I am going," she said nervously touching her flicks of hair unnecessarily and for a couple of seconds, he still saw her as if he didn't hear her or he wanted her to understand the reason behind his silence. Coming to the reality, he started his car and she turned back and walked straight rapidly. He was behind so he rushed to her and stopped his car "Wait!" she was on her house's road and turned to see him lastly. "Come online as soon as you reach," he said sternly in his typical tone. She then gave him a sad smile making her eyes heavy and he smiled back in a way which could fill all the colours of her new imaginative scenery in which only he lived with that hanaemi and she with those eyes to see it.

"Kyara, what was that?" he messaged her after five minutes.

"Nothing and can we talk a little later?" she said sadly.

"No, what was that? I mean, we met and you were sad. Do you know? Even I am. I mean what is happening?" he asked confusedly.

"See, I don't know and we should not talk," she said having tears.

"What is wrong? Even I am trying to figure out and how can you say that? Just shut up and calm down," he wrote.

"Hmm," she said.

"Actually it is just that we like so much to be together that distance makes us lose our mind," he said. "You know that we are in love and this is fine, okay? Don't be cheerless."

"Hmm yes," She sent.

"In fact, we will have to meet. Now smile my love," he said.

"Why? I don't want to meet," she said.

"Hmm, but I want to and you too. That is what made you sad and now you are speaking contrast," he said irritatingly.

That saudade that had turned out pessimistically was making her dejected and there was no cure for it. She just wished for being with him, chatting, laughing and doing all those things which gave her overall exhilaration. He was her charm and that space and the punishment of so many years apart were check by jowl for both.

"Tomorrow is twentieth and so our anniversary," he messaged.

"Yes, I know. I am so glad."

"Even I. This one year, I wonder how it passed. I feel as if we just met one week before and all this happened. Did we ever know at that time, when I saw you and you turned with that killer expression that it would be this way? You know, I got really scared at first but then I thought that the little Kyara was not ill- mannered. I was assured that you were not that girl whom I knew and when Maisha told me that you are her sister then I was like, "Ahem- Ahem! Little girl is not little anymore," he wrote.

"Was I scary? I didn't know. Actually I was very irritated that day so maybe you added to it. Seriously, we never knew that we would be like this; I mean we knew each other since childhood. Did I ever know that a normal guy who was in the high school and I was like eating dirt at that age Ha-ha would become my life? Funny that is and and I literally ignored you the first time, I was like, "Whose he?" such an over involving personality," she sent.

He sent a surprised emoticon and said, "And I thought your cousin, Aroosh to be Maisha's sister."

"You thought total opposite," she wrote.

At three of clock, when summer was at its peak in the lake city, a thought flashed that only ten days were left for her holidays to end. After that from the second of July to the sixth, her tests would begin. She had planned to study one subject for two days and in this manner, her syllabus would get finished with no trouble. It is so obvious, when youngsters get involved in relations whom they name as "love" forget everything and pay no attention on their careers and studies but she did not lie in that section. She knew that her education was essential and getting excellent grades made her image and she had no option of getting out of it. Fairly showing her advanced sensibleness, she was skilled to keep her personal and student life separately which indeed told an indescribable story of her diligence and astuteness. She had switched off her phone and kept it aside to learn her first chapter of English literature, her most beloved. After memorising it, she switched her phone on and she had mistakenly turned off the internet so Rehaam's messages were not giving double ticks on his sent messages. Puzzled and enraged, he had been wondering the reason of her behind not using the communicating application for so long. He had text messaged her on her number two hours back, "Why are you not online?" She hoped for his calmness after seeing her late reply, so she messaged, "I am sorry, I was studying so for fewer disturbances, I switched it off and even turned off the internet. You know, Filiz and Amirah then keep on texting. I needed to concentrate."

"Oh, you should have told. By the way, carry on. We will talk when you will be done," he replied.

"No, I am done. Say *na*."

"Send me your picture," he wrote and she sent it in a black and pink chiffon *kurta* and black bottoms.

"Wow! Your suit is so pretty."

"It is not a suit, it is just a *kurta*," she explained. "Okay, I was saying that we will meet today," he wrote.

"How? It is going to be dark soon and where will we meet, are you serious?"

"We are just going to. I don't know how. Tell me, Is Maisha at your home?"

"No, she is at uncle's house and she will come, I guess tomorrow," she answered.

"Great! So you say in your house that I have to give a phone sim card to Maisha but as she is not at home, I have given to you."

"What if Maisha gets to know this?" she asked hopelessly.

"She will know of course. See, she wanted her previous sim card for the phone numbers and so I will tell her that I will give at Kyara's house. How is it?"

"Funny. But what will happen in a meeting for some seconds?" she asked sadly.

"Not for seconds but for one minute. And you come at that road of mango trees. Isn't it vacant?" he laughed.

"Yes and lucky for us, Do you remember that we met on that road," she replied.

"Love you," he sent suddenly. "So I will text as soon as I get free, I am in the Thar Lagoon right now," she smiled and asked, "Why?"

He ended, "Work!"

It was seven thirty of the evening and there was no message from him. She was hesitant of their meeting but somewhere within, she believed that it will come about. First time, she was not making herself up because she just wanted to be herself and she knew that he loved her, the way she was. Wearing the same clothes, same hairstyle, she just applied a lip-gloss as she was fanatical for it. Her phone was kept at the table in her room, where it was getting charged and she went out to drink water to freshen up her mind and keep calm. She thought that if she would not be able to meet, she won't panic but just hope for some another day. The droll part was that she never knew that what would she do?

Are we just going to stand there on the road and keep on smiling? Am I going to talk to him?"

She gave a weird expression in the mirror and she forgot that her phone was on the silent mode. She went to Akira's room to ask when her mommy would return from the aunt's house and told her, "I guess, he is coming to give a sim card for Maisha." "Who?" Akira asked.

"*Wohi*! Your future brother in law," she said uninterestingly.

"Oh Rehaam. Then you go and take it." Akira replied normally.

"Huh! Why doesn't he go to Maisha's house directly? I mean why I have to go always?" she said too dramatically as if she was irritated by his frequent arrivals to make it look usual. *"Oh you drama girl."*

"Hmm, you don't have to go to his house. Firstly he is coming and you are behaving so harshly," she said.

Kyara went to her room without replying to her and saw her phone finally.

"Kyara!!! I will come in five minutes," he messaged and she got markedly edgy.

"Oh okay."

"Hmm, so why are we meeting?" he asked.

"How am I supposed to know? Don't get too happy," she messaged smiling.

"Ha-ha why? Am I not allowed to?" he asked.

"*Han?*" she said naively. *"What do you want? Both, Baddie and Elf are standing with their heads upside down."*

"Come fast to that mango road."

"I am."

Again sauntering all the way, she never looked up to know who was around. Being vanished in her own formed cysium, she glistened in that night of no luminosity. An anonymous author of this story of her was not revealing the future like any other. Howbeit, all which counted was that she saw him in the centre, where there were trees and an anti- established pale white house having a windowpane with old, off-white curtains. She kept on walking until she reached the left door of his car, where he was sitting in a black t-shirt, all spanking new. A shadowy atmosphere was there as if the moon intentionally hid itself for them. This time, they were disparate ere as they had undergone the woe of gawking. Without goggling, he handed over that tiny reason of their togetherness to her and she had admitted that it was all for this day but he was just waiting to speak more lovingly to his love! Hankering after a trivial cue of warmth, he spoke which was poignant and scrape. She gave him a peck on his right cheek.

At another flash, he had what he wanted but not really so he expressed his melancholic suffering. An only known time, when he showed his sombre and she smiled at him in coyness. But then too, she could not endorse even for a flash, his eyes to lose its glimmer. So having that feel of accismus, she bowed in the bounds of his blunt sight and that caress which was ectopic in the night fall came up. She could feel his divine smell getting entangled with her fragrance and his enticing tang taking turns in her mouth was uncontainable. Nonetheless erasing the restiveness, it satiated him and startlingly her too. She came back running and fell on her bed with lights off. Her pulsate was not high with him, but in his absence, she felt the most astounding feeling which was so latest in her. She felt close to him, in fact too much to illustrate. Her love was getting higher and it was following a particular pattern which truly everyone else chased too. It was nothing great but yes, isn't it great to feel so? Nobody knows what was in her mind at that time but one can effortlessly know that in her heart, there was a name which was solitary and her first and she wanted it to be the last too and that was of HIM.

"Kyara, have you come?" Akira said in a funny tone. "Yes," she went and hugged her. She said astonishingly, "Is everything all right?"

She said gladly, "Yes, isn't it a beautiful day? Everything is so wonderful in this world. All the people are so good."

She replied, "Yes, you know let us have dinner then I will be busy."

"Are you going somewhere?"

"Nah, I will be busy with T.V. Shahrukh in *Bazigar*, I just love and so I don't want any kind of annoyance which means I don't want you in that room." Akira winked.

"Haw, mean woman. In fact, you will not be needed in that room so just shut up," she said with anger and ran to grab the remote.

"Oh god, give me the remote else I won't tell you the channel," she demanded.

"Ha-ha! As if I don't have eyes to see the schedule. You are so dumb."

"Huh get lost," she ended and both began to watch it together.

"Your lip-gloss," he messaged with a heart sticker.

"Ha-ha!" She sent. "What?" *"Can we just not discuss what happened?"*

"It was good."

"Thank you."

"What? Really Kyara really?"

"Stop! Gone mad?" she asked.

"Yes, with you," he texted. "So finally we met."

"Yes, dangerously met," she replied.

"Why? Affectionately met,"

"Oh, I see. No more discussions on that meeting," she joked.

"Why? Tomorrow also we will meet. After all, it is going to be a year and we need to."

"Han. Just one hour left. Couldn't you buy me a present, huh?" she joked.

"Why are you behaving like those typical girls who demand expensive gifts from their boyfriends?" Good Elf scowled.

"That was simply a joke."

"Oh! Present. Well, what do you want? Silver, diamond, platinum or gold?" he asked in a serious tone as if he was just on the shop.

"Richie rich.. I know you own all the valuables minerals. Gold? Do I look like an aunty who will wear gold?"

"Gold? That's funny," she laughed.

"Ok, you want it? I will get a ring."

"Please no!" she replied. "You know what I really want?" she wrote and he asked what.

"YOU. Nothing else," she typed blushing.

"Ha-ha, I am already with you. I will get a ring."

"No, you will not. I really don't like all this. My biggest gift is when you smile," she replied and he sent her a kiss.

"By the way, will that be a marriage ring? If yes, then I will love it and when you will insert that in my finger, I am sure I will faint and if I do, then don't stop. You just make me wear it and when I will get up, I wonder what I will do," she said and he laughed and agreed.

When the clock showed twelve, he messaged, "Happy anniversary my cutie pie."

"To you too," she messaged.

"So what are the plans?" he asked.

"You know, talk to me. Please don't sleep," she asked innocently.

"Yes I am sweetie. We both shall not sleep today; after all it is so good. See it has just started and I am feeling so calm," he replied.

"Hmm as we can never celebrate our marriage anniversary ever so I will have to get happy in this only."

"Huh! Feel as if we are already married. See what's the difference? I, as your hubby and you as my wife," he said and she directly went on cloud nine after this. She never knew when she was this much happy last. Her incorruptibility and simplicity was that thing, which used to impress everyone but still was not so harmless. She believed in every word of his and it was not that he was lying, yes he was true, he loved her and so he said that. He did name their unknown relation as 'marriage' and she didn't want any ceremony to accept it but just his words on which she blindly depended.

"Ha-ha, insane you are," she laughed.

"No, I am serious so always listen to your husband."

"Okay, as you say," she ended. They talked and talked and talked whole night as if the day was ending in the morning. It was like a mania, where they just wanted one thing and that was each other. Their day had ended up in their eternal chat and they did not meet due to some of her reasons and that was the day, which has been memorable in her life and which was not cherished that much but still was a manifest testimony.

It was the most beautiful camaraderie and it appeared that none would see its closing stage. There was an idiosyncrasy which no one could ever put in plain words and even if he would try, it would never finish. It was comparable to that book which the reader doesn't want to close in any way. It was a love story which was beyond the lines of imagination, which no one could approve of but it was love which never works on our will, but takes its way and even forces two people to tread that. There were times when they both waited to see each other even for a second, when they were not alone but still enjoyed at looking at each other whenever it was a clear way. When others used to talk about him, she used to keep silent but still somewhere inside; she was convincing herself that no one could ever know him more. No one knew it but it was obvious that whenever he used to come, she used to get happy, her eyes did smile all the time with her lips and no one really noticed them ever because it was so conventional that they were no one and who doubts on something which is so clearly uncertain? Unlike any other couple who usually have so many eyes to scout, so many ears to snoop and so many mouths to tittle-tattle. They were becoming hedonistic in a phase which was ephemeral.

A clear definition of a love story, what is it? Belike enjoyment or togetherness for all or maybe it would be too colossal to say. For her, it was like those in the pictures, where love at last finds its way no matter how many problems cross it. She always wanted a prince charming that would come with the lost shoe to marry her or who would climb up the lofty towers. Tagging him to be that, she always found her love story the best but little did she know, that sometimes it's not about the happy ending but about the story.

"Ramadan is starting over morrow. Excited?" he asked.

"Yes. Do you fast on all the days?" she asked.

"Of course, you know, it is a big sin to leave any fast. You also fast right?"

"I haven't even thought to leave food in my dreams," she thought.

"He is going to think that you're a sheer atheist." Baddie discouraged. "Leaving food and water for so many hours is near to impossible."

"Then why did you fall in love with a religious person? He's not going to respect you if he gets to know that you're a non- believer." Elf stated.

"I am fasting tomorrow. That is final now!"

"Okay. We will fast for thirty days together. Won't it be fun?" she wrote.

"Yes, it will be and it is not just about fasting but prayers too. So I guess, you will pray five times and then you will be habitual of it. Okay?"

"Did he know that I was in the darkness of atheism? Prayers? Oh yes my mum taught me when I was seven. Zzzzzz. I haven't prayed since then." Her heart came in her throat out of fear. *"What will you think of me when you will get to know that I haven't prayed for so long?"*

"A pious Muslim boy will go away from a disbeliever." Baddie grinned.

"Oh please! It's not late Kyara. Pray now." Good elf sighed.

"Yes, as you say," she typed after two minutes.

"And in it, we must also see our behaviour. You know, we will not meet much." "Oh why? We can see each other at least," she got tensed.

"Aww my baby. We will meet tomorrow. Happy now?"

"Okay!" *"Happy? My blood rate has already speeded up."*

"So tomorrow, you go to Amirah's house and then we will meet, I can drop you home."

"Okay, cool!" She replied and they talked almost whole night without stoppage.

Chapter 4

Her school had begun twenty days before and her tests had gone shockingly fine. She had never thought that Rehaam would not come between her and her books. He always wanted Kyara to study best and get a lot of success because he knew her capabilities and intellect. Whenever there were tests or something, he did not talk much and even if he did, he talked about studies and always encouraged her to study more. It was so cute of him to do so and sometimes she even disliked his sudden behavioural change but he always knew how to convince her.

There was love, there was respect and there was trust and still it did not really complete itself and some where it was out of favour, as it could not be so undemanding and straight forward.

"Amirah, I am coming home," she said on the phone.

"Oh, when? I have to go to a party in the neighbourhood."

"Okay, so don't go because I have to come."

"No, I will have to. Ha'ameem's mother personally called mamma to invite and she is not going so I will have to go."

"Oh can't you understand? You are not going and it is clear now." Kyara spoke harshly.

"Why don't you understand? I have to go and I will come till seven so you please come then," she replied.

"Listen Amirah, he is going to pick me up from there and if you will go then we will not be able to meet afterwards. Try to understand," she insisted.

"Oh! But mamma is saying to go," she said and Kyara began to cry and started pleading. As she could never see her crying, she said, "Now don't cry else I will also begin. You come here; I will tell mamma that we have to do homework."

At the spur of the moment, she changed her clothes and tied a sideward braid, put her Armani perfume and asked Akira to drop her. Everyone at her house was mesmerized by her because she looked so dazzling in that loose, neon green palazzo and white shirt. She had already told him that she had reached Amirah's place and he told her that he would come by seven to pick her up. She quickly convinced her mamma to let her not go to that party and they both began to pretend doing an important work in her room. Amirah was asking her the reason of meeting him and she was behaving as if she was a new bride who was being asked about her married life. Amirah started to believe that something was cooking as whenever Kyara's lips moved, they talked about him as if there was nothing else left to talk about for her. When she told her those things he said and did, at first Amirah was just smiling listening to a tale but later she realised that it was not unreal but an actual drama happening with her sister. She even told her to be a little careful in this and she knew it was wrong and illegal but she was seeing that sparkle in her friend's eyes which stopped her to say anything which could make her lose it. Amirah heard her who was confused, happy and of course in love!

"Kyara, just fifteen minutes are left for seven. Ask him and get ready." Amirah said worriedly. "Yes let me," she texted him and he had last checked his messages one hour ago so he did not reply. She was panicking so much but she never called him for no reason. She thought that he must have got busy somewhere. She messaged him one more time at seven forty five but still he did not reply. She was sad but she knew that he was busy with his work.

"You know, I will ask Akira to pick me. Maybe he is busy," she said and being unpleased with her sadness Amirah said, "At least call him. I know you are upset, don't act fake."

"No, I am not. He is busy I know, else he would have come. I am calling Akira," she ended and in five minutes and she came to pick her up.

"Why are you turning that side?" Kyara asked Akira sitting in the car.

"Maisha has called us to the ice-cream shop." Akira replied.

"Oh! But how did she go there?" She asked and Akira said, "I don't know, some friend maybe."

A sight which was the most irksome and hurtful, when her heart actually stopped for a second and that was it. She could have never imagined in her dreams that she would see such a scene in her ages. Entirely frozen, it was so deplorable that he was there at that place. She remained sitting in the car seat just thinking of her reaction to this wicked happening. She opened the door and with her high heels, walked straight and confidently towards them because no matter how hard it was for her, she continued her faultlessness. She died a little inside but it never came on her face. Giving a pleasing smile, she greeted him but whatever it was, it was obnoxious and tactless. He did not even look at her once which was so wounding and all his attention was on his first, second, third or number _ love. His eyes were telling some other story this time and like a dim witted, she just saw down and never looked him again. She had known him a little more this time and at another moment she asked her sister to get back home.

After reaching home, she had many questions in her mind and that was the first time when someone else was given more importance than her. She was actually shattered and dispirited and she came to know that it would repeat too. She agreed that she was not so important in his life as he was in hers. He was her life but was she his? It was the most terrible feeling which was constantly hitting her and for some time, her tears did not stop falling.

"Happy Ramadan!" He messaged her after seeing the moon. She had no feeling of replying him because he showed her something which was shattering and she did not know how to express it to anyone. Starving on her worst day first time because of someone, she was in so much pain that she couldn't find anyone to share it with. All she had, was a pen in her hand and all of the sudden, she got a diary and just began to write.

A day, which was never before,
Alas! I don't long for it anymore.
Lying on the ground, feeling insane,
Praying to the providence to never show it again.

Questioning the world that "Why me?"
But who could change the decision of thee.
Strongly bonded by the threads of destiny,
Totally thoughtless in calamity.

I was a little hurt inside—
because nothing was left more to decide.
Gasping in a nonsense pain,
I was waiting for the happy rain.

Somewhere in bits, something I felt,
My eyes saw the heart melt.
It was a feeling less feeling,
But my heart had to go on dealing.

Beneath my skin, I heard a cry,
All because of that heinous lie.
Controlled all emotions with a sigh,
Was it better to live than to die?

The end came up with rolling tears,
I had to answer in deep fear.
Mercifully, it has passed away,
As I could not take it anymore, anyway.

"A day which was never before"
Alas! I don't long for it anymore.

Few minutes of penning, and there she was sitting with her first poem. At first, she could never believe what she was seeing as she was just captivated by her wordings which truly described her feelings at that time. A dream which was in front was pleasure giving but still she did not feel like showing it to anyone. She did not want anyone to read it because that was because of someone whom she did not want to talk. Like a success that hits in private, it was special beyond any doubt but all she required was to share that with him. She wanted to complain and having a thought that maybe he would read it, she put pen to paper. Being too quick to make things memorable, she was the one who always cherished past. She had written it on a rough paper with a green ink and then she copied it to a red one with a silver highlighter and even typed it in her phone.

There she was having her first fast of her life which had certain reasons. A hectic school day was ignored and all she concentrated on was to pray five times as it was being told. In practicality, she was wounded at heart but still she was following him as if there was someone watching her and marking her on her obedience. Someone who never took her lord's name ever, was standing for prayer and observing fast for fifteen and a half hours. The Morning Prayer was missed by her as she had to wake early due to school but without any negligence, she prayed it with the noon one.

They were not in any contact that day and she never wanted to talk to him but still she was waiting. For what? She wanted his name to appear on her phone's screen with an apology but it was not so. Being in a misery, she had cheerfully ended her fast with the members of her family and began to pray again. She made a prayer, *"Oh lord! Please guide him and make him know that I am hurt so much because of him. Not only because he lied to me but also because the whole day has passed and he hasn't realised that I'm angry. Please accept all his prayers and accept my prayers for him too. This was my first fast and I promise to fast for the rest twenty nine days too. Give me strength and bless my family and him"* She was in tears after that.

It was a selcouth and the kind of contentment; which she could feel afterwards was too wonderful for words. The night prayer was missed by her due to its length and all she knew was that she was a writer and a religious person from today. The day which was disregarded and was said to be the nastiest one changed her positively. Throwing off the invisible crown of ego which she wore all the time, it made her understand the imperfections of her life. First time ever, she did not have what she wanted and that was an instance of a change which was waiting.

Next afternoon, the same pattern followed and she had lost all the hopes that he would ever talk to her and suddenly her phone which was on the silent mode blinked and she saw, "So, you will not talk to me." Without replying, she locked it again.

"Oh so you will not even reply, right?" He asked and with an annoyance she said, "What?"

"What? Why are you behaving like this?" He asked and this maddened her more as she knew that he actually did not realise his mistake and so with all the intentions to make him know she said, "What? Please go to the ice cream parlour, do you get it? For god's sake, don't think to message me again."

"Kyara! Is this the way to talk?" He asked.

"Oh look who is teaching the values. You know just shut up," she said despite of knowing how much he hated if someone said to shut his mouth.

"Look even Maisha doesn't talk to me like this."

"Oh god! Am I Maisha? What do you think of yourself? And who cares what she says to you and it will be better if you go and listen to her and leave me alone. She doesn't say that actually means I can't say, right? I mean, people think twice to compare anyone with me and just look at your bravery. How could you even think to do that? You know, just forget it and I can't take this anymore," she wrote and began to cry with her head buried in her pillow.

"Oho sorry. Okay? Sorry, I am very sorry. I love you," he sent and like always those three words made her forget everything but still she did not stop to show her fury.

"You did not love me yesterday. Why can't you love me when there are people? Why only on phone or in private?

"You have started ignoring me so early and I wonder what you will do when you will get married."

"Forget all that. How can I ignore my life? I am sorry. Whenever you will say we will meet. Okay?" he typed.

"Hmm, you know I have been crying and do you even know how did I feel? Wait, read this," she sent her the poem.

"Wow! Whose poem is that?" He asked. "I have written it Huh."

"Really Kyara? It is so good; I can't tell it looks as if some well known writer has written. Mind blowing, I just love it," he wrote and being happy with the appreciation, she answered, "Hmm, it is so sad and I was in so much pain and you love it. Disgusting!"

"Oh no. I mean to say that I like your writing skills but I am also sad that you were sad," he justified which pleased her and she laughed.

"So is my Kyari fasting?"

"Yes and praying too."

"Good!"

Normalcy which couldn't be waited for was back. She was no longer falling in that category of lovers who have been deprived of it. Everything once again was flowing in the way she wanted. As we say a perfect love has fights, has tears, has envy and but obviously love. It is when that person takes all the efforts to see a smile and there is nothing called ego in its part and on its arrival, it gets everything faded.

"So dedicate a song to me!" She sent.

"Hmm, 'you are my heaven and the comfort; you are the coolness of my eyes and my beat. I don't long for anything but I say that I see god in you and I don't know what to do?'"

"Aww ha-ha. Why are you singing it in English?" She asked as that was a Hindi song.

"Ha-ha because I know you can translate and doesn't it look good? One more okay and you find which song this is. 'Your eyes are so beautiful that I desire that you may allow me living in them. Your talks are so beautiful that I smell flowers when you speak and your hair are so beautiful that I want to reside in its shadow.'"

"Aww, I am blushing. Well I know which song is that. I have never watched this film."

"Oh why? I have watched it a number of times. So we will watch together."

The evening was spent shopping with her mother and an aunt. Preparation of *eid* is one of the major parts of the month. Despite of fasting, people don't leave a chance to do compulsive shopping.

"Oh I am sorry," she crashed into a woman.

"It is alright beta," she smiled wide and she smiled back.

"Wait Aunty, your polybag is going to tear off, I guess. The crockery is too heavy maybe. Anyway you can take this cloth bag," she said in her sweetest voice.

She Laughed and replied, "No *beta*. Even if it will then I will hold it. My car must not be far. I will call the driver if required."

"I don't have any problem to give this. I don't want you to be troubled. Please take," she said helpfully.

"You are so sweet. What is your name?" She asked gladly.

"It's Kyara," she smiled with joy.

"Such a pretty name and it suits you. Have you come alone?" She asked.

"No Aunty. My mom and aunt are in the changing room," she said.

"Oh, it is such a pleasure to meet you." She said and kept her things in that bag and Kyara bade her bye by saying Salam in Arabic.

"Baby, come online. I want to see you." Rehaam sent at nine.

"No. I cannot because there are people in my house. You know, aunt and her small kids. The house is in a mess. They make so much noise."

"Just for five minutes please. Close the door," he sent with a sad emoticon.

"Oh. Just for five minutes but Maisha will come. I mean, it is too risky now because anyone can come and it is so not possible to close the door," she replied frantically.

"Huh! Send her somewhere out," he said grumpily which left her astounded as his grouchiness was on whom he would marry in sometime. It was an unusual sight or mood or maybe anything else because he wanted her to go out so that she couldn't disturb both of them. All it depended on him actually and she thought that if he could say like that about her sister so he can also say same about her to someone else but all these false thoughts evacuated because it could clearly show his devotion for her. It won't be a fib if it will be said that love is self- centred as it alters the most altruistic because at a point it comes, where egotism is not watched out.

"Come!" She sent.

"Where?" He replied with an angelic emoticon.

"*Grrr. Don't you?*" Good Elf gasped.

"What? On video."

Their talks comprised of a few seconds of formal question which were done for humour and then they used to forget all the correctness to become cosy lovers. He never smiled but there was an expression of attentiveness which was on his face and there was not much need for his lips to curve but his eyes were enough. It was her habit to start touching her hair and open them to bring them in front because in some means, she did not want an eye contact and he was aware about it so he always disliked this and urged her to tie her long hair.

"Listen," he said and she asked, "What?"

"I love you," he said suddenly and she started smiling looking down and typed, "I love you more."

"So after your marriage, will you forget me?" He asked.

"What? Whose marriage?" she asked.

"Your marriage," he said.

"Huh! Is it needed to talk all this now? Someone's knocking, I will text," she said angrily.

After one hour, he messaged, "Tell me. I asked something."

"What? Don't talk senselessly. Ok do you want to know? Then listen, I am not getting married to anyone else," she typed.

"You will have to, for me,"

"Oh really? Just some time before you said that you love me and now you are saying to me to marry someone else. I mean, how can you even think that? You know I can never see you with someone else but still I am seeing. Do you know how does it feel? You can never know and I don't want you to feel that way because of me," she replied.

"Kyara! Even I don't want to see you with someone else but that doesn't mean you will ruin your life for me. See, I will get married and I want you to get married too. At least for your mommy,"

"Oh, so we can never get married with each other, right?"

"We will my love and I don't know how. We will do something about that," he answered which made her calm.

Maybe Someday

"You know, I don't want to think all this now. Why are we arguing? When the time will come then we will see. My grandparents are coming tomorrow and mommy; Akira and Maisha are going to Delhi day after tomorrow,"

"Oh that is wonderful so we can meet easily,"

"Hmm yes," she replied.

Two day had passed and Kyara was all busy with her grandparents. Helping Akira in packing up, she was cheery to know that it will be unproblematic for her to meet him. They had left in the noon for the airport and they had to board the plane at quarter to four. There were just three people left in their house now and Kyara had got all the easiness to video chat with him day and night but Rehaam had no time that day which had left her low-spirited. She was going to a boutique where she had given her Indian dress for stitching with her grandmother. Dressed up in a white kurta and black bottoms, they both left after breaking their fasts.

"Kyara I am so sorry for not replying because I was in a business meeting, you know some businessmen have come from Kolkata and so I was with them since morning,"

"I am at Millicent's boutique. I will text as I reach home," she replied.

"Okay and I'm going to drop my cousin to the railway station so I will be back at nine of the clock so then come online."

"*Doesn't he get bored of video chatting all day long?*" Baddie said putting her pointer finger on her chin.

"*My Richie rich goes to the railway stations too? That place is too low for you. Lucky are those tracks and passengers that will see you.*"

Three constant hours chat was like a shower after a drought and it was ineffable for the pluviophiles. A glittering infection of his smile when he had seen left and right and then in front left her with a fortuitous series of happy thoughts. She loved him in white as it always emphasised his

103

fugitive intangible charm. Her bushy hair which were open, hindered him to see her and he showed his aversion by saying to keep them tied in that quixotic manner leaving her with a curious and inexplicable uneasiness. It had been midnight but that familiar and endearing intimacy couldn't find a break and he had a glance of extra ordinary meaning and she just sat there suffering agonies of shyness.

"So are we meeting tomorrow?" He asked.

"Yes, if you have some time," she said.

"All of my time is for you, my baby," he smiled.

"Wear white tomorrow."

"Why? Today also I am wearing," he asked confusedly.

"I don't know. Just wear white. I can't really say how you look in it. It leaves me wordless," *"And breathless."*

"Whoa! I don't look good in any way whatever I wear." he typed.

"Oh! So any other men could be better looking?" She asked herself.

"Noooo!" Elf and Baddie screamed hard.

She laughed and replied in a flash, "You know, I have seen you much more than you and I love you in every way. Now a person who has made me mad has to be good looking aye, it is obvious,"

"But you are better looking and the most beautiful," he said.

"Beautiful because your eyes see me which are beyond any comparison," she said and he laughed.

The dawn broke out with a dream which couldn't be dreamt of. It was something really strange to see a person whom you haven't seen before in actuality. She was unsure but she believed that it was his mother whom she saw and she couldn't really see her face properly but that was certainly seen somewhere which she wasn't able to make out. To share this appetence she thought of Amirah as for sharing it with him and telling this tale of his own mother would be nothing less than gobbledygook and she considered it to be tacenda. Giving all the attention to her talks, Amirah said to her that it was a connection by nature and maybe she would look same as she saw. Struck by a sudden curiosity, she was already in love with her second mother who came in her dream without meeting really. She just wished that she meets her soon and all she wanted to discuss was the childhood of her so-called life and the mischief of his early times; the super week day and the précised time when he came; his first words, his first injury and his first day of studies. She imagined everything which she would like to do with her mother- in-law because for her, she had that distinct respect and adoration which she had for no one else.

"Mistaken. I am reading," she sent.

"Wow Kyara. Go on and I have not read it so will you recommend?" Filiz asked.

"Well I can't say right now as I have just begun. I was so bored so I thought to read," she sighed.

"Well, Ayan was asking about you. Please call him," she typed.

"Oh me? Yes I will. Should I now?"

"No it is four now. You call at nine because he is always busy at this time,"

"Oh! It is four," she wrote thinking that today also Rehaam would get busy and they wouldn't meet.

After five minutes, she received a message from him.

"We are meeting today,"

"Yes, we are," she replied calmly.

"Send me your picture. What are you wearing?" he asked.

"I am wearing purple and white kurta with purple bottoms," she said and clicked a picture in the side pony tail.

"Pretty! Come online," he sent at another moment.

"Oh but we are meeting today so what is the need of video chatting?" She asked.

"Whatever I say, just do that, Okay? How many times should I repeat? Huh."

"Why are you saying like this? I am coming; I was just asking,"

After an hour she again messaged him to ask, "What should I wear?"

"Wear anything,"

"No, you tell me," she insisted.

"Hmm, wear black,"

"What black?" She asked.

"Kyara, wear anything. Wear a simple jean and top,"

"Hmm no, jeans is so casual. I will wear a palazzo but on what?"

"Hmm, wear anything. No one is seeing you."

"You will see me,"

"Yes and I know you have a very nice dressing sense so what is the need to show me?"

"Hmm. If I look bad then remember that 'Fashionistas need fashion disasters too!'" She joked.

It was seven of the clock when she was all dressed up in a pink loose palazzo and a small black inner with a full-sleeved shrug. Her hair was tied in his favourite hairstyle, a side pony-tail with some flicks on the right side of her fore-head. Looking at the clock, that minute hand seemed to crawl. It was a magic of fascination which made her live somewhere else.

"I am coming in two minutes," he texted and the swiftness of her heart was unexplainable. She said to the two that she was going at her friend's house for a project. To make it look real, she held her geography book and copy in her hands though they never questioned her. She ran down with her phone, books and her lip gloss. Being smart enough, he did not stop the car in front but a little forward below a tree of orange flowers. She was walking and there she opened the gate, "Please don't look at my clothes,"

He just smiled. "I didn't even get time to apply my gloss," she said in a normal tone. "What did you have in the evening?" He asked.

"I had *papad, pakode* and all," she replied looking at him.

"Okay, I too had all that and fruit salad," he said.

"Yes, I had that too. Oh my god! You are not wearing white," she said widening her eyes.

"Yes, I didn't get time," he said smiling and she ignored his excuse. He had worn a dark pink shirt with dark blue and white lines with a pair of blue jean. His hair was different this time as there was no gel but still didn't lose to look ravishing.

Where are we going?" She asked seeing his perennial charm.

"Somewhere.. Outlying," he replied without seeing her. She gave him a dulcet smile and said, "Hmm why?"

"So do you want to be with me in this traffic where we can't hear each other?"

"Not really,"

As they went towards east, she saw a nursery. It had no light and was hushed. At some distance from the main gate, lied a corroded bench. There was a small space between the two. Heedfully, he stopped the car. She got up a little and got stuck to the door and looked at him. The normalcy in the atmosphere was out and anticipations were in!

"You're going far from me?" He said grabbing her hands.

"Oh no... I was being comfortable," she replied touching her tongue to her upper teeth. As the winds whistled, he held her shoulder and she moved closer. The stars winked and a faint tremor of amusement was on his lips. She saw him, she could see just his eyes and as she continued to see, she saw his nose and the skin between his nose and lips, deeply. His frigid touch of the hand made her smile. Soon they breathed one air in!

After a minute, he smiled and asked, "You're okay?"

"Ya! Ouch!"

"What happen?" He said holding her lightly.

"Nothing! I can't sit this way. It's hurting,"

"Oh ya! Don't turn your waist so much. It is delicate," They both laughed and she hugged him while laughing. Her eyes were closed for some seconds. A half breathless murmur of amazement and incredulity, she heard. "Hmm," she said incompletely and a quiver of resistance ran through her and she thought to get back from him. "No! Stay..Here," he said clutching her and she heard his sigh.

A shiver of apprehension crisped her skin as they were buffeted by all the winds of passion. In their world of fantasy, with no air gap amidst, they stopped to look at each other and smile.

"You look pretty," he said running his fingers through her hair. She laughed again and kissed his nose and cheeks at last. "Well!" He spoke in his humorous tone. "That's all you know, right?" She said shyly and went back to the place where she sat. "Let us click a picture," she said.

"NO!" He said.

"But why? I want," she said raising her eyes and arranging her hair properly. He took her phone out and clicked a picture.

"Show me. It is bad. Another."

"Kyara, I have to go to office. We don't have time," he said annoyingly.

"Wow! You do not listen a thing."

"Don't be stubborn, I told you," he said giving her an irritated look.

"Are you fighting with me?" She said putting her head on his shoulder.

"No, don't be sad baby. We will meet during day time and then click as much as you want. There is no light. How will the pictures come properly?"

"Hmm okay," she said pressing his hand and bringing back her on himself; he kissed her again and again and again for minutes until he could see lights coming on his car.

"Get up. There are people here," he said.

"This is so deadly embarrassing. Telling me to stay at one moment and ordering me to be straight at another."

She sat straight without another tilt. "You want chocolates?" he asked.

"No, I don't feel like having," he stopped the car on the mango tree road. He gave her the books and phone. "Bye!" she gave him a soft kiss on his left cheek.

What actually happened in those minutes is too much to understand by simple minds. Peace brooded over all and it was a redamancy. Later that night, she sat on her wooden chair and thought. A constant stream of rhythmic memories was flowing as if it was very long ago. She did not know what to do and there was no one with whom she could share her feelings, her trust, her devotion and how she just surrendered herself to that one man whom she did not know some time before. Her love was making her eyes melt because she loved him, she loved him very much, very very much and he did too. She understood that her life is been made for him and she is because of him. There could be nothing else but just a paper to which she emptied her heart and core.

Zulfi Sayyed

A perfect Tuesday this had gone.
Brought happiness like a huge cyclone.
The time was mine and a great allure,
It was a disease and it was a cure.

Happy, curious, joyous, and obliged,
I could not accept but neither denied.
Existing in this world but somewhere in my own,
I met myself whom I had not known.

The time tick-tacked and flew like balloons,
Wanting to sink in the calmed up lagoons.
All it appeared like a beautiful dream,
The light of the moon began to tickle and gleam.

I behaved as if I had "lost the plot,"
Undoubtedly, a clever shot!
Shouting, annoying, arguing and being carefree,
I can't believe it was actually me!

Saw myself from someone else's eyes,
It was a truth but seemed like lies.
I wish some truths could last forever,
And this is impossible in this world however.

Luckily, that whole time was all mine,
Thinking about it and feeling imperfectly fine.
I wish it was water and I could freeze—
As it was really " bee's knees".

People pass away; good times come to an end,
As missing the yesterday is a futile trend.
The happy moments are like sand in hand,
When the end is disheartening but the beginning is grand.
The time was mine and a great allure,
It was a disease and it was a cure.

She sent it to him at another moment and he replied, "Kyara, it is wow. How can you write all this? It looks as if a very mature person has written but my Kyari is so small," he replied. "We should publish them."

"No, you read them. I don't want anyone else to."

"Why so? Won't it be great when everyone will read and then all will tell you to write poems for them?" he said and she thought that at some point he was right. Her dream would come true if she would write professionally and she tried to write about some other topics like a moon. She held her pen but not even a single word came in her mind. She was just not interested in it and she never felt the way she was feeling when she wrote her last two poems. When she tried again to concentrate on it, she just had one thought and that was of him.

"No, I can't write for everyone," she sent in confusion.

"But why?" he questioned.

"I do not know. My Writing Is For You. I can't write unless it is about you. I don't know the reason but I am unable to," she messaged calmly.

"Kyara all this is really for me, I can't imagine," he said lovingly. "Hmm, I guess whenever I will write; it will be for you till the end," she ended.

Chapter 5

"Hi," she wrote.

"I cannot reply," he sent after some hours.

"Why? What has happened?" she asked fearfully.

"Do I need to tell you everything?" he said.

"Oh my god! Don't talk like that baby"

"Listen Kyara, don't keep on messaging. I am a very busy person okay. When I will have time, I will talk to you,"

He wrote which blew an appalling soft air. She could never imagine him talking to her in that way but she even knew that there was something which had hurt him or had an emotional impact but whatever it was, it had rendered her heart as it was a new-found thing or maybe a behaviour which was not so needed but still she was keeping her hopes high and waiting for him to say something. Though he never messaged for two days, she cried and prayed endlessly for him, for her, from him.

An engagement ceremony of one of her cousin sisters was on the next day and Rehaam's family was invited too. She was not at her home but was all busy in gearing up for it. Clothes, shoes, jewellery and stuff were on her mind and the small flat in an apartment of the central city was jammed with people. Her aunt's mommy, daddy, sisters, their husbands, their countless, every size kids, paternal families, maternal families blab blab blab were there as if it was not tomorrow but at the very moment. One word was for them in her dictionary and that was "Typical". They screamed, they shouted and they spoke that standard Hindi which she never even heard by her maids and not only Hindi but some so aghast words or phrases which made her say a word and that had to be "Eww". It is not always so important to speak in English but whatever one speaks; he or she must keep in mind or just have a little pity on the person's ears who hears it. It takes nothing but it is a form of charity. She hated those who had bad tone of speech because she had been taught to be polite, to be soft and to be girlish. Maybe the reason of being a convent student but it is not that way. They think that convent girls are egoistic and bad tempered and some might be but not all. Why is it that if one girl of a family runs away, every other girl also has to suffer? If one fruit rots, it does spoil the basket but we are people not fruits or veggies to be thrown away or just washed off. Convent itself is a brand which has a lot of revere and they are different, they speak stylishly and they pride on their education but hospitality is something which is taught before anything else. Humbleness which one finds in them is discrete and the emphasis on the character is beyond any comparison.

She sat there wondering of such people and she was not like those who became cruel or forgot manners and make frustrated faces if they don't like anyone. Showers of her blissful smile were for all. A dignity could be seen in that small girl who had suddenly started to think about her good and bad deeds which were constantly being written by the two angels on her both shoulders.

All that was running in her mind and was being on and off but something which never flew was him. The entire world was on one side and that one person was on another. She could leave everything for him and she even wanted to. Always urging to prove her love, she just wanted his sadness to go away from him but she was unaware of what was yet to come and how would it turn out. After some time she saw, "I am sorry."

"No, don't be sorry but do me a favour," she sent and he asked about it so she said, "For my sake, please tell me what is going on?"

"Hmm, it is too bad," he replied.

"I know baby but I plead to you. I can't tell how sad I am because you are not talking to me. Please, for me, tell me."

"Okay, don't tell anyone. It is pathetic."

"I won't." She said in a hurry."

"Hmm Maisha is involved with someone else. I don't know why did she do this but I am broken, I don't know what to do," he wrote which gave her a sudden shock. When we hear or see something totally unexpected, we feel a jolt and so did she. She couldn't trust his words that her own sister who always claimed to love him did so.

"What?"

"Yes, I hope you believe me. Do you?" he asked.

"Yes. Is it really true? You must have misunderstood or some other confusion might have occurred," she wrote.

"No confusions. She told me. Can you imagine? Someone can do this even after being in such a serious relationship. I mean our families have got involved," he said and she just consoled.

"You tell me, will you forgive someone if he'll do this to you?" he asked which astonished her. She thought that even if he would have done this with her, she would have forgiven because love means forgiveness.

She said, "Yes, I will forgive."

"Hmm, you tell me as a sister, should I forgive her?" he asked which had totally shaken her. Did he say "sister"? Was she his sister? Was she in love with the one who considers her as his sister? That word was like an itch. How can someone say that? Being totally involved with a girl mentally, emotionally, physically and then stating her as a sister? She just did not know how to respond as she was so badly hurt and miffed that she did not have any words to exchange. Still she managed and said yes despite of knowing how much pain she was giving to herself. Her love, whom she considered more than her life was talking about some other girl who was her sister and he was calling her, his sister. What was happening? It was a sister war or some puzzlement which had no meaning but still was going. She thought that maybe Hitler was right to say that war is actually better than love as at its end either we die or live but in love we neither die nor live.

"You know, calm down now and forgive her and no more discussions on this topic now. Forget it."

There was some sort of pain which was thumping and she never knew that her own cousin could do this with him. She could understand his sting clearly and she was sympathetic but in all this, it was she who was suffering. He did not talk to her the way he always did. He was in grief and he had forgiven her but still the paper never gets straight after being crushed just once. Undeniably, it was Maisha's mistake and he loved her very much that still he was ready to be normal and continue with their relationship. She never wanted them to end up and there was no good in this thought for her but that is what made her someone who was his but she was suddenly knowing that it was Maisha who was important but not her and she was being okay but she knew what was inside. She was showing her love all the day round but he was just replying her with 'hmm' or 'yes or no'. Handling him who was so much more mature, she just wanted one thing and that was his happiness in any way.

It was eight thirty in the evening when all the guests had arrived at Miraj hotel's lawn and she stood there at the main gate dressed in a yellow and pink Indian wear, making her curls fine. The ground was wet due to rain and she saw his white car at a distance. She moved a little backwards making her facial expression cheerful. Being totally worried to meet his mom and dad, she gave her hair a final touch and brought a smile as soon as her mother moved out of the car. She moved forward with the prettiest smile she could have and greeted in her most pleasing voice. His mother was much more appealing than any other woman and she knew her. They both gave each other a very common look as they had already met before. Breaking an awkward silence, his mother said, "Kyara! Rehaam I have met her. I told you that I met a pretty girl in the market, I forgot her name. So finally Kyara, I am so happy to meet you. You are Maisha's sister. That is beautiful."

She just thought that his mother was that lady of the market. Giving a confusedly glad look, she laughed a little and went inside with them. His father couldn't come because of some work. They both talked with halt and shared everything like friends, who were lost long before. Kyara behaved at her best as she always looked upon her as her mother-in-law. Rehaam also met some friends and he remained busy with them. She made all her friends meet him one by one and she was happy that at least he talked to her. Leaving his mother with Amirah, she came to him and said in a proud tone, "How am I looking? Do you even know that there was no electricity at our home and I had to dress up so quickly? I didn't even apply eyeliner or anything. It was so hectic and by the way, have you had food?"

"So many questions," he said formally moving his eyes from her head to heels.

"Yes, so why don't you answer?" she smiled. "Well, I don't have time for you. I am going to mommy. Good bye!"

That life-changing night ended up so well that when they had left, she could not wait for his message to tell her that how did his mother find her? She constantly asked Aroosh and Amirah about her behaviour and they both optimistically gave her hopes. Being unable to concentrate on her food, rice or anything which was on her plate was not going down her throat. All she was thinking about was him and his mother and at another moment she saw his message.

"Are you there? Have you come back?" he asked.

"Yes, I mean no. I am still here," she replied nervously.

"Okay, so I will text afterwards," he said.

"No no. First tell me, what your mommy said. Did she even like me? I am so tensed," she sent.

"Ha-ha, why are you tensed?" he asked.

"Oh don't question. Tell me please. I can't breathe," she said.

"She just loved you. You know, she has been talking about you since so long. You have become her favourite," he said which gave her wings to fly.

"Really?" she asked.

"Yes, she even said that you should come home soon," he said.

"Aww, you know I am feeling like a queen. I am so happy today, I can't say. You know she has always mattered to me so much and finally she liked me. I just can't state that feeling in words. It is out of this world," She said and thanked her lord.

"Hmm," he replied. "Don't curl your hair again."

"He hated me, I guess."

She hesitated and asked, "Why? Didn't I look good?"

He said, "You did but straight suits you more."

"Okay, I will not. Aroosh is saying that we just met some time before and again we have started talking. By the way, she liked you very much," she said.

"Ha-ha she also played with you in sunder land apartments. Didn't she?" He asked. "You remember so much," She said. "Why don't you sit while drinking water?"

"Oh," he answered.

"You should. It's good for us."

"Okay I will next time," he wrote. "So I want you to find a girl for me."

She thought that he doesn't he think of her while talking of any other girl in front of him. She did not say anything for two minutes but then she thought that if she would reply negatively, he would feel bad. Already he was depressed and she didn't want him to feel that he had to live within the boundaries of her love. She was possessive but her maturity was more than that moving emotion. Having a great control on herself, she said with a heavy heart, "Hmm, what kind of girl? You have Maisha,"

He said, "No, she has cheated on me. Someone else, you know a pretty girl. I wish you say that I have found a girl for you now you talk to her,"

Both of her eyes were heavy and she could barely see her screen. It was all blurred but she did not close her eyes. She was sitting with all her family members at the dining table and her nose changed to red but she couldn't control. She closed her eyes and they fell out enormously. Hiding her head with the help of the table, she put it down and wrote in anger, "Huh. Bye."

He messaged, "Ha-ha-ha." and sent a kiss.

She said, "What? Go and talk to someone else."

"I wanted to see you like this," he typed. "You must be looking cute."

"Oh so you wanted this. You know I'm crying," she calmed down as she got to know that he was joking and doing it intentionally.

"I love you," He wrote intensely.

"If you will even have a thought about any other girl, I will kill her. Understood?" she sent and he agreed.

"What are you wearing?" he asked when she reached home.

"I am wearing a one piece night suit," she replied.

"Kyara, you look very beautiful in Indian. You should wear it more often."

Being felt in love once again which was lost somewhere, she could not stop herself from being happy. Her love for him was not because she was getting something in exchange but just because, he was someone who made her smile even while she cried. She started to believe that she was married to him and she never questioned him back once he told her to do something. Surprisingly, she did leave all those lavish and expensive clothes which were her pride and the greatest part of her life. He never ordered her, but she only took his simple statements as compulsions. Wanting to get mixed with his colours, she wanted herself to be the way he wanted her to be and as she was gaining little knowledge about her religion, she knew that a wife must dress according to her husband's orders and the truth was that they were no one to each other but the teeny girl's mind had made every relation with him. She belonged to him despite of knowing that he did not belong to her. Her love was not having limits but every time, it was on her mind that whatever it was, it had to end somewhere, sometime and in some way. Even after being told by her friends Amirah and Filiz the harms of this relationship of no meaning which acted as a source of her life, she knew that they were right, they were genuine and their explanations were the outcome of their undiminished care.

Somewhere on this stage, the two pair of eyes will meet and it`ll be known that it was waited for but it`ll be even known that it will be cruel and mortal. I know that it is going to be terrible but so do I know that it may be so mesmerising that it will blow away the calmness of that quite place which will sink in the beauty. The maple leaves will not stop blowing. The wind will be devilishly rapid. All the inhumans will begin howling and chirping and soon the droplets of water will touch the stage and at the spur of the moment we will be lost in its rejuvenation. I will be joyful forgetting about its end, feel happy forgetting about the other players and I am assured that the cast would be concerned but I can never want anyone to understand the quietness of that place, the simplicity of the rain, and the wraith of the wind and the wonderfulness of that whole atmosphere. As the weather will change its mood, the distance will be the same but the decrement will be faced, the unit of life is going to be the same but the increment will be placed!!

Its imaginary and its unreal but I believe in its occurrence as it can be felt despite of being lifeless. It lives in my imagination...it lives in the very cell of this holy stage!!

Speedily packing up his necessities, he boarded a plane to Shimla in the evening. He was uninformed about every detail but just knew that some business problem had come about. He was calm as he knew his powers and petty crisis have come across him too frequently. In the mean time, Maisha returned back to the city and she knew that he was not there due to some reasons. He didn't tell Kyara because maybe he did not consider her important enough to let know each and everything. That was something inconceivable that why did he consider her of so less value? She got to know of this and for a second she had a thought about not notifying her but sanguinity filled a larger space and so she thought that perhaps due to the rigidity of the period, he could not. She messaged him whole of the evening but got no reply and his last seen was of much before time so she thought that he must have got busy with his Himachal family. The night was spent coolly in his thoughts but the noon had another flavour.

"Good day." She sent as she saw him online. There was no reply which made her hassle as she hated late replies.

"Are you there? Why are you not replying? I have been messaging since yesterday." Five hours passed and she never saw his answer. His last checked was of fifteen minutes before which could easily make her feel agonized and concerned. Uneasiness in her heart which could not stop her to say, "I am saying something. Why are you not answering?"

"Are you mad? I told you not to message me continuously. I am very busy. I can't talk to you all the time. Every time you do this," he messaged.

"What has happened? I am just asking normally," she asked in fear.

"I am in a very big problem and now please stop irritating me all the time."

"Don't talk to me like this please. You know, I start crying when you speak in this manner. You tell me what the problem is," she said in hopefulness which made her feel guilty.

"Hmm, there are some problems at work and I am tensed. I don't know what to do. Everything is in such a mess."

"Oh, don't be tensed please. I know everything will be fine. Just have faith," she said in order to motivate but consolation was needed by her too. She was restless and worried. It was the time of night prayer which is the longest and was always ignored by her. She offered every prayer but not this one as getting up early made her feel sleepy before time and today it was different as she had to pray and she was too twitchy to wait until dawn. She made ablution and stood with all her heart. After feeling the comfort to complete her part, she went to Maisha as she knew that she would discuss something related to it. She told her that market crashed and all their shares were already in agreement with a company who was paying a huge amount but as yesterday the stocks went down so their business was at a risk. After saying some words of empathy, Maisha began to talk about her friend's coming marriage but Kyara; her mind was somewhere far, towards the north. Her mood was miserable as she did not know anything besides this. Her night went thinking of all this and the next two days went without any conversation. At eight of the clock, when she was at her aunt's house, she messaged him, "Are you fine? Did you have food?"

"Yes I had and what about you? Some people are coming and wish that everything goes well. I am tensed because their deal will prove to be helpful," he wrote.

"I didn't have. Really, *In Sha Allah* it will be good. Tell me as soon as you get over with it," she wrote and directly went in an isolated room located in the inner portion of the big, old house. She along with Aroosh began to pray and everyone there started calling them so religious seeing their devotion and commitment. After twenty minutes, she was not finding comfort in the worldly talks and was always thinking that what must be happening there at his house. She went in another vacant room where she could see the noblest book kept at a corner. Without any second thought, she covered her hair and put it on a pillow and sat thinking that "if you want to talk to god then stand to pray and if you want god to talk to you then read his *Quran*." She had already talked to him and now she wanted him to answer. People say that you may find every answer in it. Every word has a blessing and read it slowly and not hasten.

She read one verse and fifth and came to the end of one Para. Her aunt came inside and asked her that why was she reading? She replied that she was uncomfortable and so now she feels fine. Her aunt gave her a very bad look which she did mind but then had forgotten.

"By the way, why are you reading it? Tell me at least. Before this day, I never saw you being so interested." Aroosh asked.

"*Woh,* he is in problem," she spoke softly with her eyes falling down. Her cousin who had been seeing her since years and claimed to know her best was suffering with motionlessness. She couldn't bear that more and so she said, "What? Are you serious? Maisha should do that. Why are you doing?"

Hesitancy made her pale and she sat there nodding gratuitously. At eleven, when she was there at Aroosh's house, he didn't message her. He was online and Maisha was typing on her phone. She could make out that there was another conversation going on so she stayed away. She messaged, "What about the deal?"

"It is done. *Alhamdulillah* I am so happy," he answered.

"Thank god. I was so tensed."

"So sweet of you," he sent a kiss.

"You know, Kyara reads Quran when her Rehaam has a problem. Has she gone mad?" Aroosh said to Amirah in a group chat which had three of them.

"Yes I am seeing that she is not even leaving a single prayer these days. Whoa! Rehaam's effect is at its top," she replied.

"Aye Rehaam's love is at its finest point. Ahem-ahem." Aroosh taunted.

"Oh please. Will you both stop? It is nothing like that and don't say his name so directly," she interrupted.

"Oh! Now we can't even talk about him ha?" Aroosh said.

"You can but not like this. By the way, it is time for *namaz* so I will talk to you guys later." Kyara said.

"Seriously, I mean I haven't seen this kind of love ever."

"What do you mean by this kind of love?" She questioned.

"She means that you love him excessively and be calm, don't just draw in so much. Kyara, don't forget that he is going to be your brother-in-law, in fact our brother-in-law. When he will get married, I don't want you to be ill with." explained Aroosh.

"Ha-ha you both keep calm. We both love each other and it doesn't matter at which point we will reach. What matters is that how devoted we are at this time. You may call it love but I call it my soul, my presence and my belief which connects us heavenly. I don't know why we can't get married but maybe I believe that if god has written this part of us together then he will manage it afterwards too," she said.

"My Kyara has become a grown up now. I feel good to see you like this. You know, it adds to your beauty. You always called yourself perfect right? See now you are, with him. May god save both of you from any evil eye." said Amirah.

As the season of three months altered, Rehaam was in Himachal since five days. He had not talked to her for whole one day which made her livid unequivocally. In anxiety, she did not even want to say a word to him because she thought that he was not bothered and maybe he wasn't in real. His mind was made of some unhinged layers which did anything at any odd time and that was a time of total ignition. A coating of babyish behaviour could have seen which over shined her mellowness.

"Why are you not talking to me? Do I have to ask you this question thousands of times in a day or are you least bothered?" she texted.

"Hi Kyari! I am sorry, I was busy," he replied at another hour.

"Hmm, Oh!"

"I was busy," he said.

"Just shut up okay and don't you even think to talk to me again in your life. You just know how to be busy for me and nothing else. So now also please, don't do a favour and just shut up," she said and threw her phone.

"Kyara, I told you that I won't tolerate this kind of behaviour," he said.

"Oh really? You know, I can't tolerate you. What do you actually think? I mean, what is happening?" she asked in exasperation.

"Okay bye," he wrote and she didn't reply a word. Beginning with her tears, she understood that she was so bad. Despite of knowing about his problems, she behaved with him in the most undignified manner. She had messaged him later but he had not replied. She was unable to find any way as it was all her blunder and she never knew that it would affect him so badly that he wouldn't mind ignoring her. At that moment, standing in her balcony she had a lot of distinctive thoughts enveloping her and that was of his marriage. In her sight, Maisha and Rehaam were happy together and they never fought as much as they did. Maybe peace is what makes marriage and she blamed herself for being Rehaam's secondary choice!

A heavy phrase which consists of the word "secondary" joggled her mind. In that faultless life of her, she was being defined as a "secondary choice" and she couldn't have known this before that a person of simplicity which took an unnatural entry in her flawless world, made her ascend in some way but even placed her at a secondary position. Could she ever know that her life of pride was not at all upright? Nothing was falling at the right place and actually that love which she possessed for her existence was clearly fading. She did not have any reasons or complaints but in veracity, there was no peace or tranquillity in their love which was in the past.

Her tears dazzled and there was nothing explainable. If it had been said that there was lack of love, it would have been chauvinism.

"Listen, I am sorry," she wrote.

"Well it is not okay," he replied after a while.

"Yes that is why I am saying sorry," she said with annoyance.

He said, "Oh thanks for your favour. I don't need it actually, you see."

"Great. It is not a favour. I am sorry. I know I shouldn't have spoken that way."

"Hmm," he sent.

"What?" she asked.

"Nothing," he said.

"Why are you behaving like this?" she questioned.

"Like what?" he said.

"This is also not tolerable."

"Great then, bye," he said.

"Oh god! Are you having some problem with yourself or do you have any problem with me? Please justify and then leave. It is needful," she wrote.

"Hmm, Can I ask you a question?" he said suddenly. "Do you talk to someone else?"

"Of course I talk to people. What kind of question is that?" she said.

"I mean to say that do you talk to any other guy?" he said in a sudden. "If you do, then please tell me. It won't make a difference." She was perplexed and said at once, "What? I do not," she reacted as if a judge had made her live in the prison for no reason. *"Do you think me to be like Maisha? Being with someone and talking to hundreds and thousands of people."* She gave a very bad look facing the mirror and then he said, "Can you take swear? Take on me."

"Yes, swear upon you. I do not," she replied.

"Okay."

"What made you think so?" she asked.

"That day, when you had come to my house with Maisha, I saw you talking on phone inside a room alone for a long time and what was so important that you couldn't wait to reach your house? Whom were you talking to?"

"It was Amirah. You know she becomes excited so frequently and then she calls anytime and I am not allowed to cut it. You see," she justified.

"Oh okay. Why don't you both get married?" He joked.

"Ha-ha seriously. I wish she was a boy. We would have been a perfect one," she said. "By the way, you said that it wouldn't make any difference. Why? Doesn't it matter?" she asked in a serious tone.

"Of course it will make a difference. I said to make you comfortable or else you could have lied."

"Ha really? I never lie. Make a note of that," she said.

"You know, when I was talking on phone, you were passing by the room and you took a pause to see me and gave a very bad look. I was telling that only to her at that moment. Then you went away and again after two minutes you passed and again you took a halt. It was so funny and I was wondering that why were you staring at me for five seconds each time. Now I know, there was a possessiveness bacteria creeping in."

"Ha-ha yes," he said.

"You know, did I tell you? One guy proposed to me," she laughed.

"Really? Who?" He asked in suspicion.

"Ha-ha Filiz's friend. Zain Dastur, a model currently living in Delhi," she wrote.

"So? When? You know quite a lot about him," he said.

"Okay so for Mr. Re Al this intro is quite a LOT." Baddie pouted.

"Yes because he is her good friend. Not much before, during *Ramadan*," she said. "Ok, you didn't tell me. So what was your answer?" He asked casually.

"Err. I didn't find it important." *"Did you leave time to think about it?"*

"Answer?" he asked again.

"What do you think it to be?"

"How would I know?" he said.

"I didn't say a word," she said.

"Why?" he asked.

"Because I am with someone else *na*," she said.

"Oh with whom?" he asked.

"That one who lives in flora line and is so deadly insecure about me," she wrote.

"Ha-ha *acha*," he said and his "*acha*" was not same always but it occurred only when he was in a good mood or it was after something which he liked. Making out about his temper by his one word, she could simply mould herself in that way.

Lying on her bed at night and gazing at the fan, she was starting to believe that he had not changed that much as she thought him to be. Once again, it was into her that he did love her but not like he loved Maisha but in some other way and she was compelled to feel gratified with whatever she had. In her mind, rolled up that she could have answered to the proposal she received and her journey would have become without any glitch and he could have married her even. A thought which leaped was that how laid-back it could have been with him and he wouldn't even need to be shared with anyone. He would have been hers but could she be all his?

And that is where life becomes demanding and that ease gets away in next to no time. She thought that couldn't her life be as simple with him as it could be with Zain? And then she remembered 'Romeo and Juliet', 'Heer-Ranjha' and then 'Kyara- Rehaam'. They were together but couldn't express to anyone. They did die together but couldn't live for a second. In all eyes, they were unknown but still their names are taken together. There may be millions of stories like this which are inexpressibly painful but what if it has been said that if a love story ends then it is not one in real. It was unstated but she remembered how improper it was of her to love him. It was so frightful that she was lying to her own sister and she feared that if anyone would get to know this, her life would end. At the back of her mind, it was that is it a crime to love him as she knew that she loved him more than anyone could ever. Some may say, it is cruel, some may think it to be a scam. Others may regard her as characterless and shameful. And for the least people, she was somewhere right as she was in love and it doesn't see situations, relations or any comfort. If god writes it then it happens without coming to light.

The winters had fired up in the early January and she was spending her weekend at Amirah's house. Her mother, sister and both of them were watching a religious channel on which they told how Mondays and Thursdays are the best days to fast. Though, it was not compulsory to do so but it was for our own good. What we call *'Nafil'* fast is for our own good as God says, that the closest person to him is not that prophet who was able to talk to him but that person who fasts all day for his sake and prays just before the time of breaking his long day fast. He says that he is so close to that person at that time that there is only a distance of one curtain between him and his believer.

She thought that if she would begin to fast on Mondays and Thursdays as well then God will accept her prayers. And that prayer, but obviously about him who was in crisis but it was she who thought about those problems all day, maybe much more than him. Abruptly she saw that the next day was

Monday and she was all set to fast so that all his problems come to an end. She told this to her friend and she ignored her with a valid reason.

"And what about crisis?" Kyara asked Amirah's mother when they were discussing about the holy sentences which one should read at some times.

"Problems!" she told her some group of words which were to be said hundred times each after morning and night prayers. "Wait a second! Why do you want?" she asked.

"Ha-ha actually..." she stopped to think. "Because," Amirah said making her eyes wide. "Her aunt is having some problem. Kyara, you told me, don't you remember?"

"Yes exactly." Kyara replied. *"Oh god! Please forgive me for this lie,"* she said slowly.

"Oh, I will pray for her and read these wordings too." Her mother said and wrote the wordings on a paper. "Five hundred times a day so hundred times after each prayer will be easier." "Perfect!" Kyara smiled.

"Baby, how are you? I miss you," she sent to him.

"Hmm," he replied.

"What?" she said.

"I am in no mood. TTYL."

"Why? Talk to me now. I am missing you," she said and he didn't reply.

"Come, have food." Amirah said.

"Kyara Kyara, come *na*."

"I don't want to. I am going home. Bye," she said walking downstairs.

"Why? Just five minutes before you said that you were hungry. What took place in this short span? Wait, show me your phone." Amirah said strictly.

"What? Please," she said in a lament tone and she snatched the phone.

"Oh wow! Your Rehaam is doing this with you, right? I mean, look at the way he talks to you Kyara. How can anyone talk to anyone like this?" Amirah said closing the door.

"Don't interfere. He is having a bad mood so what can we do? I can't force him, is this some job going on? So please stay out," she said heatedly.

"Bad mood? Because of what? You haven't done anything and it is actually his duty to forget all his problems and talk to you. I mean, you are fasting so that his problems get over, reading what not without any particular relation and he is treating you this way. I can't stay out of it but I will bring you out of this. You will end everything with him. I can't see my sister with such a man who treats her on the basis of his mood. Huh!" she shouted.

"Amirah, don't you say a word now. Relation? Oh god, I love him; and his problems before anyone, even before him are mine. My god will ask me that what I did when he was in crisis and I want an answer at that time. He will ask me that did I only claim to love him or was I actually in love with him then I will have to prove to him. What are you talking about? Leave him? I love him Amirah and you know, you can't understand so just forget it," Kyara said without a pause.

"You love him, okay fine but does he love you? I can't see."

"He does and he doesn't need to prove to anyone," she replied. "Whoa! You need to prove and he is free from everything. Kyara, don't make it tough. Already it is late and what will you do when he will get married? I know you will not be able to live. I am your sister and I know you love him and even if he does then what is going to be the conclusion of all this? Don't forget that he is going to be your brother-in-law. He will be your sister's husband. Are you a betrayer? Just imagine, how Maisha will think if god forbid she will know." Amirah hugged her.

She became emotional, "I don't know."

"Don't you love your sister?" Amirah asked. "Have you forgotten all that love which she has given you since your birth for a man who has come in your life one year ago?" she remained silent. "Answer me."

She said helplessly, "I never decided this Amirah, it is destined. I am helpless and there is no way to come out of it."

"Kyara, what kind of love is this? You will get so many people. He is not the only one in this world. I can't see you living a life waiting for someone who is not even yours."

"I don't know what this is," she laughed with tears. "I know I will get many but not him. I can get the most handsome men but not that innocence and shine which comes in his eyes when he smiles at me. Not that feeling which I feel only when he is with me. I could have said yes to Zain but I am not like that. He is my first love and he will be my last. It has started with him and my life will end at him and I can't change it. If god has planned this for me, then let it proceed."

"Wow." Amirah said crying. "Am I in a fairy tale? My perfect princess is having an impalpable story. "Lucky you,"

"Ha-ha, you are calling it good luck? Well, at one side, it is and on another, let us not think about it," she said.

"By the way, are you serious? I mean, you will be loyal to him all your life. Did I hear that?" Amirah said.

"Yasss," she said with a wicked smile.

"Don't tell me. All your life?" she opened her eyes broad.

"Yes so do you think I have been talking nonsense all this long?" asked Kyara. "Haw, I am dead. Your marriage? What about that?" she asked.

"That... in heaven," she said superiorly. "By the way, have you looked him when he smiles? There is some weird fascination that he has in his slight curve and when he speaks softly to me when I am so close to him. Oh my god, my breathe stops at that time."

"Smile? Yes that day, I saw. Only you can see all the Magic in him, not everyone. Wait a sec! Close, what did you say? Say again." Amirah said doubtingly.

"What?" she asked looking at the fan's speed. "Why is it slow? Regulate the speed."

"Ahan, you said close? When were you close to him? Kyara, should I beat you now? You never told me," said Amirah.

"Do I need to tell you everything? It is my personal life," she said putting her lips tight in order to make an expression of irritation.

"Yes you need to. I am not a part of your professional life, okay? And don't forget Kyara, to be in your limits. You are not married to him." Amirah explained.

"Oho baby. I am *toh* married to him," she said closing her eyes.

"What? Kyara, get up. Are you mad? Should I talk to him? Is he exploiting you? I mean, what is going on? I am talking to him now," she said picking her up phone.

"Hey are you mad? 'Exploitation!' Where did it come from?" she said innocently.

"Kyara, you are sixteen, are you forgetting? What's up with you?"

"Stop over reacting at all times Amirah, for god's sake, it really irritates me. I just said about the way he talks to me when I hug him. Simple. That doesn't mean anything else. He also knows how small I am and he is very protective. So without knowing the whole story, please don't make up your own," she said furiously. "it is not just with you but it's a societal problem. Love doesn't mean exploitation or something illegal. It is the most beautiful form of life and I wonder what is up with people like you who define love in this way."

"Hmm, I am your elder sister. Don't forget. It is my right to ask you everything." said Amirah speedily. "By the way, you were on his smile. So how does my Kyara's Rehaam smile? Continue the explanations. I know they won't end."

"Don't take his name so directly," she said smiling. "You know, I never take his name."

"Ha-ha of course, alike a typical Indian wife or I would prefer calling you a '*Dharm patni*' who is so small and married. Ha, call the police, crime taking place."

"Don't tease me. Already I am tensed. God only knows, when he will talk to me," she said.

"He will, one fine day. Don't worry."

Hanging her outfits in the cupboard, she had put her phone on one of the lower sections of it. She folded some stoles and wraps while everyone else had gone to sleep. The clock was about to strike twelve and as she had school the following day, she had taken her dress out for ironing. She had to wake up for *suhur* at four thirty and she didn't find it right to tell anyone that she was about to fast the next day to avoid questionnaire. Still her mind was not calm as the day did not end well and the day was said to be good only when he was good to her, while the other days, were thought to be without the good luck. When he avoided her, she lived with his memories as total abandoning, was just not probable. He was not talking but still her mind was talking to him all the time. She lied down thinking of all those things she would say when he would talk to her and she thought to talk about his smile but the thoughts she was getting then, were diversely divine and she began.

When I have that thought of a smile;
which leaves me so much shaken.
An epitome of divine charm and perfection.
I do know that it was created in heaven.

Having the least idea about one and all.
It's a rapid, obvious cure for me,
From all d universal troubles and falls,
Abundantly it sets me so free.

Today it is, maybe tomorrow it vanishes.
I'm concerned for it more than anyone.
It creates a spark and moistens my lashes.
Its ferocious ashes burn everyone.

Those eyes get filled with lusty pearls.
When that mesmerising curve passes through.
Filling me with gifted blue curls.
I wish it was a shell and I could have lived into.

Thinking it to be alike that dusk breeze.
For a moment which adds on inert lives.
There`s an ideal door and that smile has its keys.
As if I'm a bee who constantly searches for its hives.

When you smile, the air does change its flow.
All those pains in the world too become low.
Do all feel that wonder or am I having all the luck?
I then feel to foresee, pause, stop and chuck.
I have it in my eyes and its forever in my mind.
Cause in this world none can ever get its kind.

I`m scared to know its life is transitory.
Can't it just be with me till the end?
It so resembles to the whiteness of ivory.
It has all the reasons and answers to mend.

That smile which you have has totally blown me away.
I wish it was grass in which we could lay.
Always wanting to be the reason for it to arise,
I closely relate it to d glimpse of paradise!

Her fast had begun before sun and after a frenzied day in school, she reached home at two and completed the afternoon prayer and the recitation of verses. Thinking that he had almost forgotten her, she just could not wait to talk to him. Suddenly she grasped that their fights had become so frequent that their love was trailing. The main part was that when he was with her then she never realised of his substance but when he did not talk to her then even her image in the mirror reminded her of him. That way when she would change her braid into a pony tail when he said to her was not put behind. Those nail colours which she would apply according to his likings could not be passed over. When she tried to forget him for a moment on the beg of her Aroosh, she looked down and saw that dress of which she had clicked her picture to send to him. Miserable she had been and then she was taken to the front balcony for passing time and she sat there staring at a mango tree. Putting her fingers on her cheek, she took the support of a cemented railing and sat for three minutes without blinking. There was silence between the two and it seemed intolerable tragic to her cousin who wanted to speak but looking at her despondency, she remained quiet and looked at her with sympathetic eyes. She kept on looking at her and then she saw that she was exquisitely simple. Tears of reminiscences blurred her vision but Kyara did not change the view. After half a second, her left eye gave out a drop which ran down speedily and before its finish, Aroosh said, "Hey, have you begun again? Why? Don't look there. Has it made you sad? What happened there? Tell me or common get in. Will you say?"

She kept on ogling and tenderness breathed from her and she spoke, "We met there first time." her voice was no less than a new born baby and her eyes looked alike doe. She thought to remain mature enough to deal with it but until when? Her eyes were that of an explorer of answers. Aroosh was wordless and she heard, "What have I done? Is it my fault? He is distancing himself from me. What have I done?" She began to lament at another second and Aroosh tried to bring her back. "No you haven't done anything. You can never go wrong. See, the world says that you are perfect. I am imperfect, he is imperfect but you are not. Why do you think that it is your fault? You know, people give examples of you; they discuss your brilliance and your softness. You are an ideal. Don't ever think in life that you have done anything wrong."

"No I must have done something wrong. That is why he has gone so far from me. I remember when he couldn't live for a minute without me and now he doesn't talk to me for so many days. Should I change?"

"No, are you mad? Kyara don't be a child. He is no one to you. He is Maisha's and he is talking to her. I am telling you to let him go. Just end it." Aroosh said and she began to cry again. Her tears didn't stop for five hours and her eyes had become red. She had got her eyes puffed up and a white thread like layer was seen below her eyes along with the dark circles.

"Please stop it Kyara. Think about your mother and your sisters and your grandparents. Don't they have any importance? You are ruining your health for a guy who met you some time before. I won't call it any love but this is sheer madness. Leave him and just move on." Amirah messaged. "Aroosh told me about your foolishness. I mean, really? Five hours? Are you still crying? Should I talk to that person? Seriously I am going to now. Just wait."

"No, don't. He must be busy. I don't want him to worry," she said.

"Worry? Madam, he doesn't even remember you. These boys are all same, you know. They just play." Aroosh said.

"Aroosh, mind your words, get it? How dare you? And who are you? Okay fine. I am his and these tears are for him, so it doesn't make a difference." Kyara thundered.

"Fine, keep up your behaviour. It will take you nowhere. Bye." Aroosh said and left the room.

Two days had passed and there was not a single word from him. She kept on checking her phone but he never called or messaged. She saw him online repeatedly but she thought that if he had really forgotten her then she would also end all up.

The times when his memories flew from her mind for some minutes and that was when she stood to pray. It was captivating and powerful that only her prayers had that power to outshine him. Not actually they flew but that woe used to take a form of hope and optimism, that "Maybe Some Day". She started to find him in her prayers as she was comforted and her soothe meant him. She believed that she was very close to her lord but along with that, praying for her love brought her closer to him too despite of the detachment. Her love was illegal, despicable and mean but if it was that way certainly then why did it make her closer to her lord? Why did her love make an atheist into a believer? She was filled with questions and she thought that how she could leave a person who made her understand her priorities and amplified her spirituality. Undoubtedly all do not experience this love, and if it had to be a normal love story then god must have rolled it that way but she believed that it was still being written and it was just not ending. It was taking twists but finally treading the right one.

"Hey, this is Amirah, Kyara's friend. I hope you're keeping fine." Amirah messaged.

"Hello. I am good. How about you?" he replied after half an hour.

"Well, I want to ask that what has happened?" she said.

"I didn't get you," he replied.

"Kyara has been crying constantly from three days. What is wrong? She is literally in her worst condition," she texted in an utmost anger. It appeared as if he had been in front of her, she would have really killed him.

"See, crying is what she likes the most. I fail to understand that why does she do that. You tell me, what should I do? I have to talk to Maisha also. If I reply Kyara a little later then also she begins to shed her tears. I am in so many problems and I work from eight in the morning to eleven at night, I don't get time. When I return then I have to talk to Maisha else, she will doubt on me. I am being chaotic as she starts her drama at all times," he messaged in a single breathe. Seeing his untouched manners and boorish words, she was mentally traumatized for some seconds. Facing hardships in reading what he sent to her, she could never believe that her sister chose to love a person who doesn't get disturbed to know about her struggles and torture. He showed an unnatural trait of diplomacy and abhorrence at that time which had left her immovable. She wanted to tell that to Kyara then and there, to leave him and forget all. She wanted to shout loud as there was something rapid going on in her mind and stomach. She was so badly hurt to see him who had become her friend's life. Knowing that how difficult it would be for her to forget him, she just wanted her to skip that one year of her life in any way because she could make out that if this insincere relationship would continue for some years, her sister would be filled with sorrow with time.

After thinking for one hour, she tried to convince him one more time.

"I don't know what's up with you two. I really request you to talk to her. Just once, talk to her please. She is crying so much so that she will make herself ill. I am sorry on her behalf if she gave you any inconvenience. Please talk to her."

Despite of seeing the message, he never replied. Amirah could not control her antagonism which was at its highest point. She hated him and she just wanted him to know how corrupt it was of him to do this with the person who loves him the most.

"Listen to me now, you will never talk to him. Even if he messages, you will not reply. Promise me and I don't want any arguments on this," she said when Kyara came to her house.

Kyara laughed and said, "Now what has happened? Already he has forgotten me and he will not message me so why are you telling me this."

Amirah stared in her eyes and held her hand, "I can't see you like this. I just can't. You know, how I feel when I see you crying because of that person. Please Kyara, forget him. Your lord is with you. He will help you in forgetting him. He will give you patience and today you are crying, tomorrow you will but he won't let you cry for always. I know, one day you will totally forget him. Just try once. He is not; you know he is too imperfect for you," she said and sniffed back a tear.

"Oh my goodness, I am seeing you crying. Why? Are you mad Amirah? Just stop all this. See I am not crying then why you are?" She said rubbing her cheeks.

"I am crying because of you. I know you are not crying but look at your eyes, you have become like that shattered person who has forgotten to smile. Kyara, you don't know what you are. Value yourself because in this world, none can be like you. I just feel sorry for that man who doesn't know your worth and when he will get to know, I am sure he will regret this time."

"Ha? Okay so let us forget him. I will live my life thinking that "Maybe Someday", we will meet there," she smiled and blushed.

"Where?" asked Amirah.

"In heaven, where else?" she said.

"No, you will meet your future husband there. He doesn't even deserve to live in Jannah with you. Huh." Amirah said stretching her lips to the right side.

"Ha-ha, why do you hate him so much?" she asked.

"Because you love him so much." replied Amirah and they both laughed.

He had chosen of not to come back but she chose to keep on waiting until her last breathe, when she will become tired of waiting. It was all destined as this is what life means, one keeps on waiting while the other moves on. She wanted herself to be that one memory of his which would make him smile at all times even if he forgets of all the love she gave to him.

Quite lost in these few years of mine, I am suffering with some heinous facts. Rather feeling so less who adds no glitters in the monotonous roads of yours. Roads on which I have walked upon, the sights which I dreamt of and that path which was my ultimate destination. Some senseless wind blew there and it took me away from you. I feel as if I don't have any sustenance. I agree that I breathe, but do I live? I listen and see, but do I feel? No less than a body whose soul has been taken, who doesn't have any mind but it shakes its parts at the last time.

My mouth has a graveyard of words to say and my ears are dying to have a word! To whom am I going to say them? I feel as if I am amidst an empty darkened tunnel which doesn't seem to end. Both of its ends are fatal so where should I go?

If you come there with me, even that night will see a sun rise and those creatures of the deserts will have a drop. I feel as if all that we had was just a story. Our love, our sentiments and our bond has been eyed upon. I seem like a prey which runs for life and the hunter does not bother. It is like that comedy which entertains you but the clown is always said to have a bad past!

I then see your happiness, your unconcern, your ignorance which makes me more of a sick. My tears which fall for you for days, my agony which finds no cure and my heart which discovers that it does not matter to you without me. I know you forget, but what about that first glimpse, those long hours and those smiles?

Suddenly is that all gone?

Being punished for what was lesser, I feel like an imprisoned bird. Seeing my mate rising high, we are distanced by destiny. They say, we write on our own but how can I write to be apart from you? Have I written my pain with my own hands? It's so hard to believe these beliefs. Leaving no other way for me, I am enforced to feel this way. God doesn't burden a soul more than his bearing capacity, I agree but is it not proving itself wrong? Seeing all this so soon, I fear what is yet to come? Now you live in my imagination and they say to move on but it is not easy for the heart to forget its beat?

It did stop, I shivered for long, I was thoughtless and in that state you were not there who promised me for ages. I just thought to end myself but then you came in front of me facing god. He will ask you someday the reasons behind the salty liquid of my eyes. What will you say? Your childishness will take you nowhere and maybe that was it which made me fall. This wicked time where you don't wish to see me, they say death comes once but will it come the second time too?

Sans touch which makes my hair smoother and my cheeks more pink, sans smell which I fancy and sans the taste which swirls in my tongue and then I don't want it to go. So you think all this is as easy as we met. This time gone, filled me with you and I don't need to find you but you exist in me, I have become your part. Can u deny it? Disability of my soul will follow up and if this is it then I disapprove of the time when love came in this world.

Chapter 6

She was in dormiveglia as the small hand went on to six in the evening. She felt magoa but stopped to sob more. It was fourteenth day of the month and she could remember that he stopped to talk to her on second. Disregarding him, she went out in the living room where her mother was changing the white curtain. She sat there and had a talk with her about her recent tests. As soon as she switched on the television, Maisha came out of the room and sat beside her. She touched her hair and brought her closer to herself. She hugged her and spoke something funny. Kyara loved her loving gestures and so she began to talk to her about her day at school. They both were so relaxed as they chatted with each other. It was ironical to see that Kyara never brought any change in her relationship with her best sister despite of so many problems in her life due to her because she knew that it was not her mistake. She was her sister much before he came and maybe the sisterly bond was so strapping that there was no change in them. Whenever Maisha talked about him in front of her, she always smiled and joined the talk as she used to do before. She never showed her displeasure or never complained about what he did with her. There was joy in her speech but some pain was seen in her eyes which was just not ready to leave. Nobody could see it except some of the species which were sent down only for her.

"I feel like having a soft drink or some juice." Kyara said.

"There is nothing in the house." Maisha tickled her.

"But I want *na*," she said stubbornly.

"If you both are going somewhere, then bring some cucumbers." Mommy said as she heard their talks.

"Okay, let us go Maish. We will get some snacks too. I am feeling hungry," she said and stood.

"You are such a hungry person." Maisha said uninterestedly.

"Get up! We will just go till that 'fanny' shop," she said.

They both stopped and she went inside to buy some chips and biscuits. She heard a car's horn outside and she turned half to see through the glass door. As soon as she saw Rehaam walking towards the shop along with Maisha, she turned back and breathed high. She didn't know when to turn and what to say. Feeling to get invisible, she kept on facing the shopkeeper as that was the first time when he was around and she had no feeling of seeing him. Within one minute he said, "Hello Kyara."

Firstly she decided of not replying or reacting but then she thought that she would look ill-mannered in front of Maisha. She turned half and smiled swiftly and again turned back. He saw her unpleasant smile and he drove off. They both came back home around seven. Without uttering anything, she went straight to her room, performed ablution and stood to pray.

She cried, *"Why did you make me meet him again? I was trying to forget him and again he came in front of me. Why? I never wanted to see him then why? He had no regret in his tone; he was all fine as if nothing happened ever. Does he regret me? But he is not my mistake." Her nose was filled with water and its tip became red. "How will I live without him? Will he never talk to me? I can't say to anyone that how am I feeling? You only know it and I know you don't like when I cry then don't do this with me."*

She got up in a better condition and went to her room to wash her face and apply some talcum powder on her nose to hide the redness which could have led to the questions by her family. Her phone was getting charged and was on the silent mode. She saw a message and dispassionately opened it without thinking that it would be his because whenever she thought so, it made her sadder.

"I am sorry, I never meant to hurt you," he messaged after two eighty three hours since the last time he messaged.

Her heart pounded in her throat and she looked intently on it to cope up with the veracity the moment. She threw her cell phone on bed and locked her eyes for ten seconds. Again she opened her phone lock and saw his message. Without another thought she went and stood to pray. As she completed her two *rakah* prayer of thankfulness, she said, "Oh Lord, you were listening to me so much so that you made him message me right now. I don't have words but I guess my tears can express how I am feeling seeing your immense love for me. I am left with no way for thanking you and I don't know whether I am going to talk to him or I will not but for now I just want to talk to you. I know, he doesn't love me but I know you do, a lot and I don't need anyone else. I am not crying for him or I am not thankful because he remembered me but my emotions have come out because leaving the whole world at that moment, you preferred to hear me. Thank you so much. My whole life will be less for thanking you."

She went back to her room and did not say a word. After five minutes, he messaged again, "Say something. I am sorry; I was busy so I couldn't talk to you. I am really sorry. Please say something."

Hope was far and dim in the curious irony of fate. She wanted an answer despite of all this which she had suffered. His apology looked bona fide but what if he would forget her for so many days and again come back with a five letter word. It is so crucial for a person to make up things after hurting you. What is the need of someone who is just good with the word "sorry"? She had some thoughts which afterwards were regarded as tacenda by her. It was not at all serene as she had no thought of her forthcoming response. After half an hour, he again said,

"Please reply. I promise I won't do this again. I really apologise, you know I am feeling so bad. I was busy in work and I have hurt you so much. Give me one last chance to make you happy, please."

She kept silent and did not shed any tear. She just looked at his messages without any blink.

"Please reply to me. I love you," he wrote, which again compelled her to lose her control on her sentiments. Belhevi dominated her and she said, "After twelve days?" "I am sorry Kyara. I was so busy that I did not talk to anyone. You know about my problems. I wanted to talk but time was not supportive and I just couldn't message you. I was not in the city till eighth and when I came back, there was so much work that I did not even get time for myself. You know how much I love you,"

"Stop it please. No more lies. I am sorry. Please don't message me again," she sent.

"I am sorry. Can't you forgive me? Do you even love me? Is it so easy for you to forget everything?" He asked gravely.

She started disliking this word of love because it didn't mean to everyone same as it meant to her. She set great store by it, more than anyone could ever understand. "Do you even love me?" his statement was no less than a gibe as he had so much valour to put it in front of her. There was torpor in her mood as she saw his way of conversation. It is so dunce when one questions something whose answer is so obvious that it can't be put into words. Some facts do have beggaring descriptions and that was it. She wanted to write on this globe how much she loved him. She wanted those small fragments of air to go to him and speak of her love. She wished for her each tear to have tongue to express about how she felt each second when he left her. She desired him to ask his lord to tell him that how much she loved him each second in this time. Regardless of his ruthlessness and callousness, she wanted him to be near her. She wanted him to make her or destroy her but remain with her.

He had altered the colour of her and she wanted him to stop wherever he was and whatever he was doing and smile because her every second could not be completed without thinking of him.

Horrendously, she managed to reply after two hours. "Do we have anything left that you are asking me all this? I wonder what you think of me. I know you don't love me so stop fooling me. It has been enough,"

"I am sorry. You are everything in my life," he said.

"Will you shut up or should I block you? Listen, I am not that type of a girl who will stay with you despite of seeing your true colours. You were my mistake and god knows what happened to me that I trusted you so much. So end this fake speech of yours and leave me," she sent and then she thought that she was being too rude to him.

"Hmm end? Do you want to leave me?" he asked.

"You have already left me," she said.

"I can't even imagine it for a moment. You are leaving me," he wrote.

"I am not," she said.

"Then talk to me properly."

"I don't want to. You will again get lost for another twelve days when your mood will be bad. I know you more than you know yourself," she said.

"*Acha!* If I will get lost then you will be there *na* to find me. Push me towards yourself as you see me distanced," He sent with a wink.

"Why would I? I don't have so much time."

"Then for whom do you have time?" he asked.

"Don't try to convince me okay. I am not talking to you," she wrote smiling.

"I am not convincing. I am just talking normally to my love after so many days," he wrote and she smiled. "Hmm, what do you want?

"You."

"No," she replied.

"Baby you can't say no to me. Have you forgotten the rules in these days?" he said. "You did the mistake and you are scolding me now," she said.

"Ha-ha, ha so I am scolding you, I have all the right," he said.

"Hmm," she said.

"Listen! Love you and I'm sorry. If again I will do this then you may leave me but not right now, I need you," he said.

"Why would I leave you? If you will leave me then I will kill you," she said.

"Ooh, I see. How's your friend Amirah? She messaged me. Do you know?" he said.

"Yes I know. She told me later," she said unresponsively.

"I thought you would get angry if I talk to her so I did not reply her," he said.

"Why would I get angry? You should have at least ended the conversation. She didn't like your behaviour," she typed.

"Hmm, I thought you would get angry on me for talking to her. Okay, I will talk now," he taunted.

"No need,"

"Why? She is pretty," he sent with a grinning emoticon.

"Cool, go ahead. Bye," she said heatedly. "Ha-ha you're nuts," he said.

"Oh please. Go and talk to everyone okay? I am also talking to Zain. By the way, you haven't seen him right? See, he is just so marvellous looking."

"Hmm, he looks good. So you talk to him and I will talk to her," he said.

"Great! Go on. I am not like you," she said and he laughed.

As the sun was ready to set, she sat in the living room, watching TV. There was no one in the house except Meera, her maid who worked from the afternoon until evening. She was wearing a purple and orange Pakistani dress. Her hair was tied in a form of a ponytail with the help of a large clip. The clip had got loose it got pressed against the couch's cushion. In her sluggish mood, she asked Meera to make a cup of coffee for her. Yawning at her best, she heard the doorbell at another minute. She went to the door and opened it softly. She peeped out through her heavy eyes. Initially, she couldn't see who was at the door as her eyes were half closed. As soon as she made her eyes big and got back her senses, she saw him!

He was standing smiling for no reason and she was giving her worst facial expression as she was puzzled. She didn't ask him to come inside and said in a loud voice, "What?" He smiled and said, "Your mommy has called me."

"Why? She is not home," she said arranging her hair properly and bringing them to one side.

"Well," he said and she smiled unenthusiastically as she never wanted him to see her in such a bad condition. She was half asleep and her eyes did not like the light coming from outside so she managed to keep herself normal but she hated the situation in which he saw her in her not so good attire.

"Mommy has gone to the neighbour's house. Oh, there she is," she said as she saw her coming to the front gate.

"*Assalamulaikum,*" he wished her.

She replied, "*Walekumassalam beta.* How're you? Come in. I will just go and get the papers," she said going inside the room.

"So?" he said.

"What?" she asked raising her eye brows.

"I think I should do a loyalty test on you," he said at once. "These days messages tracker applications are also coming up. I shall install."

"Han?" She said in a puzzled tone.

"Yes, who knows whether you talk to your Zain or not," he said which made her think that how mad he was. It was appearing so funny that he came into her house and started blaming her. She felt like laughing hard and she replied, "Yes please install but I fear you will read our chats. It will come under bad manners okay? They are private." They both laughed. "Yes..." he began. "Ssshh, slow," she said looking here and there.

"Okay, on text baby. By the way, be alert," he said and mommy came and handed some papers to him.

"Oh god, I wish I was looking good," she prayed as he went.

After one hour, he messaged, "Looked too happy."

"Yes, of course," she sent with a happy emoticon.

"Hmm, happy with your Zain right?" He said intensely and she laughed.

"Acha, give me a kiss. Fast," she said calmly. "Go and ask your Zain to give. Okay? Bye," He said and went offline.

"This is what I don't like about having sisters. He thinks that I'm like her."

"I am a one-man-girl! Can't this get in your business typo mind? How do you think that I can hurt my love by cheating or even just talking or even thinking? My thoughts, my words, my eyes, my mouth are just for you." Good Elf and Baddie said to her.

"But I shouldn't say all this to him else he may take me as granted." Baddie giggled.

"Ha-ha, no. Are you mad? You think anything," she said.

"No, I know, you talk to him. Don't lie," he wrote.

"Ahmm, why would I? I don't want to get killed by you."

"Hmm how should I believe?" he asked.

"Hmm, you want a proof now. You don't even trust me."

"I do," he sent.

"Then, why are you wasting time? Forget it," she replied.

"Zain Dastur is so lucky to be on my Re Adl's mind"

"Oh, happy propose day," he sent.

"Oh really?" she wrote making a pout.

"Yes," he replied.

"How can people celebrate such days? I mean, 'get a life'," she said giving an arrogant expression.

"They do without any reasons," he answered.

"Wait a second! You haven't proposed to me," she said and thought for another few seconds. "Whoa! Why haven't you? Isn't this ridiculous? You never proposed to me like all others do. You know, sitting on the knees with a ring. Okay, that is something too high, but normal proposal is also cute."

"Ha-ha, you are with me without any proposals, isn't this too great? What's the need of all this formality then? I don't understand this. When two people like each other, they are with each other. Why do people connect such relationships with some formal invitation? Should I courier to you now?" He mocked.

"Oh please. It is so cute. A gentleman does that. By the way, it is so my mistake that I didn't give you a chance to propose to me. Poor thing," she sighed.

"Ahem-Ahem," he sent.

"What?" she asked.

"Go and study. Tomorrow is your Science pre-board and you are here talking to me," he typed to end the conversation.

"No, I have studied. You don't try to change the topic. I am sad now. You didn't propose to me only. It is such a horrible thing," she wrote.

"Hmm," he replied.

"But what can we do now. Can't we change the past?" she regretted.

"Will you be my forever?" he sent at another second. She stared at her phone in wonder. It came to her with a stab of enlightenment and she bit her lips. Being obsessed by the modishness of a moment, she was overshadowed by a vague expression. Luminous with great thoughts, she soared into a rosy zone of contemplation. The deepest wants and aspirations of her soul were to shout loud to him about her consent.

In that purple vaulted night, she shared her rapture with Amirah first.

"Oh my god, oh my god, oh my god...." she kept on messaging her until she said, "What has happened?"

"I am dead." she said which made her respond furiously, "What has happened Kyara? Has he again talked badly to you? Huh. Will you tell me now what kind of destruction has he done?"

He has made me eternal. My breath has stopped and see I am living," she replied having some happy tears.

"What are you saying? Will you tell me properly?" She asked.

"He just proposed to me. Oh my god Amirah, I am dead now," she replied jumping.

"What? I thought something bad has occurred. Goodness! Kyara, be calm please. What did you say to him?" she said.

"Nothing. Gosh! I forgot to reply. Ha-ha. Do you know how happy I am today? Wait, I will be back," she texted her.

"Yes! Even more than forever," she replied to him feeling sheer superfluity of happiness.

I wish I could stop that moment,
I wish I could count it all.
A second which had taken away my beat,
For it, I wish to see myself again fall.

The story had begun yet so far,
Still I find it as if it was at the last blink.
It had gone all through the storms and shines,
As if it was a wave in which I had to sink.

It had shined all through the curious holes,
Calmed up to feel it to be psithurism
Like brook which comes to play divine roles,
Causing light everywhere and scattering like a prism.

The beauty of questioning and the silence of meanings,
which had left me wonderstruck!
Fact, destiny, postulate or fun,
Needed to pinch myself that I wasn't daydreaming.

Blindly feeling the world to be below me,
I was the one on the seventh cloud.
I wanted myself to be engrossed with thee,
Had to shout it loud-
but got scared to know was it real or foul?

A Lotus of grace that floats all the way,
A swan of love that has me anyway.
A brightness that outshines each worldly affair,
A blossom which is an ideal of care and is stupidly
sincere.

All those words, all that you say,
Will you believe, they make my day?
When I smile, you are the only reason,
When I am down you favour in the way to lessen.

All the worlds' joys, all those glitters.
I shall leave them but without you my heart shivers.
Like those childhood fairytales-
you are my only truth and only lie,
I shall live all with you in a single sigh.

My heart, soul and every little thing,
Someone rules on each and all.
With you I'm flying upmost with my wings,
I wish it to be forever and not just in Halcyon.

Forever is knowingly a lesser time,
I would like it for much more and more.
I wonder, is this madness or are you a dime?
I would be so obliged with you to soar.

I wish to be that scent that could have totally involved,
Maybe you would have seen in my eyes.
I wish I could be your good past which helped you
to evolve,
Maybe, you would have known that with you, I rise.

I wish I could stop that moment,
I wish I could count it all.
A second which had taken away my beat,
For it, I wish to see myself again fall.

"So, how was your exam?" he asked the next day.

"Great it was! I was humming songs all the time," she answered smiling.

"Hmm," he replied coldly.

"Why do you talk like this? I mean, as if you're so not interested," she wrote expecting to get a convincing answer.

"Hmm," he said again.

"What? I am asking something."

"I will talk later. Bye."

"Will you excuse me? I am talking right. Answer me."

"Excused," he sent impolitely.

"Listen Kyara, I am in no mood for your stupid fights for no reason. Okay?"

"What? Have you gone mad? I am not fighting alright. I am asking for justification."

"Ha? I don't even justify to Maisha."

"This is the second time you've brought this in."

He wrote which made her tear to roll on her left cheek, ending on her lips. She thought nothing for few minutes and said, "Even Maisha means what?"

"It means nothing."

"I know what it means, very well. You are passing your time with me, aren't you? Whenever you feel like, you become nice and whenever you feel like you insult me."

"See, the way you talk. You just begin to fight always, I wonder how someone can be so aggressive all the time," he sent.

"I wonder how someone can be so inhuman all the time," she replied.

"Thank you."

"You just told me about my place in your life. You know what I feel; I am a product of your mood."

"Hmm listen; I can't hear your abusive words all the time. So it is going to be better if you don't talk to me. Huh,"

"What Abusive words? Are you out of your brains? I am just saying that you don't have time for me and even when you have then you just say these words, 'Hmm, okay, what.' That is all! You don't even talk to me."

"Hmm. Don't message me constantly, I get irritated. Please," he messaged.

"Yes, I am an irritant in your life; I am getting to know everything now. Bye!" she ended and he didn't reply.

"*His proposal was also a lie!*" She began to cry.

Subsequently, after some hours, she said, "I am sorry." He didn't reply to her even after seeing her message. "Will you reply?"

"No, I don't want to talk," he replied.

"I am sorry. Why are you behaving so badly?"

"Because I am very bad. Bye now." she was traumatized to see his way of speech.

"Hmm, okay. I have a solution for this. Let us end it. As it is we fight all time and see it's of no use. You don't listen to one thing of mine. We are having communication issues so let us get apart," she wrote lightly to make him serious.

"Huh! Again you have begun," he wrote.

"No, I am serious. I am sick of you. I can't sit and cry all the time, right? There is no happiness in our lives. I have even started getting dark circles due to you and I feel so weak. I was not like this before. So end it up."

"Fine, do what you like. Bye," he said.

"Are you leaving me?"

"Oh God! Kyara! What is your problem? Should I block you?"

"*What am I doing with him? No, this was not me.*"

"Hmm" She said and started crying again and he blocked her. She lied on her bed and turned her face towards the wall. She covered her nose with a pillow and was weeping noiselessly. Without any ground she imagined herself without him. She believed that he would leave her and what would she do then. It would be nothing but some woe and nitpick. Some words go out and prove to be very effectual in a dire way. Although it is right that if one wants to know the love of someone then see the behaviour of the other one in rage but that never held true for Kyara. She fought with the ones whom she loved and there were just three people who actually saw her annoyance recurrently. She spoke, she felt and then she cried not only because she was hurt but because she often hurt him naively. Picturing herself to be a less deserving one, she made up that she was not so worthy to be with him. She supposed that he had started hating her for her vindictive conduct. She sat on thorns to write despite of being empty of thoughts as the day went off.

Comical that part is when those phrases come.
I get so broken in that depressing humdrum.
My heart suddenly goes through an unidentified pain.
I wonder by all this, what do you really gain?

And we know there are no feelings between us.
Don't you think parting ways will be helpful thus?
Arguments, wars, conflicts is all we do,
you in this way for me, is certainly new.

The time has come to bid a good bye,
I know with that you will never lie.
I will have to live whole without you,
please tell me all this is not at all true!

I accept that I am no one in your eyes.
I am similar to that sun which doesn't rise.
If you hate me so much, then why don't you go?
All your problems which start at me will be low.

Today I want to say, please leave me,
forget me; I plead and set yourself free.
Then you will have no one to hold, to fight with.
It will then become for you alike any myth.

Do you know why I am so much into?
Because I am deeply in love with you.
It's hard, it's tough and it's so not working.
Still I will keep on endlessly waiting.

My soul tells me to love you much more,
to the stretched extent and to the hardest core.
But, if you don't love me then why am I here?
To know that you will leave me, I am in so much fear.

My prayers on you begin and end.
All your agonies to me, I wish to send.
Do you know what can I do for you?
I can ask god to change everything for your good view.

If I had to ask one last thing from the lord,
it would be your happiness, I am assured.
But what can you do in real for me?
You are not even having interest after so long to see.
All your care suddenly flew.
Is this all I mean to you?

Possibly for you, I have mistaken.
I did not think and now I have to reckon.
All those heart beats at the spur grew.
Was it a fault to fall for you?

Everyday you make me feel my weak place,
I can't really see it and nor can I face.
Erase those memories from your brain veins,
and don't ever let them bind you in chains.

I don't know why I am doing all this.
I just know that you, I will certainly miss.
My life has all your true meanings.
I have no thought about my future dealings.

My last words, my last bye.
Please, do rise yourself high,
My love for you will be there till the last day,
and maybe you will then too have nothing to say.
The least sight and words of few,
Was that all I meant to you?

"People who treat their books as dustbins," she said to Amirah, sitting on the second bench of the first row of her classroom and seeing an unnamed science book lying on their table.

"What?" she asked.

"Yes, have a look. Blue pen, pink and which colour is not been used here. She has used every ink but couldn't use a pencil."

"Ha? People are mad." Amirah replied.

"Not really mad but I would like to have a silence of two minutes for such masters. Do they even prefer studying from such books? They look dirty. I am unable to see," she said.

"You leave this. By the way..." Amirah began.

"Kyara, how're you? Can you please pray for my maths register?" said one of her classmates.

"What?" they both screeched.

"Yes, I heard that Saheel lost something and you prayed for it and then she found that out. Please, pray for my register too," Hurmat pleaded.

"Okay, don't plead..." Kyara said sympathetically and Amirah interrupted, "Are you serious? That must have been co incidentally. You search it properly, you will find it. Phew."

"I will pray if she says," she said formally and Amirah laughed and said, "Well, are you any saint?" they all laughed and Hurmat said, "Maybe because she is very good at heart so she is too close to Allah."

"Aww, I will surely. You will get it *In Sha Allah.*"

"All your good heartedness is seen by everyone but not just one." Amirah said as they both went downstairs for another class.

"Hmm leave, don't talk about him," she said in a low pitch.

"Why? He must have done something worse than before again, right?" said Amirah making an irritated face. "Not really," she replied.

"Leave him Kyara."

"I have," she said, opening her book.

"You haven't. Have you noticed that when you hear his name, your eyes shine and now also they are shining?"

"Haw, not at all. Don't say anything," she said supporting her chin with her palm.

"It is not anything. I have said to you so many times but you don't listen." Amirah said.

"He was in Shimla since so many days and he didn't even meet me after so long," she said.

"I am saying something else, right?"

"Ha? Yes I heard," she replied to look attentive.

"His behaviour is contradictory to his name. It means mercy *na*," Amirah said.

"Chuck," she said, putting her forefinger on her lips. "I love his name."

"Oh please! You love him." Amirah said and exhaled noisily and she nodded mutely.

Her impending fate was hidden and there was an irrational awe in her irremediable sorrow. Her days were conquered by an intermingled gloom in the absence of her ingrained love. Her infantile simplicity obligated her to talk to him just once. She didn't want more than that but only for a single time. Her impotent desperation was unable to stop but she was blocked and she couldn't message him. She thought of calling him but was petrified of the coming abandonment.

She called him after five minutes. He picked the phone and remained silent. In her influential voice, she spoke, "Hello!"

He replied, "Ha."

"Talk to me," she said helplessly.

"Hmm," he said.

"What?" she said. "Nothing," He said and she cut the phone irately.

"How can he be so egoistic? Huh. I won't ever message or call again. First of all, I have been apologising since so long for no reason and he is talking to me as if I am annoying him," she wrote to Filiz.

"Kyara calm down okay? Why do you get so hyper? Take a deep breath."

"No. I am not hyper. There is a limit for everything and this is being so horrible that I can't even tell you," she said.

"Hmm stop talking to him then. Forget it. He is an unpredictable man and why are you being so attached. Leave him or should I talk to him? Really I want to ask him that how can he behave like this."

"No you don't talk. I have nothing to say more about him," she wrote.

"Did you have dinner?" Filiz asked.

"No I did not. How can I? I can't think of anything else right now," she said helplessly.

"Oh please! Go and have right away. I don't like all this Kyara. You have begun starving for that person now, huh."

"Hmm, I don't feel like eating. In fact my head is aching and my eyes are also in pain. I am feeling dizzy," she replied.

"Whoa! This was left for me to hear. Are you mad? Please stop behaving like this. He is just someone who is in your life since one year. Why are you forgetting yourself for him? I mean, you have a life Kyara. Please don't ruin it for him who doesn't even care a bit. I hope your health is fine or else visit a doctor or if you need then consult a psychiatrist too."

"Filaaa, don't over react. 'Psychiatrist' did you say that? I am not crazy," she said shockingly.

"If you're not that then don't suffer. All this is no less than craziness. I think I should talk to your mommy also. Maisha will also go through all this. Their marriage and all, I don't find appropriate."

"Hmm I have no thought about that," she said in a fussy mood. "Don't talk about their marriage."

"Hmm. You have medicine." Filiz wrote.

"No, I won't have until he talks."

"Fine! Continue with your idiocy. Die without food. I don't care and nor does he. Okay? No need of talking to me, bye! He has made you so mad that now you don't even care about me. That is alright." Filiz said.

Grim and sullen after the flush of the morning, her temperature was high. Having her hair open, she had not even changed her night suit until twelve at noon. She thought of Amirah and her friends who were in school at that time. "*The middle of the sixth class, it must be.*" She said to herself, lying in her bed and looking at her phone's clock.

"Get up and have breakfast, please." Her mother said strictly.

"I am not hungry," she said turning to another side.

"Why but?" mommy asked without a pause.

"I don't know," she said.

"Then let us go to the doctor." Mommy spoke.

"No!" she replied.

"What? You'll have to. Don't argue with me." Mommy said with a creepy look which made her remain silent.

"Hey! This is Filiz, Kyara's friend. I wanted to tell you that please talk to her. Actually she is not well and she has said that she wouldn't eat anything until you talk to her. You know, she is a little emotional type and she has not had anything since yesterday. Her fever is high and she is not listening to anyone." Filiz messaged to Rehaam at two at noon. He didn't reply to her but he messaged, "Kyara, Are you mad? Eat right now."

"Hmm why? How do you care?" she replied crudely.

"Huh! Eat right now, means eat. Understood?" he wrote.

"Hmm," she replied.

"I ates" She messaged after ten minutes and he gave her a phone call. She picked up and remained silent.

"What did you have?" he asked.

"Chicken and chapatti," she said.

"Okay now eat a medicine and visit a doctor in the evening," he said.

"No."

"Why? I am out due to some work and I can't talk much. Please go to the doctor," He said dependently.

"You have no right to order me, okay? Order someone else whom you love and talk all the time. Oh I am sorry. I have no right to say this so please leave me alone and be interested in someone else," she said cold-bloodedly.

"What? I was busy Kyara."

"Yes you were, but only for me. For others you have all the time. Am I not right?" she said.

"Hmm sorry," he said.

"You just know this word, that's all and after some time, you forget everything. All your apologies and your convincing statements are useless in your eyes," she said in a breath. "In fact I am useless," she said in a sorrowful tone.

"You're most important," he said happily.

"Oh so you treat your important people in this manner. Wow, impressive," she said. "Sorry Kyari. Sorry, Sorry, Sorry," he said stretching the words.

"Hmm," she said.

"By the way, why fever?" he asked.

"Ask yourself," she replied softly.

"Because of me?" he laughed.

"Who else, then?" she said.

"Oh! See, we have been talking since half an hour, now it must have gone. Hasn't it?"

"It doesn't go like this," she said smiling. "I want to see you."

"I am not at home, not even nearby. I am at Glare corporate park and I will be late," he said.

"Cool, I'll go to the doctor only after I see you," she said. "What's the point to visit a doctor when I know I will be fine when I will see you?"

"Kyara you're so stubborn. You know, I don't like this."

"Start liking," she said at once.

"Hmm no," he spoke frigidly. *"What the hell? He said no to me."*

"What?" She asked.

"Come online and see me there. Only this can be done for now. Now don't act obstinately," he said on which she replied, "I am not obstinate."

"You're," he said. "Now come fast," he cut the phone.

"Love you *na*," he wrote as they both began their video call.

"I love you more," she wrote and smiled looking at him.

"Remove your hair from the face. I can't see," he typed.

"Don't see me. I am looking ill, not good," She wrote biting her lip.

He saw her with a stunned look and said, "You're always good." Seeing to his left, he paused for two seconds and turned his head to right and again halted. It seemed as if, he was about to cross a road with heavy traffic. After all, he looked in the front but not in the camera. He was somewhere else in order to look for someone. She sat there, wondering about his weird actions. This whole process took about five seconds and he at last, looked at her. He blew her two kisses. At another moment, she started looking down and gave a smile. "You look so cute," she wrote.

"Ha-ha and what's for me?" she was au fait of what he said and she also did the same.

"Now go to the doctor," he said. "I have to go for a meeting. We'll talk as I get free and you eat and drink properly. You will not do this again," he said.

"You know, I have no fever now," she wrote.

"Mad girl!" he said and smiled. "Now go."

"Akira, I am fine now. I don't think I need any medication," she said to her. "No, mommy has said to me to take you. That is all. We are going."

"What wastage of money! I am fine! Why are all over reacting?" she said as they reached the clinic.

"So what has happened? Dr. Saran asked. "She is having fever since yesterday night and she is not eating anything since then only." Akira explained.

"Why you? Can't she speak?

Confronting an over smart personality again, she couldn't tolerate him even for a moment. Some people have dissimilar and abnormal thought process which inclines them to think that whatever they say or whatever they do or even think is all right. When in real a wise one always thinks himself to be a fool while an insane is flushed up with pride of knowledge. Sense of humour which is often underrated is also an outrageous feature of such type of models. Silence is expected when there is nothing beautiful left to speak but in some cases, their dense and dim brains give signals to speak about inept and pathetic stuff. Making a stranger uncomfortable should be regarded as a sinful act when every second person in the crowd is waiting to make someone embarrassed and mortified. *"Can't they be in their own lives?"* She thought to herself after self debating on this issue with Baddie and Elf.

She stared at Akira and gave her a bad look and she heard him speaking again, "Well, what has led to this? At least this much you can say," he gave a wicked smile to Akira as if she would join his daft ridicule. Kyara had no answer of this question of his which had its validity. *"Only if I could say, I am in love with a person and when he doesn't talk to me, I get ill, I would not be sitting here and seeing your shallowness."*

"As far as I know..." she began and he interrupted,

"As far as you know? Then who else knows? Your sister?"

"No, I mean," She said in fear and discomfiture. "It rained day before yesterday and I got wet in it. Maybe due to that,"

"Why are you so indefinite? Of course it is due to that only. Anyway, you pay a lot of attention to your clothes, right?" he spoke insolently.

"Excuse me." she said looking at him and then Akira, who was amazed at the doctor's question.

"Yes, I can see. You don't look ill but you're. That means your illness is not so severe for you but your dress-up is a priority," he said which made her fuming and she replied, "Yes, I believe that be sad or depressed but be well- dressed."

"Really? Nice quote, is it yours?" he said writing the prescription. "You should pay attention on your studies more than this. Clothes won't help you much."

"She is a topper," Akira finally spoke and Kyara smiled droopily. "Shall we leave?" Kyara said in a high pitch. "Yes," Akira said thanking the doctor. "Visit again. Nice to meet you." He said as if he had forgotten his nastiest behaviour some moments ago. *"Never."*

"Yes this is the reason why I severely hate doctors."

"What was he up to?" she asked Akira.

"I was guessing. He was so weird," she said.

"No he was low class and unrefined." Kyara said sharply.

"Yes, leave him. We're not going there again,"

"I doubt his medication. He hated me. I hope he has not given the wrong medicines."

"Ha-ha no. He was just annoying not a killer. Forget him; such people need ignorance nothing else." Akira said.

"Seriously! I am sorry for him. He doesn't have his own life."

Chapter 7

There was patience in that night of fathomless blackness. She was feeling tranquil without any incentive. She overlooked everyone when he was good to her. As if her life was controlled by 'A single frame of divine work'. She wrote in her diary, and he was an element of her life without which no reaction could take place.

Bareness chased if he was not there and even that single word which came from his side did make her smile which was most factual and staunch. He might not regard her that portentous but her life, it did begin with him and would finish on him only. It could give an impression of a charade for many, and it's no offence to regard her as imprudent or immature. Practical thinking could possibly say that she was just a teenager and it was impossible for her to decide all her future just due to a person. She might even fall for someone else in the coming years and might treat him in the same way. She might even force him to marry her instead of someone else. In all, she could show her worst side as she was in her puerile period. She might devastate the lives of everyone and just brighten her own. It was all in her hands and she knew what she had to do. Sometimes, it has been proven by such species that humanity still exists because of which the world has not come to an end.

Selfishness was the feeling which she didn't own. Despite of being told by many the harms of her soft heartedness, she still believed in thinking of others before herself. She had an indifferent conviction that if she would do good deeds in her life, he would be rewarded for that too. She did pray for his sins to be lesser than her so that he becomes eligible to be a part of Jannah. Everyone has to go to paradise one day but the sinners first will go to hell for the punishment. She didn't want any one of them to be there. She read that in heaven, the mates will be just staring at each other for the forty constant years of this world. She was all ready to sit eyeing him with frosty calm. "He was not hers in this momentary world. They were meant to be together, somewhere, somehow, beyond the limits of timelessness. Where she will be selfish for him and there will be no one between the two who were one, even here in this mortal life, but will find their completion there." What if god only wanted their love to gain meaning there? What if their love was too ideal for this world? They could say to her to leave him and maybe she would even do that for her sister's sake. Maybe that is what her life was written for. Forfeit was her precision.

The next morning, she messaged to him, "Good morning."

"Good morning! How's your fever?" He asked.

"I am fine now."

"Okay. Have breakfast, then talk," he said.

"Yes, I will have no,"

"Hmm what are you doing?" he asked.

"Just having a look at the A*bayas*. My aunty has come from Riyadh so she has brought," she said and he couldn't see the message for the next two hours.

"Kyara, you want Abaya? Now you have become so religious *Ma-Sha-Allah*. By the way, give it a try. You'll look good." Mommy said.

"Oh yes! I will wear that black one with black beads," she said impatiently. She wore it and carefully tied up the *Khimar* with a pin. "How am I looking?" she shouted looking in the mirror.

"*Ma-Sha-Allah*! So pretty. Beautiful. Such a bright face in *Khimar*. May Allah protect my daughter's beauty from every evil eye." Mommy said.

"Oho, Kyara. Are you okay?" Maisha said.

"Yes, why?" Kyara asked nervously as she knew that she wouldn't like it.

"Ha-ha, please remove it. Full clothes don't suit you,"

"Hmm," she removed it at another minute to avoid travesty.

There was cheerlessness in her heart as she didn't like her sister's reaction on those clothes which are obligatory on every Muslim girl. Obligation doesn't mean that there is lack of freedom but *Khimar* and *Abaya* is an identity of every *Muslimah*. It helps them profoundly to say much without having to speak.

"Yes Kyara! I got busy. Say now," he messaged at three in the evening.

"Hmm nothing much," she replied dully.

"Why? What has happened?" he asked.

"Nothing," she replied.

"Something has. My baby is dull, right? C'mon tell me," he said.

"By the way, how was *Abaya*? Wear it *na* and send me a picture."

Being thrilled on hearing that, she went in her room to apply *kajal* in her eyes. She wore the *Abaya* and tied the *Khimar* too perfectly and clicked a selfie in the mirror.

"Wow! Beautiful!" he said.

"Hmm, some don't like it," she typed sadly.

"Who doesn't? I knew you were sad due to something. Has someone said something?" he asked.

"Nothing. Maisha doesn't find such clothes good," she said miserably but thought that he would then have bad idea about her so she said, "By the way, you like it so I am happy. She is different no, A fashionista from head to toe!"

"Oh, but I love it," he wrote.

The likes of those who matter and even those who matter lesser is what everyone depends upon. Personalities, habits, behaviour is what one takes from others most of the time. It is not always termed as plagiarism or stealing but this is how we are made. We follow, sometimes even those who do not have any place, and even those who are there but hatefully accepted.

She was a follower, and she followed him as she had been doing it for long. She fretfully sat, and got up, and wore it again. She saw herself in the mirror as usual and then after three seconds or more, she saw herself from his eyes and it gave her a smile. She thought that how happy he would feel whenever he would see her in it. How lucky she would feel to be that girl who has decided to cover herself up for him! The most important part of her was her hair and her mind was telling her to cover them up from every eye, from everyone but just not from one.

"Hmm," she replied to him. "If you want, I can wear it always," She typed quickly and threw the phone away in order to avoid seeing his denial which she expected.

"Hmm *acha*. Okay then, wear daily."

"Okay. Then I can't show my hair to anyone, I mean any *non-mahram*." She explained.

"Yes, don't show," he said at once.

"I will talk to mommy about it. Hope, she allows."

"What's there to discuss so much? Wear it, I am saying," he said and she could understand his tone of irritation by it. To avoid any conflict, she sent, "Yes, I will wear."

"Hmm. You will show me your hair *na*?" he asked.

"Ha-ha no!" she said.

"Oh really?"

"Yes. How can I? Are you my brother?" She asked sarcastically.

"No, I am... yours," he said showing his gladness on knowing what he asked.

"Can I do purdah?" she said to her mommy.

"What? Do you know what it is?" she said in surprise. "Maybe I do. I...I read on the internet that it is obligatory for every girl to cover herself in front of any *non-mahram*." (Non mahram is someone whom you can marry)

"Yes but think again. It is tough." Mommy replied.

"I have thought. It is for my lord, he loves it. And can't I do such a small thing for him when he does everything for me?"

"Yes, you can do anything what you like, I will not stop until it is wrong and this is so beautiful. I am proud of you."

A step was at her heels and that appreciable relief had come due to him. Her *Abaya* was something she loved not only because he loved it but someone who had made him, did too. It was for her god first and then for him. She did love him madly but could not forget her creator. Many regard their love higher than their god but that was senseless for her. Sagacity is when one has a stronger belief on the power that has made the worlds and in her world, him! An inspired ray was in her eyes and in those moments of utter idleness and insipidity, she could straightforwardly sum up all the changes in her life which had come and were yet to come. She sat to recollect all those memoirs of her past when she was a girl but with no substance. Her clothes were her life and she wanted to become one of those who sit before camera and make fun of people who do disasters of fashion and then give them styling tips. Her dreams were to walk on the red carpets of film festivals in the lavish designs of high street designers of Paris and Italy. Her plans of Alexander McQueen's floor length gown, Donatella Versace's pencil skirt and Elli Saab's off-white up-low-hem, were fading and she could imagine them going away in a cloud which was going to burst in a second! "*I think in Jannah, I will be allowed to wear all of them. I will flaunt my hair everywhere. I will even change their colours every other day, actually every six hours,*" she said to herself.

"Amirah! I have started doing purdah," she sent to her.

"What purdah?" she asked back.

"Purdah means purdah of *awrah*," she typed bringing lines on her forehead.

As soon as she understood what she was trying to say she called her in a state of extreme shock and said, "Is everything fine? I mean, you know what are you saying, don't you? You're joking, right?"

"Is this a topic about which one would joke around? I am going to wear *Abaya* in school too, and everywhere. Even in my house if some guests come. This is a final decision and I want you to appreciate me instead of going in a setback," she spoke in an infuriated pitch.

"Yes, I am going to appreciate but how has it happened? I am so happy. From where have you got this thought?" she asked.

"I was trying it and I sent him a picture and he loved it," she said slowly.

"Ohh!" Amirah said. "Wow! Congratulations to him."

Her face got lit up by a glow of inspiration and resolve as if there was a light which was being showed to her. Before was dark, like a shadow which was due to the shadier side. There was imitation and falsehood to find glee and placate in this world of some time. Imbued with a vernal freshness, she could not stop herself from thanking her lord to make her feel the best. She was for him and not for everyone. Her dignity was at a level where one couldn't reach without toughness. There was mellowness which made her believe that all love the covered chocolate and not the open one. Pure women are made for pure men and not for every other eye. It brought poise in everything she did. From her thought process to the way she walked, everything was changed, though she did not modify her sense of styling. She loved the ramp walk and so she walked like those models even when in *Abaya*. She wore the latest designs of it and her *Khimar* was one of the best tied ones. That neatly assembled piece of cloth on her head was much more than any crown or tiara.

"You see this picture," she said to him and sent a picture of a girl wearing Khimar and the boy was arranging it properly. "You should also help me in tying my *Hijab* if it is not fine, like him."

"Hmm. Okay," he sent.

"So what are you doing? Aren't you missing me?" she asked sending a sad emoticon and went outside the room putting the phone on the corner table. When she checked her phone after half an hour, there was no reply from him.

She thought that he was busy so she didn't message again. "Akira, give me your phone for a second. I want to make a call," she said.

"Ya, wait. I was talking to Rehaam. He and Maisha had a fight." Akira replied.

"Oh! Sad," she said and thought that despite of being free, he had not replied to her. She frowned perplexedly and went in her room without making any call. She decided to get him on the right track by showing her anger. For that, she picked up the phone and she saw his reply.

"Nothing," he said.

"Hmm," she was somewhat calmer and wrote, "Can I ask you something?"

"Yes," he replied. "Can't we get married in anyway?"

He replied, "NO!" An utter depression of soul could be felt after his dissent. She took a breath and asked, "Why? Don't you like me?" her face was pale at that time as it was expressionless.

"Of course I like you but you're young," he answered in the most displeasing manner.

"*This is no excuse.*"

"Hmm, age doesn't matter," she typed.

"It does. You won't understand. You are immature."

"Immature? I am not. If I had been then I would not be talking to you right now,"

"Hmm," he said.

"So if you won't get married to Maisha then will you marry someone else?" she asked in panic.

"No, I won't marry."

Either way her fate was cruel. She accepted herself as his second choice but he did not regard her even that. There was no glint of hope anywhere but bleak loneliness. The pictures of his marriage ceremony were taking rapid turns in her forebrain. What is she going to do?" she asked to herself. Bringing candles and flowers for decorations, seeing where the stage has been placed, plainly listening to the Indian wedding songs being played, arranging sweets in the plates to be served among the guests, taking gifts to the groom's house wearing heavy dresses, deciding the jewellery for the different functions which would occur, applying henna on her sister's hand and writing "R" letter and then seeing both of them giving their signatures on that paper which would make them married to each other. She closed her eyes to stop to see all that but it was her mind which could not stop her. Her tears fell continually as she felt all those things happening. For some time, she could feel perpetual gloom and seclusion of life. That marriage will take her life as it would prove to be an imbroglio. She could be formed into a misanthrope but she chose to be a believer. Giving up on life was the only option left by him for her but taking up life was something which was for her god.

Courage made her up and she had subterranean dependence on her Lord. She believed that He would not show her that day which would take her life. He loved her; more than anyone and He would not do that and if He would do then she would get relieved that it would be his choice to let her live or not!

No matter how much maturity and forfeit comes but at some point a person is tend to be selfish and think about oneself but this love was anachronistic, it was of some other era. She wanted her love to be together with someone else. She wanted them to be married without any problems and live. She wanted to be a godmother of their kids and would love them with all her heart and soul. It is sardonic that she never asked her lord to break their relationship. She could hardly imagine doing any humbug to win him. Her love was as pure as first smile, as true as the first cry and as strong as the first breath. She left him for the world, as she had better plans up with him. She did not want to end herself because that would make him repentant. His brown eyes would lose their glimmer if they would show his regret. His face which added her lives would be down with ignominy and she could never approve of it. He was her decorum and an honour to behold. A thunder which lived with disguise could be left away but still its subtle remains would be with her.

I would never like you to be me,
And then feel how you, I see.
That would give you a pretty agony,
Then you`ll gaze for me in the canopy.

If I won't be there, then how will you go on?
Won't you search for me from dusk till dawn?
Will you ask those lands and skies?
Will you turn to small herbs and flies?

I won't ever like to come before you,
like an angel which touched and flew.
I know you will hear me swinging,
Swear, you won`t change your hope to wailing.

I know your tiny heart will not believe,
And this life, then it won't receive.
Will you recover and go on?
Will you live for me so on?

Near and far I will be there,
The sea you will sink and the hills you will tear.
Will you not deny your lovely sleep?
Will you not wish me to again sweep?
In the highlands of yours I will begin to reap—
and I will meet in the years of leap.

My journey will be higher than you!
Undeniably it shall be so true.
I wonder, will that distance be good for us.
Don't know about you but I am going to be in a fuss.

I will surely see you every time,
There too I won't ever find your any rhyme.
I suppose, you will be fondly restless,
And so I will be gladly cheerless.

I believe, I am not possible without you,
akin to the cold without any dew.
And then when I will come, will you not begin to sigh?
Will you not wish to see me cry?

I will not be sad but rather fortunate,
I will show up and then illuminate.
Will you ask me to slowly sit?
Will you ask me that why did I do it?

I won't ever have an answer to give,
but if you can't be with me then what's the need to live?
The few words I will listen and rest I will say.
Then I will wait for you to pray.

I feel you will hate me so much for that,
but how can we question our predetermined fate?
I know, you will want us to be together,
and so we won't be able to reach farther.

This is the role which we have to play—
one in this world and one in the heaven's bay.
Won't you want me to again live?
Won't you ever try to forgive?

And so..
I would never like you to be me,
and then feel how you, I see

La douler exquise occupied her as those ill-assorted views revolved in that night of meanness when she felt like an unrepentant criminal who had been wrongly judged and blamed. It was another day, fresh enough to start living. The evening sky was as green as jade. She had been waiting for Amirah in the nearby park looking at the white flowers hanging off a tree. There was no sign of her and she began to walk towards the gate to leave. Looking down, she was quite slow and before she reached the gate, she saw his car through the white fence. His car windows unhurriedly opened and their eyes met like crossed swords though he was wearing black glasses. She could see a decorous and well-intentioned person coming towards her with a burning sense of shame and horror.

"I am getting married," he said and then dropped into an eloquent silence.

"So? What should I do?" she said simply.

"Won't you ask with whom?" he said in his typical tone of sarcasm. She raised her eyes to show her nonchalance and said, "I know." She started walking speedily but she did not know where she was. She stopped to look here and there and then arranged her *Khimar* to tighten it.

"WITH YOU!" he spoke in a slightly higher pitch. Over shadowed by a fretful anxiety, she was strangled by the snare of words which were pure as the azure above them. She turned her head half to see him but couldn't see him fully. Being motionless like a plumb line, her pulses fluttered. She could sense him coming nearer. He sat down on his knees mannishly and then it made her turn to him like a thunder cloud. Finding something in his pocket, he took a box out. They were vastly dissimilar but her holy love like a vestal flame had burned him completely. "Will you marry me?" Her lashes were denying blinking. They were heavy with fluid appearing to be beads that glistened. A ring, he had which he offered to her with eager heartedness. It cut like knives, that air so chill made her made her stare at him blankly. The history was forgotten and presently she thought and spoke, "Yes." He tenderly took her left hand which was cold and white as if it had no blood. Touched with a bewildering and elusive beauty, he made her wear it. She blinked and dropped a tear from both of her eyes which reached her cheeks parallel to one another. A blank gaze of his indolently handsome eyes chilled her. She wanted to speak but her tongue stumbled and was silent but his mouth could not stop to send waves of pleasure.

Glowing with haste and happiness, she got up and sat straight. There was thoughtlessness for half a second. Pragmatically, she was gloomy and sullen after the glow of the morning. *"It was nothing. It was nothing."* She said holding her head. She felt an unaccountable loathing as soon as she found out that it was a dream, rather a lie! Entangled in illogicality, with eyes closed, she slept again to go away from the moment of no emotion.

"Why did I see such a useless and worthless dream?" Baddie said.

"It may be true," Elf answered.

"Why will he ever give me any ring and that also while sitting on his knees? HAHA what a dramatic one! Though I will love it but how does he care what I like or not. He can never do that and he will never allow anyone else too to do the same. Hugh," she said in an exasperated tone.

"Kyara! Kyara!" her mother shouted. "Yes," she said from her room and peeped through the window to see who had come. She saw her mother's friend's family sitting in the main hall. She went out of the room, dressed in trousers and *kurti* with a different coloured *hijab*. "*Assalamulaikum.*" She said smiling and went towards her aunty to hug her.

"*Walekumassalam.*" She replied and said looking at her friend, "Oh my... She looks so much like you."

"Oh really?" her mother gave an obvious smile.

"Yes and what happened? *Hijab* and all han.. I heard from your mum that you have become so religious," she said to her.

"Just like that," she responded.

"Why? There must be a reason. No?"

"It is all about blessings. She is blessed to be near Allah," her mother said.

"Yes *Ma-Sha-Allah*. May Allah bless her more. You look very pretty in this *hijab*. Everyone can't look so good but you do. You have such long hair. Wasn't it difficult to hide them from everyone? It must have been, no? See we have still shorter hair but we can't imagine hiding them." Aunt said and laughed like a man.

"How're your studies going? You must have joined some coaching classes. I have made my daughter join tuitions in maple's bay though she didn't need it. Eighth standard is tough."

"They are going good. No, I haven't joined." She said. "Oh why? Your grade is tougher."

"It may be but I manage at home. I can't go to one place every day at a particular time," she said.

"Well, you are perfect. Everyone can't be." Aunty said in a tone of guilt.

Appreciation was not that much valued by her like before at that time. She knew that people saw her wrongly and she was not at all perfect, she was not even half of it. Not really sadness but an acceptance was rising within. She was losing herself somewhere in those compliments which held themselves true at one place but did not sustain. Had it be finer then what she must be doing now? Only if he regarded her at some place in his life, it could be something else, something more!

"We are having lunch with Maisha's in-laws tomorrow." Her mother stated. She didn't reply and showed as if it was not heard or she didn't pay heed to it. "You want to come?"

"No. What will I do there? You all go. Akira can go," she said and felt weirdly possessive. *"And he will be there. I haven't seen him for days. You all can't see him".* Elf and baddie rolled their eyes.

"You must come. His mother was asking that how are you doing and you even talked to her, she told. Specifically she said that "Kyara must come. I am looking forward."

"Oh! That is sweet. I will tell, later." She said and went to her room to message him. "I am not coming tomorrow," she wrote.

"Why?"

"Because I can't. What if they all begin to talk about your marriage? Then what?" She replied.

"Hmm. Come, my dad wants to see you and mommy is already waiting," he sent.

"Really? My beautiful second parents,"

"I will have to go now. His PARENTS are waiting. Awww, I don't know why but I love them," she said to Aroosh.

"Really? I have seen the first girl who loves her boy's parents so madly."

"Ha-ha yes. They made him so beautiful both at heart and soul and for me. You also come," she said.

"Oh no no. Do you want any drama there? What if they will talk about his marriage and I see you sad? Then the lunch will become too memorable to think about."

"Ha-ha... No I don't want. Thanks. Let it be simple."

"What will I wear? I wish he just sees me and I think he will. He hasn't seen me for so many days. I will wear a Pakistani dress and *Khimar* of black colour. He loves black," she said taking out her dress for tomorrow.

She carefully rolled up her mascara and applied a liquid to highlight her eyes. She sang as she chose her stilettos and then waved to Aroosh as she saw them driving away through the room's window. There were four people in the car including her mother, aunt and Maisha. As she was reaching nearer to the Flora lines, she could sense him more. His scent was scattered even at the beginning of his house's road. The flora lines had a lot of flora in it. Those trees were echoing his voice all through which was calling her name constantly. She couldn't believe that why was it appearing to be so far though it was few kilometres away. As soon as the car stopped in front of a large white coloured villa, with stoned walls surrounding it, she stepped out of the car and made it clear to walk behind everyone.

He was nowhere around but his parents had made them sit in their hall which had a fountain inside. His mother kept on smiling all the time as her mother started talking about random topics. After their thirty seconds of conversation, his mother drew everyone's attention towards her. "Kyara, you are looking beautiful. See," she called his father and said, "Isn't she pretty? She's the youngest of all. Kyara is a writer."

Kyara smiled and wondered that how did she know of her writing? *"He must have told. Mr Narrator. Well it is cute."*

"Writer! Wonderful that is! What do you write Hindi, English, Urdu, Persian?"

"English. She writes poems," his mother said in a higher pitch. "I have read some." She said in a slightly lower pitch as his father continued, "Remarkable." He said with admiration and pride.

"Assalamulaikum." He came suddenly and smiled in the sweetest way he could. The guests responded to him in an even sweeter manner. Without looking at him at first, she expected that he was already looking at her. Breaking the suspense, she looked at him with two blinks but did not find him looking at her! His eyes did tell something diverse but his gaze was describing the present. They both, Rehaam and Maisha were smiling at each

other without a pause as if there was no one else there. She again gave her eyes a second chance and saw him. He didn't see in the initial four minutes.

"Show Kyara around," his mother said to him and he gave an uncanny look to her as if she had done some crime. Fearing his conceptions, she got up tentatively to offer the juice glasses to everyone. *"I don't know him. No, no!"* she spoke within herself as he went towards the corridor. After finishing the juice, everyone kept it on the table and she picked the tray and took it to the kitchen. Unknown of the fact that why was she doing all that in someone's house, she just behaved as if he was nowhere. As she followed the directions told by his mother to reach the kitchen, she saw him sitting on a wine-coloured couch in a small room.

"Come," he said when she was returning.

"Hmm no," she said.

"Why? What has happened? You're looking pretty," he said with a wicked smile.

"Oh, you saw me. Thank you. I thought I was no less than air."

"Ha-ha. I can see you in anyway even if I am not looking directly."

"Good for you." She raised her eyes and walked to leave.

"What?" he said narrowing his eyes. "Eat this," he offered her chips.

"Hmm what?" she narrowed her eyes too and sat next to him.

"Kyara, what if your mommy sees you sitting here so close?" he said moving closer. "Oh please. We're not even that close. This is a normal distance between two normal people," she said moving away.

"Normal people! Awright," he spoke formally. "Go and join the conversation," he said and laughed. "Of the wedding, your favourite topic."

"Huh! Why don't you go? It's your marriage, your future, your life. You are needed more desperately," she said and he laughed again and said, "You get so irritated. I haven't seen you behaving like this on any other topic. Stay calm."

"You're so right. I should find another more important and weighty topic to pay attention to as this is just a crap."

"Ohh, so you want me to marry you. Should I?" he asked smiling.

"I never want. When did I say? Don't be in any misconceptions."

"Yes right! You never did," he bit his lips as she looked at them.

"Have you called me here for insulting me and by the way what did you think of when you told your mother about my writings? She asked me that why do I write? Can you imagine how uneasy I had to feel at that time?"

"Must have told then, why didn't you?" he said with a smile.

"You know, I don't want to talk to you anymore now. Bye!" she got up and went straight to the hall without a single turn. He did not stop her because he disliked her conduct. He hated to fight with her and considered silence more appropriate instead of wars. While she had become so picky about everything that she was becoming hostile with time. Pessimism triumphed over her positivity due to her tiresome life. A tangle of ugly words spoken, made him impertinent as he too went towards the dining room. The dining table had a variety of dishes, some about which she never heard about. He had a great fondness for sweets and rice maybe because his region ate wheat more. She quickly ate little without seeing him who was sitting opposite to her. She was piqued as he never looked at her again. It was comprehendible that her dissonant way vexed him. She was feeling dreary as she thought that the tussle was not called for. She was eating with him first time and she got to know that he was more comfortable to eat rice by his hands instead of a fork or spoon. She looked quixotically at his *briyani* oil's sucked lips which were glowing but his eyes were motionless and just looked at his plate. After fifteen minutes when everyone was done with the food, his mother said, "So they should get married as soon as possible. We shall decide the dates."

"Sure," her mother replied.

I am not here and I am not here, not at all. She said closing her eyes and covering her face by her thin fingers full of rings.

"What's wrong, Kyara?" her mother asked in a low pitch. "Nothing much to consider," she answered coming back to earth where there were people and not just she alone. "Excuse me!" She said and moved towards the garden area.

"Filiz, you are a saviour. You rescued me from something really fatal. Anyways, what's up?"

"All good. What did I save you from? I hope not that topic again of your Rehaam and his family and your sister. Is it that?" she said in exasperation.

"Well, something like that. He's getting married," she replied in a miserable and a soft voice. "Hmm I see," she replied in frustration which was upgraded. "Ignore him."

"I must," she said. "Come here. I will get you admitted in one of the literature colleges where there will be neither Rehaam nor his shadow."

"I hate him and even his shadow," she replied covetously. "Wait, he's here. Hold on." She saw his brown eyes turning blue again in the moonlight.

"Oh my..! How does he manage to look so ravishing?"

All carried away from head to the toe, she again fell for him! He was heading towards her straight with his hands, by his side. They were moving rashly as he walked keeping his chin upwards, but in a microscopic ratio.

"Kyara..." he said in a gentleman's voice. Even his voice could create butterflies in her stomach. Looking into his eyes dramatically, she uttered "What?" he smiled looking at her temper and said, "Do you have school tomorrow?"

"How do you care?" she replied turning her head sideward. "Tell me." He asked politely.

"How does it make any difference in your busy life? Go and ask the one who matters to you and not the tissue papers," she said as if she was a storm, ready to destroy her most loving creature.

"Whoa! You are always ready to fight because you are fond of that. You're very small that's why I tolerate every word which you speak without a second thought. Leave second, not even first! We will not talk, that's final. Just look at your behaviour Kyara. I beg of you to work on it," he said in one breath and left at another.

She came back and told Filiz about everything which had happened. She knew that it was his fault but she even knew somewhere that it was she who initiated the mess.

"Do you even know that I am crying? I mean, he is too much. He just insulted me in his own house. I never ever had expected such a treacherous behaviour." She messaged her.

"Relax Kyara! Stop crying for every little thing," she replied.

"I don't want to discuss anything more of him. I am not talking to him anymore," she typed and saw him online. She blocked him and deleted his number.

"Unblock him." Filiz said.

"Are you on his side?" she asked making her worst face.

"I am not taking anyone's side. I just don't want you to decide everything so early. I know Rehaam and he will be fine in a day or two."

"Why are you saying all this Fila? He's hurt me."

"So you have also hurt him Kyara. For god's sake, grow up! He is in love with you. Don't you understand?" *"So Mr. unpredictable is in love with me.. Crap!"*

"What? He's not. It is impossible."

"I am elder than you. He is totally smitten by you and I know that." *"Doesn't that sound like heaven? I'm flying..eeeeeh.. I am. Filiz said that first time. How could her idea about him change? He's killing me."*

"Now what?" she asked impatiently.

"Unblock him and ignore him for two days and then message him on the third day. He will be fine and don't begin to fight. Control yourself." Filiz typed.

"Okay but I don't want to be with him. What about Maisha?" she asked.

"Don't talk about her. First I thought that she was being cheated upon. I was really sympathetic towards that girl. But now I'm not. I don't want to discuss with you the reason because you must be aware of that. She is spoiling a lot of lives. She is so confused. She wants Rehaam but she doesn't only want him and Rehaam wants her but he is also in love with you. Both of them are aliens and it is going to be better if you are going to think about yourself before anyone because they are not worth it."

"Fila.. She's my sister. I love her and I want to leave him for her. Why are you saying like that?" she questioned in regret.

"I can understand your love for her but she can get anyone. She will be happy, I know. She should leave Rehaam because you both must be together. Haven't you heard of that quote? If one falls in love with two people at the same time then choose the second one because if you had loved the first one truly then you must not have fallen for the second," she replied.

"She has had an amazing study about 'Maisha's love life'. Maybe she will be happy with someone else too but who are we to decide. After all she was before me. I feel like a pendulum. One side stands Maisha and the other side... Mr Re."

"Leave it filz. I'm bored with both of them." Kyara messaged.

"MOVIE?" messaged Amirah. "Which and when?" she asked.

"Any. Today at six."

"Wait. Let me ask mum." *"Him? NO WAY!"* "Okay. I'm on," she said.

At four thirty, she got up from her bed and dressed herself up. She wore a black *Abaya* and a *Khimar* of pink colour. Putting her ear rings, knuckle rings, kohl, mascara, eye liner, she opened her drawer to choose her footwear. She wore a pair of brown wedges with pink and white beads stuck in the form of a hemisphere. Hearing the horn of an SUV, she quickly grabbed her phone and lip balm and put it in a black and pink sling. The car had Amirah's parents and siblings along with her. She sat between Amirah and Haira, her elder sister. She met Haira after a gap of ten months so she gave her a hug and a soft kiss on the cheek. "All good Kyara?" she smiled.

"Yes, by God's grace," she smiled too.

"How're you?"

"Fine!" she turned her face and started looking out of the window.

The film began at 6:05 pm. The theatre was not full but had a few people sitting in the last rows. Its start was boring but then it took a fascinating turn as it proceeded.

"Do you like it?" She asked Amirah softly.

"Yes. Why? Don't you?" she questioned.

"No, I do. It's monotonously cool." "See that couple is so much in love. That guy has brought her to see such a boring animated film." Amirah said looking at them. *"Love… I have heard of that."*

"You and Rehaam should have come to see it then you must not have got bored," she winked.

"Gosh! His name again. Can't people just stop talking about that guy?"

"Chuck it Amirah. Don't talk about him," she replied.

"Oh! What's wrong?" she held her hand and pressed it.

"I left him," she said removing her hand from her hand.

"How many times will you leave him?" She laughed.

"It is serious this time. Don't just talk about him. I have come here to come out of the depression which he has sent me in," she said putting her hand on her forehead.

"Depression, are you into that? Do you know its symptoms?" she asked in a tone of a child.

"Yea!" she said stretching a. "When in depression, one does not feel sadness even in the worst times and guess what."

"What? You also don't feel sad, right?" she asked.

"Yes, exactly. I feel nothing. I'm not sad at the thought that everything is over. I'm not sad that we will never talk and I don't even care about his meaningless marriage anymore," she said in pride.

"Well, using meaningless as a prefix to his marriage tells me something else. You still care Kyara," she says looking in front. *"Aaaaah noo! I don't give a damn."*

"Hmm, you must be happy right? You have never approved of us being together," she asked excitedly.

"Hmm, honestly I'm not." She replied raising her right eye brow which made her heart beat rapid as if it was alerting her about the damage she has caused; not only to herself but also her closed ones.

"Why? You never liked him for me," she asked and stared at her.

"It is not about my liking. It is about both of you. He loves you."

"Congratulations and celebrations! Another best friend just took his side. Was one less? Whoa! He loves you; he is smitten by you and blah blah. My friends need to fix their screws. Love is just a word for him. Why do they show that they know him more than me? First, they both hated him from the bottom of their hearts and now when I want to get over, both of them have suddenly developed sympathy, pity and liking for him. Mr. Re, you're ruining my friendships too."

"Filiz said the same. You both confuse me," she said. "If he loved me, he shouldn't have destroyed me. You know how much I cry due to him and he doesn't care. What kind of love you both are talking about, I fail to understand."

"I know that he makes you sad but you also make him no less. When you cry, you speak anything to him but he listens to you. Your behaviour sometimes is so cruel and harsh. It's intolerable but he still tolerates and doesn't say a word back. I hope you know that."

"Tolerate? Am I some pain which he bears? Ssshh! Baddie. I love him and that's what my heart says. Yes, I do, mentally, emotionally, physically and every lly"

"Hmm. I will talk day after tomorrow. He should message me first," she said.

"Gosh! Keep your ego in your pocket. You both need some communication. Be normal. Tell him that you love him and he will be fine," she ended.

I would never want you to love me as I do. It isn't your shallowness or incapability but I just deny to that enzyme of inanity which has found its place in me. It creates a complex obsession and I do fight my shadows to overcome but again I go back to the initiation. It's beyond acceptance that despite of getting everything, I choose you over all my privileges. I choose you over the rain in dry, I choose you even when I deny. Some substance of intimacy is not only one which connects and makes me yours but what takes turns in my mind is that by the agreements of heaven, all my life is not written with you but not even without you!

When in your absence, I don't feel you but still you remain—

In the air surrounding,
In the beams arising,
Within the bounds, you don't set.
Here and there you reflect.

You see our love is not homespun.
I'm with you despite of all odds.
I know, we can't be together and it will take a turn,
Still I'm faithful that it will be in place like instrumental cords.

I see something getting mixed in us, and then my love reaches to a point where I can't possess you and I prefer lunacy. When this whole world is on one side and you, on one for me, if my leave for you is bliss, then I am blessed. I believe, god won't let me go away maybe because he made us one once!

I'm yours but you aren't all mine.
Still I believe in some day's sunshine.
Full of pride that I've devoted my life to another
life—
We have come at this point with so much thrive.

I want all my life to be spent on your beat,
I would then feel it like a coin which swiftly flips.
At that time when this life would retreat,
I want my end to come on your lips.

So I sense you in my creation. I pray for your life's
elongation. For your some day's realisation. Without
you is my deterioration.
I want all my life to be spent on your beat,
I would then feel like a coin which swiftly flips,
At that time this life would retreat,
I want my end to come on your lips.
All this explicates why I say that don't love me as
I love you!
"It is not sensible though liable and not possible
though incredible"

Chapter 8

"*He is online.*"

"Hi. How're you?" she wrote. "*Offline? Why does he see my message and go offline? He didn't see that. No double ticks.*"

"*Theek*," he messaged after one and a half hour. "*He meant that he is good. Without me?*"

"If you have time, we could talk for some minutes about something critical," she sent in a not so informal way. "*Offline again! I'm disturbing him. He's got over me.*"

After two hours he came online and replied, "About what?"

"Are we breaking up?" she asked with a heavy heart. "*Yes!" Please say no,*"

"NO!" he answered.

She sighed with relief. "Then? Be normal," "*Love me then.*"

"Yes," he said.

"*I should say now.*"

"I lovvee youuuu," she sent smiling.

"Why?" he asked.

"Ah what?" she asked as she did not understand his words.

"Answer me. Why do you love me?" he asked dangerously.

"*Mr. Re Al, how could you ask me such an obvious question? It makes me so intolerant.*"

"You are my life. My everything depends on you; in this world and even after."

"So you fight with me despite of loving me. You hurt me Kyara." *"unint entionally*unintentionally*unintentionally."*

"If there is love, there are fights too. You know the best relationship is that in which no matter how hard it gets, two of them don't give up on each other," she typed emotionally. "Like us."

"Hmm," he sent her two kisses.

"Do you love me?" she asked something whose answer was obvious for him too. It made him impatient. He loved her like no one else could. Her pleasurable laughter, her glossy hair, her nervousness when he was close to her, warmness of her soul, wholly took his heart. "Yes," he replied with gladness.

"I know."

"Why don't you say that to me?" she complained.

"Some things are not to be told. You just need to understand them," he said and she smiled.

"We are meeting tomorrow," he sent.

"Oh why?"

"I will come to pick you up at two in the afternoon."

"That smile is beautiful Kyara." Aroosh said. "Oh you're here. I didn't notice," she turned and said, "What's up?"

"Sandwiches?" she offered.

"Thanks."

"So? He must be the reason behind that smile," she said winking.

"Ha hmm ya," she said nodding oddly.

After a break of twenty five minutes he sent, "You're married to me."

"What?" she asked.

"Yes. You're," he said.

"What is going on in his mind? Well, why am I crying?"

"Hmm," she replied.

"What happen?" he asked as if he could know her state.

"Nothing. I am crying," she typed and locked her phone. Putting her hand over her nose, she kept her head on the pillow. She could hear the sound of her ringtone which notified her of his constant messages. She saw, "Kyara!" "Stop crying baby." "What did I do?" "Are these tears of happiness or sadness? "Answer me."

"I am glad. Is this heaven? How can I take this? He says I am his. How can I be so lucky to be called his? What are you doing with me? You're making me mad for yourself. I am getting absorbed in your love."

"I love you," she typed. "I have been married to you since the day when you actually told me about your feelings."

"*Acha!* Love you too!"

"*Diary calling*"

My words are bewitchingly new,
which can't reside in simple minds.
They have my heart, my lord and you,
And so I don't need anything besides.

I feel to discontinue but then I begin yet again,
As if, then you will lose your survival.
I write to taste life and completely attain,
For one more time to fill the interval.

Could you beseech to know what's behind?
For opening the hardly knitted mysteries,
I can't be secretive and you can't ever find,
Anything related to it in series.

If this remains or does not,
My words will be for you till eternity.
Beyond the bounds of mortal lot,
They will have place in humanity.

Even if you forget my abiding affection,
they will make you remember infrequently-
Of all those times when I looked for your attention,
And we both gazed at each other dotingly.

In all those phrases, which portray,
Your vividness and extreme pull.
It drives off all the monotony away,
Spontaneously, it makes my aspirations full.

You act as a spring to my mind's eye.
It compels me to form you in poetry.
With every creation, I get nearer,
To you and your striking history.

With what I write, maybe you don't realize.
On that decision taking platform of good and bad,
You will go kaput; and you will criticize-
each second when you went on to degrade.

Within it, I see your image sporadic,
I wish to cling to it tautly.
As I sigh, to find any tactic,
You get poured upon me profoundly.

My words are bewitchingly new-
and can't reside in simple minds.
They have my heart, my lord and you,
And so I don't need anything besides.

"Miss writer, you write heavenly." Aroosh said and she gave her a sweet laugh.

"I, sometimes, really feel bad for mm.. Maisha," she said making her comfortable on the chair.

"Shit! I don't want to indulge in this conversation right now."

"Why?" she asked hesitantly.

"Well, you know why. She is my sister too. She's been cheated upon."

"I feel bad too." Elf said.

"What's the point then? I haven't made her life miserable. Instead, her choices have made," she said in a selfish tone. *"Selfishness.. It's not my thing."*

"That is true too. She's awkwardly flushed with pride for no reason."

"Not really pride. She's like that since birth. Whatever she has been, she is my sister. We can't do anything and I don't think we need to talk more about this," she spoke quickly and her eyes, all filled with the tears of guilt, shame, agony and every negative feeling. The reality of vindictiveness shown by her all through couldn't be shadowed. "It's been my fault to indulge in wrong love, wrong feelings, wrong MAN," she cried frightfully.

"Wrong man? No no. He loves you. You love him. No wrong in that Kyara. You have the right to fall in love," she spoke touching her back.

"Hmm." she said looking at the redness of her nose in the mirror. "Smile Kyara. Why do you worry? You shouldn't," she said crying with her.

"How can't I worry? I worry all the time. What if you are told that next year, at this time, at the very moment, you will have nothing? What if God gave us the details of our death before only? What if you get to know that on a particular day in this inauspicious year, you will see the world ending before your eyes and you, feeling it, surviving? You're been forced to live alone on this planet. How would you feel?

"You can't worry because you PRAY. You're a believer. Your lord is testing you because you're his beloved. Why don't you understand your value? He loves you so much. Leave everything on him. He's the turner of fates. Your prayers hold more weight than your hand's lines," Aroosh said as her tears flew down her cheeks. "He gave you HIM. He gave you the power to love him, to be faithful to him, to be his. Both of you, your love is giving me Goosebumps."

"My lord! I know he loves to hear me praying. Until now, my belief on him has given me beats. All upon him," they both smiled and hugged each other. *"I love you girl!"*

"Kyara!" her phone blinked. "Mr. Romeo must be missing you. Talk to him. You both have been apart since ten minutes." She said handling over the phone to her. *"ROMEO? A Boss actually."*

"Yes," she replied.

"What are you doing?" he asked.

"Talking about you."

"Good," he texted. "We're meeting day after tomorrow Kyara."

"That moment when he takes my name makes me electrified. Wait a sec! Two more days, no way!"

"Why? You told me about tomorrow. You're making me sad," she typed.

"Oh don't be sad. I can't wait to see you. I have work outside the city. I'm at the airport."

"You're going so far. This means we will not meet, right?"

"We will baby. I will come day after tomorrow in the morning. At two, as I said, just a day more. I will be present before you and you in front of me, being all mine." *"How does he do that? His flattery convinces me every time."*

"All yours?" she blushed.

"All MINE, you're," he sent giving an evidence of his dominance.

"So what about your good past? You've never told me about it," she sat on the chair. "Was it too boring?"

"Past? Well you know me more than I know myself," he said insignificantly.

"Your personal life has been vacant, don't you tell me,"

"Kyara," he sent her name to her.

"What? I'm your present."

"And future," he typed at once.

"And past?"

"Hmm," he paused. "Kratika."

"K factor, I see." Baddie got green.

"Another religion," she replied.

"Yes," he typed and she could sense his tone.

"You loved her?" she sent with the heaviest heart.

"Hmm," he stopped again. "Yes."

"I wish he says the same to others about me." Good Elf sympathised. "My unpredictable loved that girl."

"More than me?"

"No," he answered.

"Glad I'm," she sent. "You must delete that girl from your account that just followed you."

"Who?"

"She just followed you because an hour ago she wasn't there in your list."

"Okay, I will," he said coolly. "She's pretty hun."

"Good gracious!"

"Ha-ha. Have your sleep please. You sleep for so less time."

"You've made me sad," she wrote.

"No, I was just kidding love," he replied. "SLEEP."

"And you know what do the capitals mean?" Baddie asked Good Elf.

"*A powerful yell. Gosh! I love this person.*" Good Elf panted.

His less crafty ways were so much dominating that she loved how he threatened her for his love now and then. Not obeying him could have never come into as she really knew him more than he did himself. He was her star and a man of dreams with everything in plenty. His untainted gestures, glint of skin and bashful manners floated her so frantically that there was no single night spent without dreams lacking him! She had not named him as her boyfriend because that he was not. He was someone more subterranean, they were something more. Despite of all the clashes and disparity, their literal craving had not found its way out. He had touched her soul more and she wanted her every splinter to get glued with his. And he longed for her constant thoughts more than her presence because they hardly met each other. Rehaam Alhamd was nothing but an accurate devotee and an exemplary quality of all the lovers was intensifying in him. Frailty was felt when their eyes danced but their bodies couldn't. His ways of scanning her from head to toe, ignoring at first, confessing at second were carved in her mind's major part filled with him and her heart which was not beating in her chest but rather, in his. That day in between them was stretching itself from both the sides. She felt herself to be on an island, an island of him. Deserted in his humorous statements, spine-chilling romance and paranormal love, she cared for none, not even herself. For the moment, she wanted him in every way she could. Desperation? Basorexia? Yes maybe she was hankering after them. His endearing words were like asphodels, augmenting their mutual covets.

"*Saturday! You're here finally.*"

His work stood first but she was next to it. He was travelling chiefly for her from some hill station in the north to their city. He had boarded the plane at seven in the morning as it was a flight of two hours due to frequent halts in between.

"His last seen is of six forty five. Why didn't he text me in the morning? Is he even coming? It can be possible due to his unpredictability. I shouldn't think so much. Today is another normal day," she spoke making herself calmer.

"Good morning kiddo," he sent her after half an hour. "My phone was switched off when I was up in the air."

"Well, you could message me before boarding," she replied madly.

"Kiddo? No one has made me feel so young than he does every now and then."

"I didn't want to disturb your sleep," he replied coolly.

"For your information, I didn't sleep all night."

"Why?" he enquired.

"Ask yourself. Do you let me sleep? You act better than coffee to keep me awake," she wrote.

"Ha-ha I see. You must have slept Kyara. I wanted you to sleep properly and I supposed you loved sleeping. Didn't you?"

"Who doesn't love sleeping? I tried to sleep but you didn't let me. You don't know how much your absence affects me."

"And my presence?" he asked.

"It makes me lose senses."

"Then get ready to lose your senses today."

"Is that a warning Mr. Re?"

"What will you be wearing?" he asked.

"Palazzo pants. I love animal prints."

"No palazzo walazzo. There is no party."

"Oh god! He just called my favourite pants so badly? Why? There is no party but there will be you."

"Oh why? What else then?" she asked swallowing her furry.

"Normal and easy clothes. Wear jeans and a t-shirt and of course an *abaya*," he typed.

"I love when he says to wear abaya."

"Okay. Yes *abaya* of course," she sighed.

"Where should I come to pick you up?" he asked. "I don't know," she said.

"Then who else does? Tell me fast," he sent. "Go to Amirah's house. I will come there."

"She has gone to her farmhouse. Her house is locked," she said worriedly.

"You know that, I know that and nobody else. Just go there. I will come after two minutes you reach at her place. Keep your phone charged. Do you have the internet plan working or are you using Wi-Fi?"

"Wireless fidelity," she said. Trr Trr. Her phone ringed at another moment. *"Message! Net pack recharge. Excuse me? Why? I don't like such favours."*

"Why did you do that? I have Wi-Fi," she wrote in distress.

"Well, I want to talk to you all the time," he answered.

"But I stay at home all the time. We could talk without it too."

"Don't argue."

"He's angry now."

"Keep calm baby. Are you being mad at me?" she asked in utmost innocence.

"Yes. I don't want you to argue with me," he said.

"Okay," she replied soothingly.

"I will text you as I reach. Later my love," he wrote and went offline.

She wanted to wash her hair which had oil in them since the previous night. Abundantly applying shampoo and then smoothing her hair with the conditioner, she gazed at her hair in the mirror which reminded her of him and his statements about its length. The drops of water which were flowing down in a rush told her about his speediness in everything which he did. His pure tenderness of holding her as if she was a seedling, still under developed, still naive and green. As she ended her bath and rolled up her hair in the towel, she turned her heels to dance softly. With her eyes shut, she imagined him holding her waist and cooperating with her steps. That music which was being hummed unhurriedly screamed to be told to him. He was not into dance, not even a bit. She could never imagine him dancing in his formal suits of mostly grey, white and black shades. It was a dunce thought but still she pictured him moving in her flow, dancing towards her or rather pushing himself close.

The relief of meeting him after so long was paramount. She did think that why was she meeting him but her gladness over shined her interrogation. A man who has hurt her distinctly, whose getting married to another girl, who is bossy and rules over her without any agreement and who has married her in the air told her to meet and she was all ready with the flowing current. Why couldn't she just say no to him? All her morals concluded at his views and desires. Why was that electricity still alive after one and a half year of this so called relationship? Nobody knew they could make it so far. Passion was still covering their hearts. It might have begun because of momentary attraction or infatuation but the gone months made them attached. Their hearts were tightened with each other. Impermanent affair had acquired some undying and perpetual gist.

Putting her kohl and rubbing the gloss on her lips, she tied the ponytail using the pink rubber band. She saw herself the last time in the mirror. Her light green t- shirt was paired up with blue jeans which she had folded outwards from the bottom. She wore her *abaya* and then her copper wedges.

"Kyari! You ready?" he messaged.

"Yes almost. Should I leave?"

"Please do," he said.

"Akira, I'm going to Amirah. Hope you tell mum," she waved her.

"Wait. How'll you go?" She questioned.

"I will go walking. I will take the watchman's daughter. I will send her back. Good bye," she said and closed the door.

"Breath Kyara! He's not an alien. He's your Rehaam." Good Elf whispered feeling her extreme nervousness.

His Bentley Mulsanne was parked before Amirah's house. A lavish Bentley was driven by the most gorgeous man on earth. *"When did he buy that? I have no account of it. If he is going to look so stunning then who will look at his cars?"*

She saw him opening his door and walking around the car's front. She stood motionlessly beside the car's door. He generously opened the door and said, "Hi Kyara! Have a seat."

"Oh my! This gentlemanliness is so pleasing."

"With pleasure," she smiled. He went back to his seat and fastened the seat belt as if he was in a mood of some long drive. It was a hot afternoon but his car's atmosphere made her feel cold. She hugged herself with both of her hands to avoid exposure to the air conditioner.

"Are you cold?" he asked.

"No! I'm just feeling dizzy," she sighed.

"Oh why? I told you to sleep," he said.

"I told you the reason," she replied sarcastically. He grinned shyly.

"Where are we going?" she asked to end the flirtation.

"Home!" he replied in a flash.

"What? Whose home? Yours? I thought we were.. I mean, home why? What about your parents?" she asked disapprovingly.

"You question so much," he said staring at her.

"I thought we were having a private meeting. Gosh! I want to cry now. He is taking me to meet his parents."

"Answer me then," she replied making a sad face.

"My parents are out. They are in Nainital," he said looking at her.
"*Wicked, he is.*"

"We are going to your house, right? But for what reason? I mean, I thought we would go somewhere to hang out," she said putting her bag on the back seat.

"Hang out? You want us to go in public?" He asked touching his forehead.

"*Public? Yes. I mean, not really. But I do want to show the world that I possess a charmer.*"

"I don't know," she said moving her head.

"We'll go public some other day. HOME for now," he stopped the car at the much seen villa in the flora lines. He parked his car along with the other cars in his extra prolific garage. He again showed his gentlemanliness by opening the door for her and asking her to come out.

"After you," he smiled like a child. She turned back to look for her bag. "Leave it here only. Just take your phone," he said and she followed.

She went inside the living room which had French couches and white wooden chairs. It looked as if it was one of those European houses which she had learnt about in the literature. Arts of M.F Husain and some other artists which she hadn't even heard about hung on the walls. She gazed at them as she had entered that area first time. Whenever she came to his house, a new place was discovered.

"*I wonder how big this house is.*"

"Make yourself comfortable Kyara. We need to talk right now," he spoke as he closed the door.

"Yes," she whispered. They had a distance of ten feet between them which was decreasing as he moved closer to her steadily. When he was five feet apart, he said, "Your hair."

"Oh I'm sorry," she said removing her stole from her hair. The detachment was lessening itself with every step. She looked down at her hands and touched her knuckles to hinder timidity. Light brown met dark brown and he sank himself deeply in her eyes. He held her delicately like before showing that nothing had changed. His expressionless face made her impatient so she whispered, "You were talking about something."

He held her close, more close. Her head leaned over his left shoulder, getting a hold of them. "Do you allow me to kiss you?" Without hearing to it, she knew that he always asked for her permission; not through words but through eyes. She didn't say a word but moved her head upwards. Her eyes were not closed like always, they were wide opened for searching his, for getting lost in his.

"There's lot of light," she said looking downwards. Immediately he went to close the four tube lights and just switched on a side lamp which emitted yellow light. Their shadow could be seen on the off-white curtains. "Hmm?" he raised his eyebrows. Upon her heels which made her not so tall, she was tip toed to reach at his level. He moved backwards and so did she. Being involved in each other, he fell on the couch, and she, on his lap. He paused to look at her and nodded once. That was his pattern of nodding after kissing her. She gave him a smile which had trust as well as hope in it. Feeling the most protected when he clasped her in himself, she snorted. He took her rubber band and slowly got her hair free. They were open, coming on her cheeks and his lap. He carried out cafune, running his fingers through her hair for some seconds.

"You wanted to talk," she said holding his face, rubbing his cheeks.

"Yes. Not now," he replied kissing her cheeks. "Why not now?" she asked kissing his nose.

"It's not the time Kyara. I had to but your presence distracts me. You make me powerless," he murmured in her ears.

"You're hurting me," she said uninterestingly.

"In what way?" He was puzzled.

"In every way. Like now," she replied.

"Now? Well, I thought you were strong," he spoke stroking her forehead softly.

"I was." *"My biggest weakness is telling me to be strong. Cool!"*

"You can put up with this. For me?" he replied like an ordering army officer.

"He is telling me to accept his ways of hurting. He loves to hurt me. I knew this since start."

"Why are you still in your foot wears? I said to you to make yourself comfortable," he said in an annoyed tone.

She abided instantly and put her wedges in the corner. He stood as if he was about to leave so she held his hand and sat on the couch, beside him as silence hovered between them. She denied looking at him in repugnance but he continued adoring her. She narrowed her eyes and turned to him. Pulling her or rather dragging her to his side, he started to spread his boyish smile. Maintaining her balance by the support of the settee's back to avoid a fall which could have embarrassed both of them, she got lifted and was kept on his lap again as if she was not a human but a doll, it was not Rehaam but a kid who holds its toys and turns them in any way.

"What're you doingggg? Am I a baby who could be twisted and turned in any direction? He's made me boneless. Why am I being so weird? He can do anything. Baddie permits him prior to my angelic elf."

After a small second, a smile came on her lips which she criticized at first. To avoid his laughter on her anger plus smile face, she hugged him at another moment. Her hands encircling his head, his not-so-gelled hair touching her nose making her live through his sweet sweat. His hands gripping her tiny waist made her lost and nowhere to be found. She felt herself going in the reverse path to that of gravity. She opened her eyes to observe the certainty of the moment. Before she could make any sound, he whispered, "Kyara. Be still."

"Man! He's holding me up in the air. Put me back on the ground. This is such an uncomfortable situation. I love it! No I don't. What if we fall? He's holding me like a baby Awwwww."

"We will fall." She uttered looking down over his shoulders as if she had been taken to the tallest tower to be pushed from there and she had to estimate the height for protection.

"Why would we? You're so light." He said kissing her hair and bringing them to the left side. She laughed and joined him in his fad.

"Breathe. Slowly," he said knowing about her discomfit.

"Put me down." She said smiling serenely and he sat on the settee having her in the same position as he had her when they stood. Taking his phone out, he opened the front camera and held it close.

"You wanted our pictures last time," he said posing.

"Last time but not now, at this moment." As she turned her eyes towards the camera, her hair looked terribly messy and cheeks as red as a cherry. Her lips had lost their lustre due to the gloss being transported to someone else. Though a small amount of red was still present, she rolled her tongue over her lips to distribute the redness all over. He sat there observing her through the front camera. "What're you doing Kyara?" he asked with a grin and took a long breath.

"What will you do with photos?" she asked arranging her hair to avoid answering his amorous questions.

"I am going to see them later," he answered giving an impish smile.

"Click then. She said touching her forehead with his. Her hands on his shoulders, which he took and placed sideward, went unnoticed. She again put her right hand on his left shoulder and again, he took it, pressed it and kept sideward.

"He doesn't like it." "What?" she asked.

"Nothing. Keep your left hand down. It's blocking the view. You may keep your right hand anywhere but not left."

'I would prefer keeping both my hands under control."

Click*Click. "You're adorable," he spoke seeing the time in his I phone which made her wonder about her phone. It was kept on the side table.

"Twenty missed calls," she said raising her brows at him.

"Whose?" he asked putting her beside him.

"My friend. Can I have your phone to call her back? My phone is running out of balance."

"Why didn't you tell me before? It would make her think that you're with me if you use my phone."

"There's nothing to hide." "I will text her and ask."

"No. Call her," he said opening his screen lock.

"No need. I will talk later," she said getting closer to him.

"Get up Kyara. Let me drop you home," he got up and went to the wash basin.

"Was this so short?" she asked searching for her rubber band.

"It's been so long. Look at the clock," he said washing his face.

"Don't wash your face please."

"Sooner baby," he said opening the room's door. "Make sure you get your things from here like your pins and all."

"I did," she replied wearing her foot wear and realising that he hadn't even removed his shoes. *"He didn't put off his shoes. His lovely feet! I wanted to see them. Why can't I stay here forever? I'm married to you."*

"Do not speak," he uttered wearing his black shades and left the room closing the door. She sat there waiting for him to call her out, quietly. She was in the centre stage of getting ready when he had ordered her mouth to be in a statue mode.

"Breathtaking eyes under those black glasses. It's a no no."

"We have to stay here for some more time. Ten minutes, maybe," he said coming in, closing the door and switching on the lights.

"Oh." *"May these ten minutes never end."* "I'm feeling dizzy. Can I share your rest room?"

"Yes. That way. You can share everything," he smirked.

"In that case, I'm using your toothbrush. May I?" *"Of course, you can. I expect."*

"Yes. You may," he spoke intensely. "Why do you have to brush now?"

"I was asking for the coming days," she laughed.

"Smart one. What else for the coming days?" he asked deeply.

"Well, your clothes. Can you share?" she asked forgetting her dizziness.

"Ha-ha. From where do you get such off the wall ideas? My shirts will cover whole of you."

"I know," she said gladly.

"Next time okay. We are running late. I have meetings to attend and tonight, I am flying back to the hill station."

"Why? You just came." *"Don't go!"*

"I will have to. I will be back in a week and going to stay close to you through texts. Don't worry," he said opening the room's door, once more. "Come out in two minutes. Not more!"

Dropping her on the same mango road, he drove off. As she started walking fast and then running towards her home, he was still in his car, on another road, watching her.

Again, their eyes met with a burning feeling as if they were never satiable and could never get full of each other, from each other. She shuddered and didn't look up again. As she reached in her room, she got herself in cosy clothes. Untied her hair and left them open. "The Hair Band", in which his fingers were entangled, a few minutes ago was no more a normal band. She kept that thing of value in a box so that it couldn't be lost.

She remembered that she had to reply her friend. Going through her messages on internet, she got one from Amirah.

"So you met him!"

"Chuck! Not even my angels know this. How does she?"

"What're you talking about?"

"Yes. You in his Bentley, beside him," she replied in her tone of anger.

Her world shifted after seeing what she wrote. *"Someone saw? Who? He will kill me if I tell him this."*

"How can you know this?"

"You were in a Bentley. Nobody else has it except him. Didn't you see yesterday's newspaper? His name has come in that. And you were beside him, thankfully Haira saw you. What's up? You were in his house. Did he take you to his parents?"

"He's news now."

"No. His parents are out. He wanted to talk to me so in his house, we were." *"Err... What am I saying?"*

"Damn you Kyara. In his house, ALONE! For what worthy reason did you go to his house all alone?"

"Hugh! Miss. Overreaction."

"Will you answer?" she messaged again after twenty minutes.

"Amirah, I am tired. Can we talk tomorrow at school?"

"If Mr. R has left you in your senses then please know that tomorrow is Sunday."

"Disgusting! Why is she doing this? She tells me to be with him and now when I am, she is behaving so sickly."

"Don't be sick. Why are you being mad at me?"

"Because I don't want you to be in any trouble due to him,"

"I am in no trouble. For heaven's sake, stop looking at him like that. It's my life and I know what I have to do with it. I went to his place because we needed to talk. You're being childishly over protective," she sighed.

"Well, I know he's good but you're my sister. I hope you are not planning any family with him."

"What? Family? Kids? I am seventeen!"

"From where has that come? I am of your age, if you can recall."

"Yes, you're but you are in a marriage with him. I mean, like you see it."

"Like I see it... I see."

"No family. Okay? Chill," she wrote miserably and went to bed.

Her eyes opened with a knock on her bedroom's door. She couldn't remember the time presently and when she had gone to sleep. She checked her phone and it was six P.M.

"Oh no! I missed my evening prayers," she spoke loudly rubbing her eyes and opening the door.

"Amirah is sitting in the hallway." Akira said. "Wake up!"

"Oh my goodness! She wants a live fight now. Nooooo!"

"I missed my evening prayer," she told her while kissing her on the cheek.

"Still you've got five minutes," she said pressing her back.

"I will just run. Wait!"

After greeting both the shoulders, she put her hands forward so that her palm lines, of both the hands, joined to make a moon. She prayed and got up to remove her stole.

"So?" Amirah sipped coffee.

"Hi," she grinned.

"What did you wear? Tell me in detail," she smirked. *"Finally like a friend, she behaved."*

"I wore a normal jeans and a green t-shirt."

"Coffee?" Amirah offered.

"No. I am just not feeling well. Due to Nausea."

"What? Nausea? Are you okay Kyara?"

"I can guess what you're thinking."

She sneered back and said, "Amirah! Please!"

They both laughed and she replied, "Kyara! Will those kids get to see their father? I mean, he remains so busy,"

"Are you serious? I will kill him if he won't give time to his family," she said winking. "I was thinking about their names. They should be ending with "am" like his name does."

"Oh I see. That's so cute but I wish they look like you," she replied sipping again.

"Even he wishes the same. But his eyes and fingers and toes, should resemble," she said dreamily.

"Oh does he wish so? I thought he wouldn't like them."

"Why wouldn't he? He is cutely fond of kids," she replied. "I'm going out with my sisters. Want to join?"

"No. I have a wedding to attend tonight. All of you enjoy. Is Hero of the era joining too?" Amirah laughed.

"No idea! Wish he does." Amirah grabbed her phone and went towards the exit door of the hall. Giving her regards to Maisha and Akira who came to greet her, she walked out of the main gate and opened the SUV door to be driven back.

"Where's the Naked eye colour box?" Akira screamed.

"I didn't use it. Maisha must have," she said tying up her *Khimar*.

"Whose gonna drive?" she interrogated.

"Rehaam," Akira stated. *"Goodness! I ought to look good now."*

"Why he?"

"What? Can't he join us? Don't be so anti-social."

"No, I meant.. I mean..Okay fine," she ended and went downstairs.

"He's in white." She inhaled softly so that no one could hear her puff. Her stomach could not bear hindering the noise of her gasp so she pressed her lips to stop the intake of air through her mouth. Nose was a better option in such a thorny state. Her stomach was moving up and then down as if someone had removed the nebulizer of a severe patient.

"I won't look at him now." Elf said. "There are people here Kyara! He will kill you if he gets to know about your not so decent behaviour."

She closed her eyes and covered her face with her hands to avoid him. "Are you okay?" Akira whispered.

"No. It suffocates me," she spoke putting her hand on her mouth. He turned a little to look at her. His look said that he knew what she felt and she didn't want him to know about it.

"I mean, if you can diminish the temperature," she said looking at him.

"No! I didn't say that. Is he thinking that I meant something else?"

"Of the air conditioner," she completed.

"Yes sure," he did it without looking at her.

After fifteen minutes of the driving, she could not feel the butterflies in her stomach as she didn't look at him but she began to feel uncomfortable due to cold.

"If you could turn off the air-conditioner," she spoke in her loveliest tone.

"If Maisha and Akira had not been here, I would have got punched. Both of my beauties have saved me."

"Decide what you want." Maisha smiled.

"I want it to be off. I will put down the windows," she replied at once and he set the air conditioner off glaring at her through the front mirror. *"Oh yes! I can tease you through the mirror."*

They reached the hotel Lebensmittel and he ordered some bratfurst, currywurst, Fischbrotchen and konigdberger klopse for everyone.

"You've been here before?" he asked Akira.

"Oh yes. A lot of time. I love German," she said gladly.

"I have come here second time with you." Maisha said to him.

"But we didn't ask that." Baddie said.

"So I hope I ordered finely," he again said to Akira.

"Perfectly. Akira loves konigdberger klopse." Maisha interrupted.

"And what do you love.." he turned his intense eyes to her.

"YOU! Elf screamed.

"..To have?" he beamed.

"Oh my! Why do you do this? Butterflies have again gone wild in tickling me."

"Whatever you ordered, it's really fine,"

"Kyara is so choosy, you know. She is not well today else she must have ordered a lot many things." Akira smiled and her eyes went rolling at him.

"Hey! Hi!" Akira screamed.

"Hey Akira! How're you? Didn't expect you here," he said hugging her lightly.

"He's Nihaal," she said to them.

"Nihaal! That guy whom Akira talked about. He's an auditor. Isn't he?"

"Kyara right? Hi! Heard a lot about you. Glad to see you today," he spoke suddenly and she said, "Hello," she smiled at the new person but stopped as soon as she saw him raising his brows.

"Hope he's fine. I just said hello."

He got up to shake hands with him and said, "You may join us."

222

"*Large hearted person is back after two seconds.*"

"No, I.." he began.

"Yes please do. As it is, we wanted to have a dinner." Akira insisted.

"Okay for you, lovely lady," he said blushing at her. She gave him a coy smile in return.

"*Is something cooking between the two new bees?*"

"So what would you like to have? We have already ordered," he said apologetically.

"Great! I will have what you all will have. This place takes a lot of time to serve." Nihaal replied.

He had dark, curly hair which was not gelled. His height was more than Rehaam's and he was a little broader. She could clearly figure out that he was much elder than the others but still in his twenties.

As the food took thirty five minutes to reach their mouth, she watched him cutting the meat balls on his plate with the knife. Managing to bring them with the fork before his lips, he exhaled without taking his eyes off her. She sat there with her mouth dropped open in wariness.

"*Intense eyes intentions don't look so generous. My eyes can see some lovely gestures.*"

He swallowed his food in the most dramatic way, licked the sauce which was on his lips and then poured the water in his glass to have a sip. As he gulped it, he laid stress so that she could see the water running down his throat. His thick brows fluttered as he picked up the spoon and sliced a piece to eat. His pinkish lips were caressing the spoon when she saw him eating every fragment of what was on it. Seeing his brows raised in passion, she made her eyes large to stop his continual romance with the food!

"Why aren't you eating?" Nihaal interrupted their distant love bubbles.

"I..." she said looking at him who was grinning to the fullest with narrowed eyes. *"Because of this distractive man seated here."* She narrowed her eyes at Rehaam and replied, "I was about to begin. Please pass me sauces." He touched his upper teeth with his tongue to celebrate his victory in off-putting her.

"Kyara, you look deep. I mean, I am in awe of your personality." Nihaal stated. "And of course your beauty too."

"Ha-ha!" She gave a tiny fake laugh. "Thank you," she smiled at him and then looked at the person opposite to her side.

"Did he just frown at me? What can I do if a person is praising me, unlike you?"

"So what are the future plans? What are you going to study further?" Nihaal questioned. She saw him first, before replying to him. He didn't react to it and showed his furry by being involved in the food.

"Please don't talk to me. I can't afford him getting mad. Just a minute before he was so loving and now, he's got so angry that he isn't even looking at me."

Giving a dull smile, she replied, "I haven't thought about it." *"This boy who is going red in anger is gonna decide it."* Nihaal smiled back and started his conversation with Rehaam as if they knew each other since pre-historic period. Akira and Maisha busied themselves in their talks and she sat there looking at her phone which didn't interest her much as she wasn't knowing whether he was talking to her or not. Nihaal gave her a smile again when she had a not-so-required eye contact with him. Feeling her hair on her forehead, she arranged her Khimar properly for five seconds. She heard from Maisha, "Let us go. It is ten." Everyone got up and he paid the bill whose amount, she was unaware about. As they went towards the corridor, she thought that she could tie her *Khimar* again so that it didn't loosen.

"Excuse me people. I will be back from the powder room," she spoke pulling out her pin.

"Where is it?" he asked. *"Thank God! He spoke to me."*

"I don't know," she replied making a pout.

"Where are the rest rooms?" He asked one of the workers.

"Towards the left side of the banquet hall entrance," he replied.

He walked towards her and stood on the right side. "Go! That side." His lips moved which she was watching carefully since a micro second. Touching her right shoulder in the gentlest manner, with his left hand, he said, "Go *na*." Electricity crawled over her body. No drop of blood moved in the skin of her shoulder for a minute and she turned towards him and sank in the well of his eyes. His hand was still on her shoulder and so she looked at his hand to tell him that they weren't alone. In a flash, he put his hand sideways and distracted his sight. She walked towards the restrooms hoping that no one watched his informal ways of bonding with her.

"What were you doing?" she messaged as they got back.

"When?"

"Mr unpredictable has an unusual habit of replying like this." Elf and baddie agreed.

"Few minutes ago," she replied.

"He was good looking," he wrote.

"I know what you are trying to bring up."

"Didn't see much. Do you give me time to look at others?"

"Oh really? You looked.." he sent an emoticon with hearts as eyes.

"Aww Thank you," she answered. "I don't know why but I felt you became angry with me. You hadn't looked at me after food."

"Hmm. I did look at you," he sent.

"Our anniversary is coming. Didn't you remember?" She wrote in disgust.

"When?" *"Okay, you may shoot me now. He doesn't remember."*

"You don't remember. That's so nice. This Saturday,"

"Oh ya! What gift do you want?"

"Why does he think that all starts and ends at gifts?"

"I don't want anything. I have got your gift," she wrote happily.

"What do you want?" he asked again. "Please tell me."

"Can I really tell? Even if you will give me a ring made up of a stem, I will cherish it and wear it for life. No diamonds, no platinum. Just a ring of any material which you will make me wear. I will live my whole life in that moment. Please give me a ring, please!" Elf was on her knees.

"Don't even dare to ask about a ring. He will think that you want diamonds or silvers. He won't understand the reason behind your wanting." Baddie ordered.

"Yes! I will go with Baddie."

"Nothing at all! I want you," she wrote.

"You have me already."

"Your presence,"

"We will meet up soon baby. I love Kyari, you know small farmlands," he sent.

"I didn't know you liked farming," she said confusedly.

"I still don't like it."

"You just said that you like small farmlands," she said.

"Yes, that is because of you," he sent with a winking emoticon.

"Kyari=small farmlands. I see," Good elf said wearing the crown.

"Because of my name?" she asked.

"No, just because of you,"

"You act so differently cute sometimes and mad too," she smiled.

"Mad? Am I? You said so?"

"And he doesn't like this." Good Elf stood on her head.

"You know," she wrote.

"What?"

"I feel scared, sometimes."

"What scares you?" he asked attentively.

"I don't know. I am a girl. This scares me."

"What? I didn't get you."

"I mean, sometimes I feel, I wish I was not so good looking. You know, I don't like when someone sees me." Kyara wrote.

"Who? A boy?"

"Yes. I don't like when someone sees me. I feel scared. You know there are a lot of people who like me and want to make use of me. You know what I mean?"

"Baby, I love you. Whom are you talking about? Don't be scared of me. Tell me the name."

"What if he kills those people?"

"Hmm. Such people have no names. But I only feel good when I'm with you, near you. You won't let anyone hurt me."

"Hmm. Name?" he sent.

"No! I don't want you to do anything. It is just that I don't like some people's way of seeing or expressing. You know, a girl can know the character by looking at the eyes of a man."

"You don't have to be scared of anyone. Got it? If you feel that way then tell me or your mother."

"I feel impure," she typed in tears.

"What? Kyara! You're so pious. How can you talk like this? A glimpse can't make you impure."

"A glimpse can't but a touch can," she wrote.

"Tell me precisely. Please! For my sake."

"What if you leave me?" she asked as her tears dropped on her phone screen.

"Oh god! Why would I do that? Who's tried on you? Tell me, I will destroy that man."

"My ex-driver. I mean, I don't find him right and some more people. You can't understand."

"DRIVER!" he wrote in capitals which seemed no less than a yell.

Sensing him beside in her utmost fears when others saw her, wanting to escape from all the foul and grubby eyes, she assumed herself being clasped by his hands out of harm's way. Believing that he wouldn't let anyone hurt her, she ascertained that he could protect her by his lone touch from all those brutes who wanted her bodily. A rescuer he was, who not only had power over her corporally but her spirit, soul and heart was even won by her "Hero". She knew that he would devastate all those fiends that made her frightened so much so that she had sleeping and breathing problems.

"You're not doing anything," she typed.

"You can't tell me what I have to do."

"Yes I can't but it is just that I don't want. We live in such a society where only a girl is blamed for everything. I don't want you to be in touch with any of such people. They're too low for my sophisticated cuddle cake."

"Hmm. Cuddle cake?"

"Yes. You!"

"Hmm," he replied.

"You can't be romantic at all times like other guys whom I read books about," she smiled.

"Ha-ha! Because of work," he sent.

"No! You are moody, unlike typical boys. Like now, I am flirting with you and you're replying one word. You know, I only flirt with you. Feel lucky."

"You're not allowed with someone else," he answered.

"Ha-ha. What if I do?" she joked.

"Someone is pleading me for a nice battering,"

"He can beat me whoa!"

"Can you?"

"You think so? Only if you create such indecent situations,"

"Mr trying-to-be-harsh cannot even hold my hand harshly."

"Ha-ha I know how light it would be and then I will only have to say to make it look real. You really think that I don't know that you can't hurt me."

"Oh so you know,"

"Ha-ha, you're such a baby," she sent a laughing emoticon.

"Huh! It is not funny. You are just mine in every way. Nobody can see you or talk to you,"

"Completely yours!" she added, "Why do you get so angry?"

"I don't like when you talk about someone else."

"And what about me when I see you talking to my sister."

"Oh. What about my liking then?"

"What kind of liking?"

"You're too clever to know it." "Nothing"

He sent her two kisses to stay away from the upcoming conflict. She didn't know what to reply to him because he didn't belong to her and was just a veiled thing.

"What's wrong?" he sent.

"Leave me alone okay. Talk to your Maisha. Isn't she free?"

"Why do I have to follow all the rules? And he is nowhere in it. Travelling, eating, living and marrying Maisha and setting the idiotic rules for me. Telling me to be within the boundaries, loving me in such a drastic manner, being possessive about me but what's the conclusion? That extraneous marriage!" Baddie said as she buried her head in the pillow.

"What?" Aroosh shouted standing on the door.

"Nothing," she replied removing hair from her face.

"He?"

"Ooh my gorgeous cousin's mind!"

"I just heard that their marriage date has been fixed," she said softly. "This year it is!"

"Oh!" she said at once. *"Do I look like I care?"* "Cool! We will have a reason to dance."

"Yes really," she smiled.

"He will look good in that groom's head gear." Kyara smiled back. "In the henna ceremony, we will have to hold his fingers and the closest sister of the bride will apply henna on his palm. Akira may do that."

"You will do that. Not Akira," she spoke.

"Ha? I won't be there," she replied.

"Where will you be?"

"I don't know but not there. My lord won't show me that, I believe," she rubbed her cheeks.

"It won't happen. No one will see it. Do you pray that you marry him?" she asked attentively.

She laughed and said, "How can I pray that? He doesn't want to marry me." She paused. "Will you excuse me? I have to change."

There was numbed stillness which led to the start of her shiver. The nameless fear took the form of tears and she was shaking, shaking strongly enough to make her hands and feet cold. As cruel as death it was which made her egocentric and there was an utter depression of soul. She managed to raise her eyes and looked at the mirror. Thinking of him to be with her at the present moment, she was searching for his words. There were none. He was nowhere to comfort her with his presence or just thoughts. Maybe he was as much in love with her sister as he was with her. Maybe he loved her more, loved her enough to let his life be spent with her. She thought herself to be a person with no allure. What did she have? A soul which had been truthful to him and a body which she had hidden from head to toe just for his sake.

Still here, people look for girls who have been untouched and had no past and that is not something to roast about. A democracy in which people have to choose what they prefer, gave rights to everyone. Certainly, anyone could choose the purest girls and that was it! An ideal girl's tagline which she possessed was a white lie. She was no clean, no blameless, and no gullible. Falling in love with him could not raise her status, in her eyes!

Seeing some medicines lying in the bedside drawer, she got up, tied her hair, washed her face and went into the kitchen to bring water. Taking out packet of medicines, she took out one..two..three..four and five but ate only two!

"Remaining three after midnight," She said and put them in the drawer again, leaving the packet on her bed.

Feeling like puking, she drank some more water. Switching off the bulb, regulating the fan's speed, she lied beneath her blanket gazing at the clock. The stillness could make her hear the tick tick of the second's hand. She knew her end was near, as her head was too heavy to make her get up again.

"Abmirah- She will miss me but will be fine some day.

Mr Re Al- He! He may miss me sometimes. I don't want him to regret.

Fila- She will miss me the most. There is someone who loves me.

Abkira- She will kill the conspirators.

Maisha- My sister will miss me. This is for her. I want her life to be great.

Grandparents- They won't be able to take it.

Mommy-

What will she do? Will she think that her daughter whom she prided upon gave up? She may think that I wasn't happy with myself. How will she feel *if she will know that I was in a love affair with my own.....? Will she ever be able to live? She said that prayers can change the fate. What if she gets to know that I didn't pray for my destiny to be changed? Will she ever accept him after this?"*

She closed her eyes as tears tumbled.

"Aroosh- She will feel same as Akira.

What about your lord whom you pray to? Elf said.

"He won't accept my soul. I will be left between the clouds. He will hate me for this."

"Don't you know that taking your own life is prohibited?" Baddie said.

"Am I dead? Should I pray for mercy? This is my first experience. I don't know how to die."

"Kyara! Kyara!" Someone shook her face. She opened her eyes but closed them as everything was blurred. She felt some water on her face which made her uneasy. She could know that she wasn't dead yet! Revolving her eyes around the room to see, she didn't want everyone to know about her suicidal attempt.

"What? Drink this." Aroosh said giving her a glass of some green water. Unable to speak, she closed her eyes again to show her disapproval. She made her sit and supported her to take in that bitter drink.

"Vomit it out. Here!" she vomited before the completion of her sentence. Aroosh sat there with red eyes due to the continual tears.

"You look beautiful with red nose," she whispered.

"You know what? I'm not coming to this house again." Aroosh threw her words.

"Why? Don't you like it my sister?"

"Don't sister me. Get it?"

"What's the time? I've to pray," she said rubbing her nose.

"Whom are you going to pray to?"

"What's wrong?" she asked in an infuriated manner.

"Yes, that is what I also want to know. You ate those five painkillers. Are you in your senses?"

"What? No I ate only two due to my headache," she replied.

"Don't lie. I saw the packet."

"No, let me show you. Here are the remaining three." Kyara spoke expressionlessly.

"I thought..Err.. Something inauspicious," she spoke. "That is why I asked you to vomit."

"Oh! I was about to but then I thought about my afterlife and my mamma."

"Can you tell me how much you will love your kids with him? Those ones with names ending with 'Aam',"

I will love them the most. In fact, I already love them, a lot." She smiled gladly.

"If you love them without seeing then imagine how much your mother loves her babies with the man who loved her."

She listened to her silently and said, "I know. I'm sorry for the trouble. I didn't mean that."

"I know what you meant. Grow up! He's just another person. If he can decide your life or death then I am sorry but you're associating him with your lord and that is completely banned."

"No no. You're taking it wrongly, completely."

"Then what? I know, you can't live without him but you will have to. Okay? If not for yourself then for him and your family and if you get time then think about me too." Aroosh exhaled.

She laughed a little but stopped as she saw her expression unchanged. "It's fine okay. I know what it is. I can't be selfish," she rubbed her back.

"By the way, are you really naming them that way, ending with 'Aam'?" she expanded her eyes.

"Yes, Obviously,"

Cleaning her bed cover, Aroosh went into the rest room to flush off the remaining pills. Uneasiness flew out as Kyara stood to pray again. Amity was in her heart, until she heard the sound of the doorbell, and her ears noticed cheerful greetings from a voice which she longed to listen forever. *"He's here!"* Elf and Baddie screamed and danced in her stomach. She couldn't change the direction of her eyes due to her prayers and so she completed them and again wished both of her shoulders, one after another. As she saw straight, Aroosh was standing near the chair kept beside the door towards the main hall. Seeing her and keeping her hand on the chair's upper part, she pouted raising her eye brows and asked Kyara to come out. Having her heart in her throat, she nodded left and right to say no. Pointing towards her eyes to show how dead they looked, she nodded again. Aroosh came into the room and said, "Apply the eyeliner fast and come. Your clothes are fine."

"No, they aren't," she said and Aroosh opened her hair and divided them so that they fell on both the shoulders.

"What're you doing? He doesn't like. There must be more people with him. Has he come alone?"

"Yea, alone. He's talking to your mum. Now come on else he will go." Aroosh sighed.

She went out in an outlandish fashion and didn't want to cause an illogical interruption. His infantile simplicity was speaking softly which prevented his heedless love to raise her eyes to see the cause of his indefinite yearning. The indolent negligence was making his influential voice, a hymn. Tenderness was lingering in the air as she went into the kitchen to make him coffee! The coffee maker began with a heavy sound disallowing her to listen to his voice, coming from a distance. At last, she sprinkled some coffee beans on the foam and went out with an uncomprehending smile. She handled over the cup to Maisha showing an unexampled sweetness.

"Why are you giving this to me?" she shuddered due to which the coffee spilled all over the floor. "Who told you to make this?" she shouted.

"I thought to." Kyara replied looking at the liquid.

"What the hell? Why has he come here?" she shouted loud enough for him to hear.

"I will just serve him. There is an extra cup." Akira said looking at the mess.

"No need," she shouted and began her insults and verbal abuse. Biting sentences flew about and Kyara remained like a stone, staring at the ground as if it was she who was being mistreated.

"Kyara your phone is ringing." Aroosh said and she went running inside the room, crying forcefully. Dying a thousand deaths, she tried to forget those appalling words said for him which made her go in an abyss of ignominy. That was an abhorrence of meanness which had withered her quietude.

"Has he left?" she whispered.

"Yes, he has." Aroosh answered. "He drank your coffee."

"Did he leave sadly? Did he hear what she said? Did you see?" Kyara spoke.

"Maybe he didn't."

"What if he did?" She said weakly.

"Wish he did." Aroosh said with a terrible sigh.

"What? He would be so miserable then. I mean, why did she say so? Did you hear what did she speak?"

"Yes I did. It was not pleasant. Actually it was heart-rending. But you don't cry. You couldn't stop her. It was just not your fault. I liked that you didn't react at that point."

"What if he gets to know?" She sobbed. "You know, he is a child. He doesn't know all this. He hasn't even talked ill about anyone to me. How will he feel when he will know this? I mean, it is so moving. I never imagined her to be so cruel."

"Don't you know her? I didn't know that you don't know her. What I'm thinking is that what led her to say so about him?"

"You have a doubt on him?"

"No not him. She must have made a small thing big, like always. I know her quite well. Something must not have been according to her wishes so she started with the drama. I still can't believe that she disrespects him and you think that she loves him." Aroosh argued. "I don't even see a bit of care or respect, leave lovvve!" she stressed.

"Hmm. I wish God gives her senses. She has someone which everyone can't," she ended and went out as she heard Maisha shouting again. This time it was Akira who was being targeted.

"You don't have to tell me what do I have to do?" She spoke egotistically.

"Maisha, I'm just saying that you shouldn't have spoken that way. It didn't give a correct impression."

She's right Maisha," she spoke delicately from behind.

"Oh really Kyara! What would you do if your fiancée or boyfriend promises to watch a film with you and cancels the plans without informing and goes with his damn cousins instead?"

"He has never promised me for any film yet." Elf groaned. *"We neither go out. Once he asked me for the movie, I still feel lucky that he did."*

"Wait a sec! Was this the reason of that?" Baddie's ears stood straight.

"Maisha, I won't hear another word. Go straight to your room." Mommy said roughly.

"They are not 'Damn cousins'. They are 'His' cousins. They possess some part of his sweet blood."

The white pillow's linen absorbed each tear which flew from Kyara's eyes as those harsh sayings took harsher turns in her mind. She didn't talk to him too as she didn't want him to know that she heard all of that which was spoken. Having no idea about his knowledge about it, she never wanted him to be embarrassed at any cost. As she heard a knock on her bedroom's door at midnight, she got up and opened.

Maisha hugged her at another second. "Kyara. I didn't mean to shout at you. I'm severely sorry."

"It is alright Maish! I know you were furious," she said hugging her back.

"But I shouldn't have talked to you like that just because of anybody."
"Anybody? Is he not more important than me?"

"It is fine. Talk to him," she smiled with heavy eyes.

"No. Only if he apologises,' she said.

"But you're getting married to him. Learn to say sorry." *"Like me zzz."*

"Forget it. You know, our relationship means much more than anything," she stated emotionally.

"Oh my sister!" she thought to herself. *"She loves you a lot."* Elf and Baddie said putting their heads down.

"I know. I love her too, a lot."

Their fights came to the end quite few days after. All energetic, they were meant to be maybe for this world. The avalanche of scorn brought about a vivid portrayal about his enigmatic relationship with Maisha. It was so petty and one-dimensional that it provided an easy access to see into it. A gesture of despair or detestation proved it all. She no more, had grimace of disappointment to know how ironical her life was but after unravelling the pattern, she could feel that intensity of faith more. Her love with him was not based upon pledges or treaties. They were no one to each other but still their love gave hue of divinity. It gave gusts of laughter, tempests of passion and hummed pleasure. Like a trance of delight, it no longer mattered whether he would remember her all his life or not. When he would see his children, would he think of those names which she pre-decided or choose the new ones. His lukewarm and selfish love might remind him of those times when he romanced her with his chocolate eyes, made her high with his trusting voice!

In the silvery winter, when it would be hard for him to remove his blanket for the morning prayers, she might cross his mind who always wished for praying together. He could complete her religion by his one 'Yes' but he rather preferred her to be incomplete. Each time when the water would go down his throat, it might take him to the time when she asked him to sit whilst drinking and eating. Seeing any girl, covered from head to top, leaving no skin bare except her face, hands and toes, he might hark back to the day when he came across her and she was, in her shortest dress. What did he do to that Kyara who dressed in the smallest clothes? He might cherish the way in which he transformed her into someone that promoted her incessant charm even under the veil!

A painful thought ought to be flooding him when she would be enforced to be someone else's. Despite of that, there would be no freedom or integrity of soul, he would forever echo in her heart. There would be questions and reasons to consider their love as sullied and no one would be able to understand the answer. Her mind froze and she recognized that occasional flashes of his tenderness and love would assist her in living with noble and sublime patience.

As I urge to see through the mist, I lose myself. The day is blind with fog and my vision gets blurred due to the complexities felt. A frail soul goes up to get mixed in the lost air. Like a dream, it vanishes. Beyond the seven clouds it's taken and placed on a podium. It's white like snow capped mountains and the floor seems to be made of cotton balls. A white bird floats there, like a drifting leaf with the rash breeze which doesn't destruct but soothes. I am then, taken to the place where there is excessive shine, enough for my eyes to get close. In the air, is the tang of spring and I manage to look forward with my body upright and straight head. A liquid of wisdom is seen in my eyes. I should be frightened by the magical light but I am calmer than ever. As what I had been seeing has taken every feeling of fear from me. The element of fright crossed its level and then I forgot it for always.

I see some humanly creatures flying around; dressed in white long cloth and a white rope is covering their head. I find hard to make out their faces and I see that they are more beautiful than the earthly beauty. They are smiling incarnations of loveliness whose skins glow as if they are luminous. Without any expression they land on the cotton floor. As the silence grows stolid, I am asked that whether I want to have any glimpse from anywhere. I hesitantly clear my throat to say the name precisely.

All those creatures have turned to me after listening to what I said. They are overshadowed by a vague expression but they have no mark of trick or artifice. I speak again honourably. They begin to talk among themselves which I can't understand. They all become soundless as soon as a big mirror reaches in front of me to give me a picture of 'You'.

Love hovers in my gaze and like a movie it is being played and the audiences are seeing me, then you, then me, then you! I am lulled by dreamy musings and I linger a few leisurely seconds seeing you smile all through and then you lose it. Sorrow prevails and I have questions but I am quite. I ask, "Why? Couldn't that smile last till the end?"

There are no answers from any direction. The creatures are seeing me but are wordless. As soon as I begin to cry, you smile! I am baffled to hear that I prayed to give me tears to make you smile. Suddenly smitten with reality, I accept it with open arms. My ears are now hearing so many voices. Some are lamenting, some are showing their condemnation by the action of their hands and some are saying "La", some speaking "Lum", others "Len". I Think "La" means no. They have different languages but they understand everything. They look at me as if I'm someone whom they know. Yes, they know my story, they know 'You'!

I look down to touch my nails in worry and at another moment they all disappear. I do not know them but still I feel guarded, even without you and I come to know that this place is not earth!

Hearing the melodies of birds and bees, I comb my hair to keep them on one side. The past is slowly drifted out of my thought. I have learnt to live without people, you taught me to live without you. I see the river singing with its lips to the pebbles from my window and then my eyes see a cloud of pink colour going somewhere with the wind. I am exhaling noisily at another moment intuiting something which makes me homesick as I remember that this is the same feeling which originated in me decades ago. I'm dreadfully ill at ease and rub my cheek to decrease the effect. A soft knock, I hear which I ignore at first, thinking it to be from the wind. The knock gets intensely loud so I search for a cloth to cover my head before opening the door but then I remember that I am allowed to show my hair here!

Being habitual of it, I cover my head with a synthetic cloth which continually falls if not supported by the hand. I open the door and it is all silent as the sheeted dead. There is a lot of light again and I close my eyes to avoid the revelation. I move outside the door and I feel that there is no light now but still my eyes are closed. I try to open them but I'm unable to. As I try to find the cause, I hear, I hear a voice, a known voice.

My beats are not stopped but are curious. I feel nothing but I feel that my head cover has fallen due to the wind. I turn back; open my eyes and my hair are hanging down like summer twilight and continue to be on one side and I try to bring them on both the sides. I feel a touch on my open hair from behind as I see some flowers like lilies falling upon me. I suddenly turn back again without a blink. I don't look down as always but in the eyes of the one who brings my hair to the right side and says, "I like this way." His lips like two budded roses smile and then he sets his gaze. I flicker to drop two tears, both from the left and the right eye and join the mania. The sky above isn't really blue but of the shade of his eyes and it bows to greet. His scent hovers in the air and I see the surroundings dancing with delight. Stars are not only white but of every pleasing colour. Glitters are raining and each drop is still slighter than his shine.

My pulses are fluttering like a dove and silence creeps between us. His eyes with lashes like fans upon his cheeks are exchanging words. We are not so close but not even so far. I am able to hear his heart's cords clearly. Feeling his fingers entwined with mine, we look at our hands and then the time. We come to know that forty years have passed! "Forty years in his eyes, I drowned." His face is glad as dawn to me and he laughs unknowingly as we talk about the past forty years which didn't even seem like forty micro seconds.

"You're of sixteen years and me too," he hisses. "You look younger."

"I'm still the same as you left me," I utter.

"I didn't. You did," he says bossily. I don't disagree but I smile and he holds my chin and whispers in my ears, nuzzling my hair, "This is for life!"

Seeing him inhaling me after so long, joy riots in my eyes and I say, "Our lives have ended."

"This is the longest life. Do you want to spend it with me?"

I don't say anything but sit fixing my eyes on him. I want to cry but I don't because this place is not made for it. He continues to speak as if I am the only one. He behaves as if he's the most fortunate. I haven't met this type of Rehaam ever. Free from work, free from the world. He tells me to not to cover my hair here but I deny by saying that I cover myself to be seen by him. His smile full of subtle charm comes on his lips and he says that he doesn't understand my love!

All the magic of youth and joy is there and events are taking an unexpected turn. A charming air of vigour and vitality is blowing which defines happiness in every form. When he comes to know that what I did in his absence, he gives me a baffled stare. The heaven's flora speaks to him about me as though my love is something too discrete. He hears the paradise castle saying, "Your love was not made for that place." I surrender myself to gloomy thought.

"Follow that tree." We do as told. The tree is shifting its position and moving laterally. His eyes stare at me unseeingly. I pull his hand to make him pay attention on the ongoing situation. As we walk a distance of some kilometres together, we see the tree's leaves flying in a particular way. I look at him in bewilderment and he nods at me giving dreamy hints.

"Look. You both were made here." The tree speaks.

"Wow!" He broadens his eyes which widens his smile. He keeps on seeing at that place but I keep on seeing at him whose face is lit up by the glow of pristine area.

"She was made from you." The soil says as he touches it. He pulls me hard unexpectedly, reaches for my hand and kisses my knuckles. "You see," his eyes again have those boyish longings and I tell him to stop.

"Like a new couple, all engrossed," he says blinking looking at the sky.

"New?" I raise my eyes.

"You're always novel to me," he says and I move my eyes off him and see the place.

"Did you know this?" he asks coming back to it and I do not pretend to explain.

"Maybe she did." The soil answers. He holds his breath in admiring silence as he comes to know more and more. I then remember some words of my mother said to me when I was small. She told me that we were made in pairs. I didn't know that I was made with him or maybe I did. If not then how could I feel him despite of such tyrannous distance? How could I continue being faithful to his heart even when he forgot me? Was only I made from him? Was not he too made with me? I erase all such grey concepts as I see his mouth quivering with pleasure.

"Happy?" he says undoing his coat as we reach our house. I press my lips seeing him wearing the same grey shirt which I got for him on our second anniversary.

"Yes," I speak. "Does it fit you?"

"Yes. Now I know why our skin type is same," he smirks.

"You do."

My pulses are leaping anew as I stand to cook for him despite of having cooked food anytime. Cooking for him is a privilege and this dream place calls for it. After quite long, my eyes are not seeing him. He is in the loggia upstairs listening to some delightful music. Music is not abandoned here, I realise after some time. This place allows everything which was barred on earth but I feel that restrictions were for our own enhancement. Putting the Mugh rice, tangy lemon yoghurt sauce and Greek chicken oregano in the silver tray, I reach the first floor and keeping it on the table near the window pane, I try to call him but I still don't know how to take his name. So I rather prefer texting him as the walls of my house are not allowed to speak like others'. He tells me that he is in my bedroom. I shyly take the tray and reach my place. His back faces me as he stands facing towards the table.

"This is incomplete," he states turning. I keep the food on the bed and catch his sight. He has a paper in his hand. Not recognizing at first, I go nearer to read what I wrote on it. As I see it, my heart pounds in my throat and I feel the land shifting beneath.

"You have written it? He speaks dimly taking my face in his hands.

"I stopped yesterday," I say sensitively.

The way he made me sit on thorns for long, suffocates him. One long torture of soul forces him to frown at himself perplexedly. He is aware of my emotions and that is what I wanted since the first showers. Being discreetly silent for two moments, he is entangled in the paradox.

"For me?" he puffs out thunderously snuggling my nose. I see his eyes are lightly closed but still he is able to take his nose to every part of my face hinting me about his awareness of every inch of it. Questioning despite of knowing the answer is his pattern since always. Anticipating for no answer but just me to lay down my arms, his eyes full of majestic tenderness are resting upon my cheeks.

"You," I gasp burying my face into his. "Only!"

Maybe someday... Your hand in mine,
Ceaselessly written in my any one fate line.
Hearing you saying, "Stay with me.
For here and later, make I as we."

That will lead me blink for one.
Then too I will find means to trust.
For what until you have done,
Inexorable is its true thrust.

Maybe some day... I will be only-
For whom your sight will gain certain distance.
For whose sake, you'll live fully,
And liveliness all through, I will sense.

Maybe some day... I will wake your sleep,
From the showy little length amidst.
Moving my fingers in your hair, too deep.
With what it will be, you'll be ready to assist.

Maybe some day... that once seen dream-
Which had taken me to an authentic Avalon.
Its trueness will find grounds to gleam.
It will delineate our comings and the gone.

Perhaps our haphazard love,
Will gain something to boot pithy.
It`s been a pure essence of verve.
As yet it is virtuous and not witty.

Maybe some day... that consistency of pain,
Will fly far like a cloud of bubble.
Vanishing each spot and every stain,
It`ll make you mine without a crumble.

Maybe some day... wholly, plainly-
You`ll explain yourself to me as I do.
My heart with bit contentedness,
Will spot the doubts to end with blindness.
With feel of being an answer to you!

Maybe someday, when the cosmos will say, He becomes
hers and she all his.
When the posterity will solicit that "May-
We too have a love like this."

They say that their bond is not for here.
As here, it contains love of material.
They ask, "Is it real or has some iniquitous layer."
Its depth is moderately so rare.

Maybe some day... some evidences of us. Every gene of
yours which will come,
Your brows, your sense, your wit and thus-
It will be you whom they will become.

Maybe someday... will be beyond,
All those boundaries of take and give.
Caring for none but my lord,
Who'll say, "Stay with him and solely live."

No phrase of guilt, no wish for more.
My state to typify will make me encore.
Time when you will be persuaded by,
My expressions in which you utterly lie.

Sometime of plenary singularity,
When you will also sympathise.
Your inamorata will wait until the day-
when no words but the gaze will say.

The impoverished moon standing there, pleading for its
whiteness from you.
It'll blubber and edgily blare,
To get its genuineness back from your hue.

Maybe some day... a closing stage.
I, with...